From *Murder, Chop Chop*

An astonishingly beautiful Eurasian girl with shoulder-length black hair cut in a page-boy bob had occupied her place. The Eurasian girl looked up, smiling. She had lovely eyes, dark, almond shaped, with very long black lashes that swept her cheeks.

"Miss Mildred Woodford?" she asked in polished English.

The Englishwoman conquered her surprise, but she was ruffled. Antagonism showed plainly upon her features. "I'm Woodford," she said flatly.

"I'm Mountain of Virtue." The Eurasian girl spoke with the rounded, pliable intonations of the Soochow accents. "I was sent to meet you. I am so glad you have come."

At the mere mention of the name Mountain of Virtue, the six Chinese officers crowded around the girl, beaming and mooning. Mountain of Virtue was well known in China, it seemed.

Mildred Woodford sank into an empty end seat and proceeded to stare with a frigid British eye. The Eurasian girl was slender. Her skin had a faint golden blush. Although she was dressed with Chinese exactness and taste, she was quite modern. Her duck's-egg green skirt, French-heeled shoes and bobbed hair gave ample proof.

What Mildred Woodford did not recognize was that Mountain of Virtue was what the Chinese poets call *hsiao-chieh*—a woman born to attract men, then retire, bestowing favors artfully, rarely and elusively. In short, a dangerous woman!

Books by James Norman

In the Gimiendo Hernandez Quinto series

Murder, Chop Chop (1942)
An Inch of Time (1945)
The Nightwalkers (1947)

Other Novels

A Little North of Everywhere (1953)
Cimmaron Trace (1956)
Valley of Lotus House (1956)
Juniper and the General (1957)
The Fell of Dark (1960)
The Obsidian Mirror (1977)

Plays

Juniper and the Pagans (1959)

Radio Plays: *Studio One* series

Television Plays: *Herald Theatre* & *Loretta Young Show*

Juveniles

The Navy that Crossed Mountains (1964)
The Forgotten Empire (1965)
The Strange World of Reptiles (1966)
The Riddle of the Incas (1968)
The Young Generals (1968)
Charro: Mexican Horseman (1970)
Kearny Rode West (1971)

Others

Handbook to the Christian Liturgy (1944)
In Mexico (A Shopper's Guide to Mexico) (1959 & 1966)
Terry's Guide to Mexico (1962, Revised 1972)
Mexican Hill Town (1963)

Murder, Chop Chop

by
James Norman

With an afterword on the author by
Tom & Enid Schantz

The Rue Morgue Press
Boulder, Colorado
1997

Murder, Chop Chop
was first published in book form
by William Morrow
in 1942.

A condensed version of this book
appeared serially in the December 1941
and January 1942 issues of
Adventure under the title
Viva China!

This edition is reprinted with the
permission of the author's son
and literary executor,
Paul Schmidt.

New material © 1997 by
The Rue Morgue Press
946 Pearl Street
Boulder, CO 80302

TO

Irv Goff and Bill Alto
Guerrilleros Extraordinary

Chinese names, to be appreciated, should be rolled between the tongue and teeth and gnawed upon carefully. To prevent them from adding more mystery to an already complicated story, I have used a phonetic key in the form of footnotes when such names first appear.

J.N.

"There are three hundred rules of ceremony and three thousand of behavior."

North China proberb

SOME CHARACTERS IN CHINA

GIMIENDO QUINTO: a gigantic Mexican who grew up with $10,000 on his head and solved an intricate crime.

MOUNTAIN OF VIRTUE: Chinese poets called her *hsiaochieh*, meaning dangerous to men!

MILDRED WOODFORD: the hardest-drinking British journalist ever to hit Sianfu in Northwest China.

JOHN TATE: portly American calligraphist who wasn't made for adventure but got it as Quinto's right-hand man.

LIEUTENANT CHI: young Hunanese patriot weighted down by the cares of China and the Brooklyn Dodgers.

WANG: a Sianfu banker with sinister boots.

SERGEANT SUN: he handles a rifle twice his size with more skill than English.

TENG FA: a pair of inquisitive ears and sudden justice. The peasants spoke of him with awe.

MR. HO: a scholar and partisan of the poppies.

JOCK McKAY: Scotch doctor; medico for the guerrilla school in Lingtung.

MIGNON CHAUVET: assistant doctor; a lady.

ABE HARROW: Ambulance Corps captain who died at three very distinct times.

NEVADA: wears his pistols tied down hard and flips coins with bullets.

MR. YELLOW COAT: an elusive stranger in gabardine.

PAPA WIER: the missionary without a mission.

MARY WIER: his daughter, and beloved of Nevada.

CLIVE FIRTH: Scot secretary to Quinto who spied and was spied upon.

SIR OLIVER QUIST: British Ambassador who felt the Empire would hold together through a thirty-six-course dinner.

COLONEL NOHURI: a Japanese officer enmeshed in intrigue and yards of gold braid.

THE MIN-TUAN: bandits of sorts; very charming and equally practical in the art of diplomacy.

GUERRILLEROS: Quinto's sixty guerrilla-fighter students; all CLhinese, and the late Pancho Villa couldn't have trained them better.

THE LUNGHAI EXPRESS: a slightly irresponsible train.

Incidental government ministers, mayors,
soldiers and a pair of illustrious teeth.

Contents

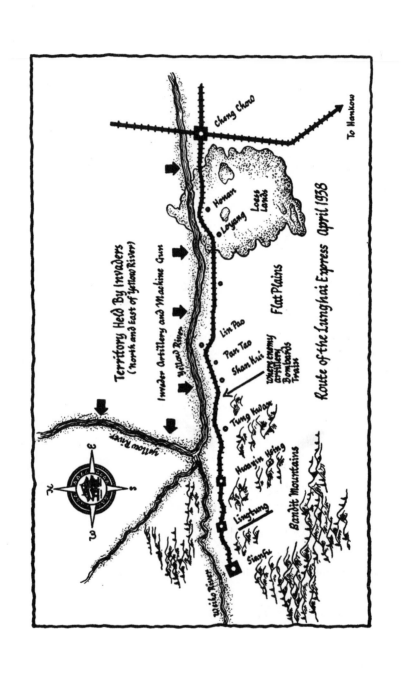

CHAPTER 1
The Camouflaged Train

THE SINGLE-TRACK Lunghai Railway that wanders between Kaifeng and Sianfu has, as the Chinese put it, "much face." Its small, Belgian-made engine chugs along the Yellow River Valley with immense dignity, picking up villages here and there with the casual air of a woman gathering bouquets of flowers. For every village it threads through, at least three of equal importance are overlooked and left behind for closer inspection by the Yellow River herself.

At intervals the train meanders along the river's sandstone bluffs, absently coming within range of Japanese cannons near Tung Kwan. The annoyance is ignored— comic-opera style. Chinese trainmen simply couple a camouflaged car to the other nine, complacently hoping Nipponese gunners will some day respect the gesture.

John Tate, sprawled upon the top of the first car, was terrified. For three days he had clung to the roof of the train, traveling from Hankow to the tune of one catastrophe after another.

Tate obviously wasn't built for adventure. He was a scholar. At best one would expect to find him puffing up the well-explored steps of the pyramids, his white, badly wrinkled Palm Beach suit bagging at the elbows and knees, his Panama brim fluttering in the wind.

He was a plump little man with a pink face and heavy-lidded- albino eyes that darted here and there anxiously. Although the war broke out when he was in Pekin studying Chinese calligraphy, he had paid no attention to it. Pekin fell and the Chinese were pushed back to Nanking, then to Hankow. With each withdrawal, Tate's supply of books diminished. At Hankow there was nothing left for him but to take a job with the government press bureau. For six months he translated military communiques into English and French.

Now, against his better judgment, he was riding on the Lunghai Express with a ticket to Lingtung . . . a ticket to troubles already begun.

The train was *full-up*, Chinese fashion, and Tate rode on the roof. At Cheng Chow it had crashed into a cow, throwing him overboard and breaking his right arm which he now carried in a sling with chopstick splints. In the Loess Lands, a bare, fantastic region studded with hills shaped like Parker House rolls and round scones, the train ran short of fuel. Four hundred Chinese scurried over the hills searching for wood, while the little Belgian engine's fiery insides confiscated six books of Master Chang Yen Yuan's ten-volume *Short Essentials of Chinese Calligraphy* which Tate had with him.

As they approached within range of Japanese guns along the Yellow River, Tate sighed meditatively, shifting his position on the top boards of the train. It was too dark to read. He let tired, windburned eyes sweep the length of the Express with a certain vague uneasiness that had nothing to do with the cannons at Tung Kwan.

The wheezing locomotive clattered over uneven rails dragging ten overcrowded cars with lumbering swiftness. By starlight, he could see outlines of the soldiers who had attached themselves to the train's sides and roof with the tenacity of closely packed barnacles. His eyes betrayed a growing anxiety as he listened to the lively betting going on among the troops as to how many would be swept off in the low tunnels before Tung Kwan.

When the train curved northward toward the river, small mountains scudded by, springing from the darkness in great leaps, falling backward into the dust raised by the camouflaged car. During a comparatively level stretch, Tate hooked his feet in the top boards and, with a great deal of maneuvering and twisting pain in his injured arm, succeeded in leaning sideways over the curving roof to peer down at the lighted compartment window below. The train lurched and he almost lost his balance. Shivering, he pulled himself back without having seen more than a glimpse of the window. "I wish," he murmured helplessly, "that she had never come to China."

A lady in tweed and six Chinese army officers sat in the compartment. The lady was a towheaded, willowy Englishwoman of about thirty years. She had a startling Yorkshire nose and a complexion resembling that of a mildly boiled lobster. Since Cheng Chow she had kibitzed a mah jong game which the officers played in a rapid-fire style, calling their shots, the bamboos and winds, like veteran crapshooters.

A satisfied expression brightened the lady's face, for in the three-day journey she had gained a number of important military secrets from the six smooth-haired officers. Cleverly, she had said nothing about the present war. The Chinese officers had not minded being politely cooperative, in that they only gave out information concerning the 1900 Boxer Rebellion.

"Perhaps the honorable lady is a historian," one of the officers murmured.

At Pan Tao the Lunghai Express halted for a half hour in the darkness, taking on a few hundred additional passengers. The station platform overflowed with strange voices, half-illuminated faces and the glitter of bayonets. There were fat, boisterous boys from the South; Annamites carrying rifles, parasols and fans; also taller soldiers, Manchurians from the 105th Regiment.

A black-and-silver-uniformed railroad policeman stopped the Englishwoman and one of the officers as they sauntered along the platform.

"Papers!" he said.

"What's that? Oh, my passport," said the woman. She handed the guard her passport and a calling card. The policeman immediately returned the passport without glancing at it. In his world calling cards were more important. He could take them home and show his friends the important people he met during the day. He glanced at the card.

"English journalist, very good, yes," he observed in passable English.

Then the lady and her army officer sauntered on. Breathing the heavy odor of the jostling crowd around the train, the woman sighed, saying:

"Beastly odor. What do Chinese coolies eat to make them smell so?"

The officer, a major, smiled complacently. "Sianfu," he said. "Perhaps we arrive tomorrow, the next day, perhaps sometime. Smell all over in Sianfu. Very strong. You like to hear about fighting in Sianfu?"

"Lingtung," the Englishwoman laughed. "I'll not go to Sianfu yet. You know, I'm stopping off at Lingtung, the hot-springs resort. It's not a resort now—during the war— is it?"

The officer's face brightened in the glow of the station's single light. "You like to hear about fighting in Lingtung? Fine kidnaping place!"

There came a melancholy cry from the Lunghai Express. A bell clanged near by. Without so much as glancing at the passengers crowded upon the roof of the train, the woman hurried inside, followed by the major. Reaching her compartment door, she stopped short.

An astonishingly beautiful Eurasian girl with shoulder-length black hair cut in a page-boy bob had occupied her place. The Eurasian girl looked up, smiling. She had lovely eyes, dark, almond shaped, with very long black lashes that swept her cheeks.

"Miss Mildred Woodford?" she asked in polished English.

The Englishwoman conquered her surprise, but she was ruffled. Antagonism showed plainly upon her features. "I'm Woodford," she said flatly.

"I'm Mountain of Virtue." The Eurasian girl spoke with the rounded, pliable intonations of the Soochow accents. "I was sent to meet you. I am so glad you have come."

At the mere mention of the name Mountain of Virtue, the six Chinese officers crowded around the girl, beaming and mooning. Mountain of Virtue was well known in China, it seemed.

Mildred Woodford sank into an empty end seat and proceeded to stare with a frigid British eye. The Eurasian girl was slender. Her skin had a faint golden blush. Although she was dressed with Chinese exactness and taste, she was quite modern. Her duck's-egg green skirt, French-heeled shoes and bobbed hair gave ample proof.

What Mildred Woodford did not recognize was that Mountain of Virtue was what the Chinese poets call *hsiaochieh**—a woman born to attract men, then retire, bestowing favors artfully, rarely and elusively. In short, a dangerous woman!

As the train moved from the station, something tugged at John Tate's bandaged arm. Turning awkwardly, he stared at a moon-faced boy who grinned at him out of the semidarkness.

"No cigarettes," he said in annoyance.

The boy-soldier shook his head. He looked most absurd stretched at full length upon the roof boards, the wind whipping his visored army cap up and down like a duck's bill.

He wore the quilted uniform and insignia of the North Army. A French Mauser hung at his belt in a great polished wooden case. A red worsted tassel fluttered from the hilt-ring of the two-handed long sword strapped over his shoulder. Tate noted the millet bag, the cup and rice bowl dangling from his belt, the pair of ivory chopsticks thrust into his puttees. This, indeed, was no ordinary soldier.

"Mr. Johnny Tate?" The words came in spotless, precise English.

Tate looked disturbed. "Who said I was Tate?" he demanded.

"But you are Mr. Tate, no?" said the grinning soldier. "I know you are. I am sure. I know everything. If I do not know everything, then I shall know. You are riding to Lingtung? You will see Quinto there?"

The strange, boyish Chinese face hovered in the darkness with a queer, disturbing luminosity. Even the cheerful grin stood out like a Cheshire mask.

"*Ayi!* You fail to recognize me?" he asked in a way suggestive that this was an old and oft repeated game.

*Hsiaochieh, pronounced *seeow-cheeay* (the *ow* as in how) is seldom ever pronounced twice in the same manner due to the fact that most Chinese get terribly excited at the mere mention of the word.

"No, I don't," Tate answered.

"A sadness. I am Teng Fa.* Now you know me?" Teng Fa rummaged in his pocket and brought forth a calling card which he handed to the calligraphist.

Tate didn't bother to look. It was too dark to read, but on one side of the card, he knew, the name was written in English, on the other in Chinese characters. Slowly it dawned on him—Teng Fa!

*Teng Fa sounds like *tung* in tungsten, and *fa* as in father.

His mouth opened slightly as he peered at the incredible young soldier. Teng Fa was a household word in China. Many natives, the more superstitious, swore that Teng Fa was just a name for a pair of inquisitive ears and sudden justice. But Tate knew better. The Chinese was chief of the *Hsien Ping* or North Army secret police.

Teng Fa glanced toward the rear of the train, where flickering bursts of light from the compartment windows brushed eerily against the walls of a narrow cutting. Again he turned toward the American.

"So, Mr. Tate. I hoped I'd see you," he said. He shouted against the clatter of the train. Then he jerked his thumb downward, indicating the compartment below, and grinned.

In the passageways below, conductors and train boys were racing back and forth turning off lights and drawing window shades. Somewhere ahead the Lunghai Express was due to burst through a tunnel, run across an open ledge along the river and plunge madly toward another tunnel while Japanese cannons fired at it.

"The Englishwoman, you can tell me about her?" Teng Fa shouted.

A nervous tremor ran through Tate's unathletic body. "What about her?" he countered.

"You tell me all about her?" Teng Fa demanded. "Her name is Woodford? You tell me more. What does she want with China?"

"Ah—" Tate hesitated, then, "She's a journalist."

"A spy, yes?"

"How do I know?"

"Yes, she must be a spy. All lady journalists are spies," Teng Fa observed wisely. "Who will she see in Lingtung?"

He picked up one of Tate's four remaining volumes of Master Chang Yen Yuan. It was too dark to read the faded titles, but the young Chinese nodded knowingly, leaving the uncomfortable implication that he knew exactly what it was by the weight and feel of it.

He leaned forward, saying:

"Mr. Tate, you were commissioned in Hankow to follow the British lady, no?"

*Teng Fa sounds like *tung* in tungsten, and *fa* as in father.

The train whistle shrieked loudly, snatching the question away. Abruptly, Tate was shoved flat against the train roof. Darkness suddenly swooped down in a hot, rushing, sooty mass. It was the first tunnel before Tung Kwan. Teng Fa's strong fingers held Tate aboard the pitching train.

Then the engine rushed into the open again, blowing its whistle belligerently. Tate gasped as the cars swept around a perilous ledge. It was like running across a stage in the full glare of footlights. Across the river Japanese searchlights riveted white thumbs of light upon the clattering Express.

An artillery shell whistled. It burst against the rocky ledge below the tracks with a reverberating shock. The cars rocked crazily from side to side, hurtling toward the second tunnel.

"Lord! We'll never make it. They're going to kill us!" Tate cried emotionally.

In the bright glare Teng Fa's broad, coppery face laughed with all the boyish Chinese delight in fireworks. Tate gritted his teeth. He looked foolish in that instant. This was war.

The second tunnel gaped blackly, a hundred yards ahead. The Japanese still had time to fire another blast. It was a race against time. Tate's fingers went white, gripping the top boards. The pain in his broken arm was forgotten.

"Soon they will see the last car, the camouflaged wagon," Teng Fa shouted reassuringly. "Then, perhaps, the invader will cease fire out of respect for our superior military equipment."

Bwwoomb! A second shell ripped into the bluff behind the train, throwing down an avalanche of loose rock. The little Belgian locomotive whistled insolently at the Japanese across the river and plunged into the safety of the second tunnel.

John Tate sighed heavily and collapsed, his body acting as if someone had jerked each supporting bone and nerve away. He was still limp when the train rode into the starlight once more and raced cross country until it reached the Tung Kwan sidings. It was then that he noticed Teng Pa was no longer on the train; nor were his four books of calligraphy anywhere about.

Conductors and train boys fought their way through the packed compartments, relighting lamps and joking about the Japanese bad aim. In the Englishwoman's compartment the various passengers had taken the bombardment with flying colors. The army officers were a bit more patriotic. Mildred Woodford was ruddier in complexion, having somehow consumed a half bottle of Scotch in the space of two tunnels.

"Lots of noise. Nobody killed. What kind of a war is this anyway?" she said dryly, meanwhile glancing in annoyance at the Eurasian girl.

Mountain of Virtue smiled—not for the Englishwoman, but for her circle of admiring officers. "The cannons are very annoying this season," she murmured. "They were not half so annoying last year. I will tell Gimiendo Quinto. Gimiendo will stop them!" She glanced through the window as the train slowed and nudged its way into a dark siding.

At Tung Kwan, the Lunghai Express paused a few minutes as if to think things over. Then, having apparently decided to desert the Yellow River as too dangerous, it chugged directly westward along the Wei Ho Valley.

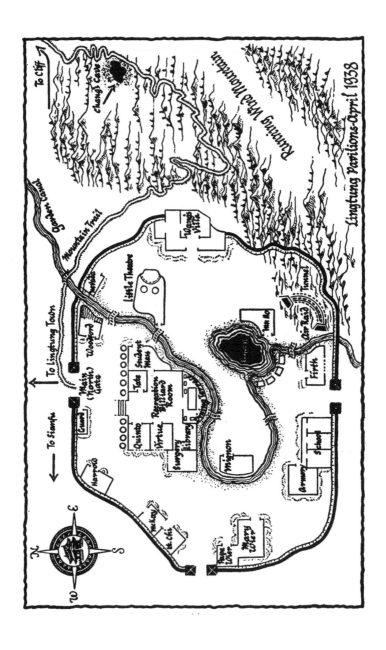

CHAPTER 2
Three Mountains of Lingtung

LINGTUNG, China's most popular watering place, is nestled in the Lishan Hills twelve miles southeast of Sianfu. Its hills verge upon the great northwest deserts, whence, over the centuries, Tartar, Hun and Mongol had swooped across Cathay. Lingtung itself is very hard to avoid, even on a map, because of the oddly shaped sacred Running Wind Mountain that thrusts its molar tooth above the pines just beyond the village and on the south bank of the Wei Ho.

According to conservative historians, the peak lost its top and gained fame in the third century B.C. when the overenthusiastic emperor, Ch'in Huang Ti, had a few hundred feet of mountain top lopped off that he might better view the sunrises without being bothered by lowflying clouds.

The neat little town at the mountain's base was an afterthought. So were the clean, cobbled streets, the several ancient shrines and the magnificent Lingtung Pavilions, a modern garden-type hotel set upon the pine slopes a mile back from the town.

In the spring of 1938 folks in Lingtung boasted that their town had three equally famous mountains—Running Wind Mountain; the beautiful and clever Eurasian girl, Mountain of Virtue; and her constant companion, Gimiendo Hernandez Quinto. Of the three, Quinto was as visible as the mountain. He was a huge, mild-mannered man whose smudgy black eyes and dark military-cropped hair further increased the idea of largeness. But all this was deceptive, for he could move his two hundred and twenty pounds with a crafty, catlike grace. He was well seasoned and could be quick and hard.

No one in China knew much about his past. G.H.Q., as he was called by American friends, had been visible in Shanghai, Pekin and Hankow for years. It was said that his blood cousin was no other than the late illustrious Pancho Villa and that his various grandfathers had fought in innumerable wars for Mexican independence, so it seemed quite natural that he should be in China on such an occasion.

The Nationalist Government, headquartered in Hankow, was positive about this, for they had put Quinto in charge of the Chinese Northwest Guerrilla Fighters' Training School at Lingtung.

His own exploits in the field threatened the heroic deeds of his own late cousin. A year earlier, Quinto had planned and led the famous raid on the Bubbling Well Cinema in Japanese-occupied Shanghai. The theater had been showing an American gangster film complete with sound effects, tommy guns, roaring squad cars and police whistles. When the epic was over and the light turned on in the theater, six Japanese majors were found dead in their seats. Four generals and one Norwegian admiral had disappeared.

Quinto, of course, was credited with the four generals but the admiral had to be returned in good condition. "It is very sad that I should have fallen into such error," Quinto observed afterward upon being presented the highest military honor of the Republic, the Order of Blue Sky and White Sun.

While the Lunghai Express gathered in the last few miles before reaching Lingtung, the same Gimiendo Quinto added certain touches to his elaborate plan in which the incoming train figured. He called Doctor McKay into his *yamen*, or office, the former main pavilion where Chiang Kai-shek had once suffered a bitter experience.

McKay, the volunteer medico for the guerrilla school, was a peaked Scot, about forty years old but looking fifty. He was a parched man with a mouth that was amiably cynical and eyes that darted beneath tufted brows.

Quinto, with a cigarette rolling loosely in his mouth, laid out his plans. "Senor Doctor Mac," he said, "I have a very special assignment today. You and I meet the train in Lingtung at noon. It brings a Senorita Woodford whom we must surround very carefully." He waved a blue telegram from Hankow. "She is undoubtedly a spy and we must see that she talks to no one but the right people while she visits in Lingtung."

McKay pulled on a dry pipe. His eyes lighted with interest although he said nothing.

Quinto continued rapidly: "Hankow has sent a man, John Tate, to watch her. I myself sent Mountain of Virtue to Pan Tao, following Senor Harrow, but Virtue will also pick up this British lady. It is always better to have a clever woman watch a spy than a man, eh? But as for Lingtung, when this Woodford arrives, she must always have Senor Tate, Virtue or Doctor Mac at her side. She must not be alone! You understand?"

"Righto!" The doctor nodded. His keen eyes wandered about the office, absently noting the things they had recorded before. The Cantonese hardwood easy chairs, a mahogany table spread with military maps, a smaller table holding model junks and pieces of marble with figures shown in natural line. On the wall there was a reward poster in Spanish offering $10,000 for one Gimiendo Hernandez Quinto, dead or alive. On it was the faded picture of a thirteen-year-old boy loaded down with bandoleers, rifles and pistols. It was dated "1916, Juarez, Mexico." The doctor's gaze came to rest on a row of cognac bottles, Pedro Domecq.

McKay smiled. His main interest in life was to be on hand when the Mexican died, so convinced was he that Quinto, as a result of his brandy consumption, must have kidneys and liver as big as a horse's.

Suddenly the doctor glanced at his watch. It was almost ten o'clock. The train was due at noon. He remembered another job he had to do. "See you at the station," he told Quinto and hurried from the room.

Hidden among the camphors outside the *yamen*, a meticulously dressed, hook-nosed man smiled his satisfaction as McKay left. The hook-nosed one wore the uniform of the Chinese Emergency Ambulance Corps and the three red bars of a captain. In his pocket he had a row of five fountain pens.

Had Quinto known the man was there, watching his every move, he would scarcely have raised his eyebrows. Lurking among trees was a Harrow characteristic. Eight years in China acting as adviser for various petty warlords had made Abe Harrow secretive and sly. It had become second nature to his smooth, ingratiating manner. The talent had been valuable once when there was a market value on warlords. Today, Harrow still had the talent, but no warlords. Meanwhile, heeding his practical nature, he had volunteered in the army, getting himself a captaincy. If the fighting on the fronts became tough, Captain Harrow contrived to have Abe Harrow sent to Lingtung for a rest.

Of the six foreigners living at the Lingtung Pavilions, Harrow was Quinto's greatest problem. He had a peculiar ability for gathering all enemies and no friends. People hated his smooth tongue, his hairline mustache, his flaunting of expensive English zipper boots in the face of a ragged Republican army. In fact, Harrow was scheduled for death—and that was another Quinto problem.

Now, Harrow shrank back among the camphors, watching, while G.H.Q. prepared to leave the *yamen*. His dark, quick eyes poked through the window, sweeping the room's interior, finally settling upon the table covered with military maps.

A moment later the *yamen* door clicked shut. Quinto was gone. Harrow lingered among the trees a few minutes, making sure the Mexican did not return; then, abruptly, he boosted himself to the sill and swung into the room. He stopped and listened. There was no sound.

His eyes again swept toward the map table. He saw the telegram from Hankow, paused, and while reading it made a surprised clucking with his tongue. Dropping the telegram, he turned his attention to the maps. They were crude layouts, mostly of territory, railway centers and munition depots behind the Japanese lines.

His attention was caught by a jade fantailed fish weighing down a corner of the map. Quickly he picked it up, examined it with the eye of a collector, then slipped it into his trouser pocket. His next move was to locate an inking pad, half lost under a pile of papers. He picked up a Chinese chop, or character seal—the insignia of the Guerrilla School—and wetting it on the pad, stamped a blank sheet of paper.

With the blank paper neatly folded in his trouser pocket, Harrow hastily left the room as he had come.

"It's late again," Doctor McKay remarked dryly. He pulled his pipe from his mouth and spat across the windswept railway tracks before the Lingtung station.

"It is always late," Quinto answered complacently. "Today it's the wind, a remarkably strong one. But always expect the train late. It only starts on time at Cheng Chow, and there many times they hold it over until the following day to start it at the proper hour. That's the trouble with trains. They are exact about little things, not the big things."

The shrill, belligerent whistle of the Lunghai Express screamed in the distance. A few minutes later the train chugged around the base of Running Wind Mountain, clattering into the bomb-pitted station with the restless air of a young stallion in heat.

Soldiers, coolies and refugees seethed around, on top and between the cars as they came to a standstill. Women ran alongside in the track bed, hawking stale rice cakes and quartered chickens. Quinto elbowed his way through the crowd until he saw Mountain of Virtue and a strange, long-nosed woman come toward him. His face brightened cheerily.

"Ah, Virtue," he murmured.

The Eurasian girl was a dream of loveliness in her bright crepe jacket with its square jade buttons and long, oldstyle embroidered sleeves.

"I did not see Mr. Harrow in Pan Tao," she spoke hastily, before the Englishwoman came within hearing.

"No. He returned to Lingtung this morning," said Quinto. He flashed her a warning glance.

"Hello, there. You're Captain Quinto, aren't you?" The Englishwoman brushed forward. She smiled mannishly, extended her hand and gave Quinto's big fist a resounding squeeze. "I'm Miss Woodford.

Mildred Woodford. It was good of you to send the Chinese girl to meet me. You shouldn't have bothered, though."

"Ah, a small service, Senorita," said Quinto. A shudder ran through his huge frame, for he detested talkative women.

"Well, I'm relieved to be here," Mildred Woodford went on cheerfully. "The train ride was so fatiguing. All through it I've looked forward to meeting you, Captain. I've heard so much about you. Fabulous stories, too. Is it true you fought with Pancho Villa in Mexico? You must have been quite young then?"

Quinto winced for an instant, then with a sunny smile such as only he could give, he offered her to Doc McKay. "Senor Doctor Mac," he said softly.

With a slight nod to Virtue and the doctor, he slipped away in the crowd surrounding the train, his eyes alert for another visitor. He caught John Tate as the latter maneuvered, one-armed, from the train roof. On first seeing the portly American, Quinto thought, "What a ridiculous little man! "

"Senor Tate?" he said. "I am Quinto."

Tate appeared dusty and red from the wind. For a moment the exertion in dropping from the train roof caused a loss of breath and he regained his voice only after Quinto had hurried him through the station and into the town. Then he began to look around desperately.

"Look here, where are we going?" he demanded.

"To the communal baths. You need one."

"But I can't." Tate was almost panicky. "I've got to be with Miss Woodford. Those are my instructions."

"She is well surrounded for the moment."

"But—"

"Don't worry." Quinto smiled with magnificent certainty. "We go to the baths."

As the two men walked through Lingtung's narrow, cobbled streets, shopkeepers and coolies alike paused in their daily tasks to greet Quinto with a steady series of *haos*. It was evident that the Mexican was very important. Everyone knew him. Everybody respected him. Part of that respect was because he religiously observed the Northern custom of bathing.

Each day Quinto repaired to the communal baths, the hot springs at the Lingtung Pavilions being out of order and unattended during the war. In the town baths he was thoroughly steamed, washed by expert muscle-pounding boys, then hurried off to a curtained section where his enormous toes were massaged for a half hour, Shensi fashion.

"It is not quite as satisfactory as when Mountain of Virtue rubs my

toes," Quinto sighed, when he and Tate finally reached that department in the baths. "*La muchacha es magnifica!*"

"Virtue—the Chinese girl?" Tate asked.

"Eurasian. Her father was Chinese. Remarkable. Did you notice
her? *Hsiaochieh!*"

Tate blushed slightly at the mere mention of classical China's most
discreet, most potent romantic phrase.

"Where is she from?" he asked.

"Sianfu. But first she came west from Soochow. She arrived in Sianfu
with an aviator who somehow got lost in the shuffle. A little thing, that,"
said Quinto, waving an airy hand. "I played a poker game in Sianfu one
night. I won Virtue."

A bath boy with the skin of a salamander rubbed Quinto's feet with
a hard cotton towel while Tate watched in silence, privately envying the
Mexican's stocky legs and barrel chest. At length the American looked
directly at Quinto's face.

"I suppose you know why I'm here?" he asked, still looking at the
Mexican.

"Certainly."

"The press bureau in Hankow is suspicious of Miss Woodford. You
know that? They sent me to keep track of her. I'm not much of a guard,
but—"

A light of utter beatitude irradiated Quinto's features. "You need
not be so circumspect," he said. "They sent her here to be shot, naturally? Just like Hankow. They know who does the most professional
shooting of spies in all China—Gimiendo Hernandez Quinto, no?"

Tate stiffened. There was a shocked expression in his eyes.

"Shot!" he gulped. "No! You can't. There's no proof yet."

Quinto's articulate face changed to a look of mild disappointment.
"So. Perhaps next time." He shrugged.

"She's not a paid agent as far as we know," said Tate. "Woodford is a
free-lance journalist, but the government suspects her of pro-Japanese
leanings. It's said that she was an intimate friend of their Cabinet Minister Mitsu. Since there's no other proof, she is being allowed a visitor's
permit in China. My orders are not to let her talk with one man here."

"Abe Harrow?"

Tate looked up surprised. "Yes."

"You know Senor Abe?"

"Vaguely. I met him in Pekin some years ago, during my second
trip to China."

"And Senorita Woodford?"

"No. Mind you, I'm not sure, but I doubt she's ever seen Harrow.

Somehow she got his name. Where? That's a mystery. And what she wants of him, I don't know. Anyway, Harrow at present is under a cloud of official suspicion—the old squeeze business."

"Are you sure?"

"No. Why?"

"*Oyeme*," said Quinto. "Three days ago, April *primero*, Senor Harrow asked me for a *salvo*, a military pass to Pan Tao. He was very anxious. So I had Virtue follow him. He succeeded in eluding her and today he returned."

Quinto dismissed the bath boy and began dressing. He looked at Tate, saying:

"But perhaps the Englishwoman will never meet Harrow. Lingtung might take care of that."

"You've arrested Harrow?"

"He is not the kind you arrest," Quinto shrugged. "That is not for Harrow. Lingtung has other ways. Remember, Chiang Kai-shek was once kidnaped in Lingtung."

CHAPTER 3
He Dead!

NEVADA disconsolately walked toward the pink brick guardhouse at the entrance of the Lingtung Pavilions gardens. His lean cowboy face was creased in thought. He was in love! A dry scaffolding of a man who seemed to have grown up only lengthwise, he found it almost impossible to convey his feelings to Mary Wier.

Mary was a missionary's daughter. She was a pretty girl and as Nevada put it, "kind of moody." He had tried to tell her about the West—Arizona, Nevada, Utah. She had been born in China. He even asked her if she would care to see the West after the war was over, but Mary had become very quiet. She changed the subject, leaving him to wonder if she, after all, knew what was on his mind and didn't want him to speak. That moodiness was very strange. It puzzled him.

On another occasion he had talked about himself, explaining in his own unadorned drawl how he had come to China, working for the government as a cattle-breeder, then deserting the model farm at Chen-kiang to join the army. He liked the Chinese people and sympathized with them. Mary had said she and her father disapproved of war. She had said that because she knew what he was going to say next—that he was glad he had met her in China.

Nevada frowned, unable to understand the strangeness of the girl. She was pretty and young; still, she was afraid of something, so afraid that she wouldn't let him say it.

At the guardhouse, the frown upon his face relaxed to greet Sergeant Sun. He couldn't help smiling at Sun*, for the latter, like most Chinese soldiers, was ragged, looked unmilitary, but still maintained an ingenuous smiling front. Sun came from Shantung province where pongee silk is made, women are handsome and 111,000,000 eggs are laid per year. With such a provincial heritage upon his shoulders the young man took his soldiering seriously and out of sheer patriotism stood a permanent guard at the Pavilions' main gate.

"Not good bad be sadden," he crowed cheerfully.

"Hello, Sun. Anything new?" Nevada drawled.

The Sergeant shook his head vehemently, answering in his private version of pidgin English which he used with a modicum of vanity even on native comrades. "Capin Queeto not commee backward. Shoo foreign missy chop chop Doc Meeki Mountain Virtue."

Nevada listened indifferently. He glanced through the doorway of the guardhouse where Sun operated a miniature farm. The place was crammed with an odd assortment of potted plants, stunted peach trees, tufts of wheat in various stages of cultivation. "Nice stuff," Nevada remarked, thus winning the undying gratitude of the lad.

"Want lookee mold from oak leafs?" Sun asked affably, pointing his captured bolt-action Japanese rifle toward a corner of the guardhouse.

Nevada shook his head and wandered on through the walled garden. The scent of fresh jasmine hung heavy along the walls where the wind failed to disturb it. Here and there the roofs of tiny pavilion houses appeared above the greenery like horned new moons with up-curling edges. He halted on the arch of a half-moon bridge spanning a small canal and thoughtfully watched a dozen white ducks run through noisy fleet formations upon the turquoise water below.

"Nevada—"

He looked up and found himself staring at Mary Wier. For the hundredth time he caught his breath. He wasn't used to girls like her. He was fascinated by her tiny hands and ridiculously small feet in their absurdly high-heeled pumps. A little Dresden doll of a girl in a fluttering white dress, talking to six feet and more of lanky cowboy! In spite of himself, Nevada wanted to laugh, but he saw that her forehead was wrinkled anxiously.

"Nevada," she repeated his name. She was more upset than he had ever seen her. "What does the army do about people who . . . ah . . . people who are suspicious?"

Nevada looked at her incredulously. "What do you mean?" he asked slowly.

"Well, what would happen in Lingtung, or here, if there were a spy? Would he be shot? Or would he have a trial?"

"Who?"

"No, Nevada, you don't understand. Just supposing?"

"It depends. Here, Quinto is in charge."

"And there wouldn't be a trial?"

"That depends again. If there's an out-and-out spy or someone mussing with sabotage, he's just plain ordinary shot."

"Who would have to give the final order, Captain Quinto?"

"Yeah."

Mary looked relieved for a moment.

"You worrying about Clive Firth?" Nevada suddenly asked.

"Yes, I'm afraid."

"I wouldn't worry about it, Mary."

"But this morning I heard Clive and Captain Quinto arguing. Clive threatened that if the army didn't shoot Abe Harrow, he'd do it!"

"What did Quinto say?"

"He just shrugged his shoulders, that's all."

Nevada avoided her eyes. "That's what I figured," he said. "I saw Harrow go up the mountain this morning. Firth wasn't far behind."

Abruptly the small spots of red in each of Mary's cheeks faded. She glanced down at the ducks in the canal, favoring them with a distressed look. The ducks ignored her and swung into battle line, preparing to engage the enemy, a black swan that carelessly chased a goldfish across the canal.

Then Mary gasped and her hand flew to her throat. Nevada's eyes followed the direction of her gaze, sweeping toward the far side of the bridge. The lines around his mouth tightened at the sight of Clive Firth.

Firth came over the bridge, limping badly. His clothes were torn and his face was scratched and bleeding. He halted for a moment, breathing heavily.

"Is Quinto back yet?" he asked.

Nevada shook his head. "He's still in town."

"Clive! What happened?" Mary cried.

She was as pale as a ghost.

Firth glanced at her and then at his clothes. He smiled wryly. "What a mess! I strayed off the trail and slipped." He brushed his disheveled brown hair from his forehead, and fishing a cigarette from his pocket, lit it nervously. Then he stared curiously at both Nevada and Mary. "What's wrong?" he asked.

With a little sob that caught in her throat, Mary turned and ran through the garden toward the small pavilion where she and her father lived. Both Firth and Nevada stared after her, astonished.

"Well—" Nevada finally asked. "Where's Harrow?"

For a man who had set out to kill another man and had returned alone, Firth looked cool and composed. He dragged deeply on his cigarette while glancing sharply at the cowboy. His eyes, however, betrayed excitement.

"The last I saw of Harrow, he was going up the mountain," said Firth.

"Alive?"

"Yes, alive."

Nevada shrugged. This wasn't his department. He was a

machine-gunner. Firth was a political director. It was Firth who had caught Harrow speculating with Chinese money a week ago. He also had the reports on Harrow stealing valuables from the Pavilions.

Firth tossed his cigarette away. "I'm going to town," he said abruptly. "If I miss Quinto, tell him I want Harrow arrested the moment he comes in."

Sergeant Sun was earnestly exhibiting his potted farm to a strange woman with a freckled Yorkshire nose when Nevada came to the guardhouse again. Doc McKay was there and Nevada started to tell him something, then changed his mind because of the woman.

"Are you Harrow?" the Englishwoman asked him bluntly.

Nevada caught his breath and glanced questioningly at McKay.

"He's not Harrow," said McKay.

"Oh!" the lady looked disappointed. "I'm sorry," she said. "I didn't realize there were other white people here besides Doctor McKay and Mr. Harrow. Well, I'm glad to meet you. I'm Mildred Woodford. I left Captain Quinto in town and came on ahead with the doctor and Miss Virtue. That's an amazing name, don't you agree? Virtue— do you imagine she really is?"

Mildred Woodford paused and looked at Nevada sharply. "When do you expect Harrow back? Isn't he generally around?" she asked.

Nevada shook his head.

"Are you a guerrilla fighter?" asked Mildred Woodford. "I'm sorry, I didn't get your name?"

"Nevada."

"Is it American or Spanish?"

"American."

"Lovely garden here, isn't it?" The Englishwoman passed from one subject to another with the ease of a gymnast swinging from trapeze to trapeze.

"Not many gardens left like this in China," McKay interrupted. "It was a hotel before the war. The big pavilion there—" he waved his hand toward a large, one-story, sprawling pavilion with crimson columns— Quinto's *yamen*. It houses the Guerrilla School office, library, dining rooms, my surgery and the billiard room. In the old days hotel guests slept in the smaller villas scattered through the garden. The Little Garden Theatre, over on the left, used to show opera. Chinese opera. It's a barracks now."

"Are you part of the school, Mr. Nevada?" Mildred Woodford asked. "And the other foreigners?"

"People just came," McKay explained tartly. "Nevada was wounded, weren't you, lad?" He glanced at the cowboy, then returned his gaze to the woman's incredible nose. "Nevada came here for a rest. Harrow sort of invited himself in. No reason. And the others simply seeped in. Whenever G.H.Q., that's Quinto, took his fighting laddies into enemy territory for a bit of field training someone moved in at Lingtung. The Wiers came that way. Japs captured their mission. Wang*, on the other hand, was here already."

"Wang?"

"The Banker Wang. He owns the big villa across the garden at the foot of the mountain. I'll show it to you later. It's just across the canal that your pavilion is on. . ."

McKay suddenly stopped talking to stare beyond the garden gate at a strange procession approaching along the Lingtung road.

"Good Lord! What's that—a parade?" said Miss Woodford.

Ten Chinese peasants from the town surrounded a Sian cart and were vociferously urging a decidedly stubborn Shensi donkey to make haste with the cart. A number of the peasants ran ahead, lighting and tossing little red firecrackers on both sides of the road.

"There's something up," said McKay after a moment. "The blighters are doing their damnedest to scare the devils and spirits away from that cart. Sun—"

The young sergeant had already run out to meet the procession. Following a minute or two of parley, he yelled for Nevada. Then he began shouting excitedly.

"Mista Harro—killed dead. He velly dead!"

Nevada quickly climbed upon the cart, looking in over the backboard.

Abe Harrow's body was stretched upon a straw pallet. The flesh on his upturned face was fishbelly white and the features were twisted in frozen pain. A trickle of dark dried blood had hardened in the corner of his mouth. His arm was bent back in the straw, oddly.

"Hey Doc!" Nevada looked back. Suddenly he saw McKay holding Mildred Woodford's limp body.

"Fainted!" McKay snapped. "What does she think China is—a tea party?"

---

*Wang needs an Iowa farmer's twang to sound like *warng*.

CHAPTER 4
Murder Graduates to Mystery

JOHN TATE was quite mellow and a little unsteady. After leaving the communal bath, both he and Quinto had paused at Lingtung's only open-air teahouse, where business went on as if there were no war. A score of citizens, mostly tradesmen and artisans, lolled on rattan chairs, taking the last hours of sunlight to sip cups of weak, bitter tea.

"Only animals and savages practice sobriety," Quinto had said to the waiter. "I will start with five or six Shanghai Sherries."

"Our Sherry is of unspeakable taste," said the waiter.

"Make it seven, then," said Quinto.

Tate had regarded the Mexican with a degree of awe; and the awe doubled as he slowly realized that the latter spoke Chinese as flawlessly as he did English.

"You drink?" Quinto asked.

Though moderate in his ways, Tate agreed. Long ago, during his scholarly probings of the Chinese Liang Dynasty, approximately 505 A.D., he had unearthed an emperor who, it is said, got high on distilled grain and painted Chinese characters with masterly strokes. It was not for Tate to flaunt prohibition in the face of such a precedent.

So he had matched Quinto's sherry with North China Whiskey, a distillation of peanut oil, gasoline and alcohol invented by a Shensi native who had once washed glasses in a Denver, Colorado, speakeasy where prohibition liquor had never been at its best.

A while later, both Tate and Quinto left the bright little village, striking out along the cobbled road leading to the Lingtung Pavilions. Quinto hummed a sprightly Mexican air, occasionally bursting into verse as he supported his companion.

> *Viva la China Brigada*
> *Rumba-la, rumba-la, rumba-la-la*
> *No tenemos tanques,*
> *Ni aviones,*
> *Ni canones . . .*

"Street's terribly hilly. Really awful hilly," Tate worried, stumbling over the cobbles at each step but nevertheless negotiating the way in a half-creditable manner for a calligraphist.

The steady, less blustery wind along the cypress-bordered one-mile road, combined with the pleasant warmth of the late afternoon sun and Quinto's hale companionship, apparently washed the bitter reflections of the past few days from Tate's memory. "Lingtung is wonderful," he murmured. "Quinto is wonderful. Everything is momentarily magnificent."

From time to time he cast admiring glances at his companion's loose-fitting, or rather, sagging pea-green trousers and cotton shirt. He openly envied the fancy jade chopsticks in Quinto's breast pocket and he resolved that, upon the first suitable occasion, he'd purchase himself a similar outfit. He might even get the bandoleers of bullets and pistols that the Mexican no doubt carried on certain adventures.

Arriving at the Lingtung Pavilions' gate in such a mood, Tate let out a sigh of utter satisfaction upon sighting the camphor- and jasmine-scented gardens beyond. It was indeed a true Chinese garden, designed so as to present an endless prospect of artfully concealed surprises, lagoons, little canals, small hills, hidden villas and the toe of a sacred mountain. Tate sighed again, murmuring, "What a perfect background for her—Mountain of Virtue."

Suddenly he stumbled back in alarm. A smiling soldier in tattered trousers swung out past the gate with a rifle twice his own size. The lad immediately snapped his gun to attention, incidentally knocking off his peaked cap in the operation.

"*Sargento* Sun," Quinto explained.

"Foreign missy commee," said Sun to Quinto. He stared wide-eyed at Tate's rumpled Palm Beach. "Missy want find out Capn Queeto got one piece wife? Doc Meeki got one piece wife? Everybody got him one piece wife?"

Tate hiccoughed. "Oh, My God—Woodford!" he groaned.

"Missy say sickee. Not visit supper," said Sun.

"The Senorita is sick?" asked Quinto. "*N'importa.*"

"Plenty sick. Spend lots time look Mista Harro get sick chop chop."

Tate quickly lost his flush of liquor. "She's started already. She's been trying to contact Harrow," he said. Sergeant Sun was still bursting with information. He curled his bare toes in the rich earth and looked gleefully at Quinto. "Missy take one look running Mista Harro—he velly dead. Get plenty sickness."

"Harrow—?" Quinto snapped.

"Yessum!" His private version of pidgin being insufficient to handle so delectable a subject as Harrow's death, Sun reverted to his native tongue and rapidly explained the details with appropriate gestures, exactly as he had gotten them from the peasants who had found the body.

Harrow's battered remains had been discovered jammed among huge rocks half way up the Wei Ho side of Running Wind Mountain. The American Ambulance Corps captain had fallen over a sheer cliff, a two-hundred-foot drop. The natives had identified a dozen prominent Mountain Spirits who might have had something to do with it, depending on exactly which ones Mr. Harrow had insulted.

"Fine accident, yessum," Sun reverted to pidgin with iconoclastic glee. The young sergeant believed only in the stock Chinese Wind and Water Spirits, rejecting Mountain Spirits as an upper-class superstition.

"A-A-Accident, did you say?" Tate put in. Although still hiccoughing in a major key, he appeared to be fuzzily grasping at some half-formed impression lost in the curtain of his memory. A look of suspicion, then clear-cut shock flashed into his albino eyes as he gazed at the Mexican.

"Harrow was murdered?" he gasped.

"Murdered?" said Quinto, almost casually. "Murder is a loose word. Accident, perhaps. Running Wind Mountain is notorious for its dangerous cliffs." He took Tate by the arm, propelling him gently through the gardens to the main pavilion.

"He was thrown off!" Tate gave vent to a whistle.

"An accident," Quinto repeated stoically. "A very fortunate accident. But say nothing about it now. At supper you shall hear more."

"But what's this all about?"

"Save the curiosity, *companero*. We go in."

Passing through a half-moon arch to the porch of the rambling main pavilion, Quinto silently pointed at the scars of bullet holes in the scarlet columns. The doorway of the *yamen* building was blocked by a spirit screen with a dragon design sketched upon it, for, unlike human beings, Cathay spirits could move only in straight lines. The screens kept them out of houses. Once past the elaborate obstacle, the two men stood in a large room, and face to face with a glass museum case. A pair of carefully polished false teeth grinned toothily at them from a plush pillow under the glass. A bronze tag, engraved in modern characters, read:

His Excellency the Generalissimo's—1936

"Chiang Kai-shek's. I will tell you about them later," Quinto explained. *"Son de on arrastrado."*

Two men were playing billiards on a slashed snooker table at the far end of the room, obviously killing time until supper. One was a gaunt Occidental with tufted brows; the other, a handsome, stubbily built Chinese dressed outlandishly in plus fours, orange and blue golf sox and brown, mildewed two-tone oxfords. On the latter's woolen sweater a safety pin held the insignia of an army lieutenant and the red star of the Fourth Army Corps. His head was bandaged.

Quinto introduced them as Doctor McKay and Lieutenant Chi.* Tate quickly decided that he liked them both. McKay's eyes were humorous and warm; his accent at times seemed more American than Scotch. And Lieutenant Chi swept aside a full half hour of customary ritual, greetings, exchanges of calling cards and incidental Oriental politenesses by extending his hand and shaking Tate's vigorously, almost in the manner of a Y.M.C.A. summer-camp director.

Lieutenant Chi spoke excellent English, salted with as many American and British slang expressions as he had been able to pick up from an untold number of foreign movies. He took Tate in tow, showing him the guerrilla school library off to the right of the billiard room, McKay's surgery adjoining that, the student mess on the opposite side, Quinto's once, Virtue's room and the quarters assigned to Tate himself. The doorway of each of these rooms opened in upon the billiard hall. During the tour, Chi unwound the bandage on his head, exhibiting a shaved spot where a wound was healing.

"Japanese shrapnel," he said succinctly. "105 millimeter shell. Not quite hard enough. I'm tough, I am."

"You like to eat? We put on the feed bag?" asked Lieutenant Chi.

"I haven't much appetite, but I'd better, though."

The lieutenant led the way to the international dining table, which, with the coming of spring in Lingtung, had been set on the garden terrace beyond the billiard room. The terrace overlooked a small canal that wound through the gardens.

"Like movies—atmosphere," said Chi.

There was indeed atmosphere on the terrace. The sky overhead was dusted with a silvery powder of clouds and stars, while a mild breeze swept the heavy odor of jasmine across the canal. A pet cricket, hanging in a cage, chirped noisily. The long dining table was illuminated by oil lamps that shed a yellow light over the setting of knives, forks and bamboo chopsticks. There was a translucent Chinese plum flower in a col-

*Chi calls for pronunciation as the *chee* in cheese.

ored pot in the center of the table.

Tate sat between McKay and Lieutenant Chi, the latter making introductions as they were needed. Quinto took his place at the head of the table beside Mountain of Virtue, and pulling his personal jade chopsticks from his pocket, made a flourishing gesture toward the food, like a cavalry officer ordering an attack with the sweep of his saber.

The internationals were a curious group, and even Tate reacted. He ran his eyes appraisingly around. The cowboy, Nevada, was an interesting type. A cool one, thought Tate. His gaze went on to Mary Wier and her father.

The missionary, Papa Wier, as he was called, was a man approaching gray hair, a man turning bitter. He was thin without showing signs of having been underfed or overworked. His type was easily recognized—Old China Hands; they were all alike.

They sat in Shanghai or Pekin legations, bars and clubs, scrupulously minding the "Don't Commandments" which regulated the lives of well-behaved foreigners in China. The commandments were simple and direct: Don't mix with natives. Don't try to speak their language or it'll make you queer. Don't be seen with any but the right people. Don't drink anywhere but in the right places. Don't worry too much about wars and revolution and bandits; everything is always upset in China. Don't read anything but the *North China Daily*. And above all, don't marry a Russian girl.

Tate's glance rested momentarily on Mary Wier. She was blond and pretty, almost doll-like. Then two newcomers entered the terrace, and were introduced by Chi. The first was Mignon Chauvet, a young and rather attractive Frenchwoman. A first impression of her was one of mystery. Her straight black hair and excitable eyes called for speculation as to why a woman as attractive as Mignon Chauvet had come to Northwest China alone.

Mr. Wang, a middle-aged, middle-class Chinese, took his place beside her. He barely nodded at the others. He was a smooth, formal man dressed in black. His eyes flashed an inner mental vigor, perhaps ruthlessness. Lieutenant Chi explained that he was an administrator connected with the Bank of China's Sianfu branch.

Word had already gotten around that Abe Harrow was dead, but strangely everyone seemed to make a point of not discussing it. The atmosphere at the table was strained. There were three empty places, one for Miss Woodford, who was ill and had taken her supper at her villa; and two places reserved for Harrow and Clive Firth. As supper progressed, the sense of strain increased. Mignon Chauvet was visibly preoccupied; the Wiers ate next to nothing; Mr. Wang gulped his food down wolfishly. From time to time eyes made fitful pauses upon the three empty places.

Finally Quinto, after expressing his appreciation for the food in the Chinese manner by belching heftily, addressed the internationals. "*Companeros—*" he began.

There was an absolute silence.

"*Companeros.* Senor Abe Harrow died today. An accident, perhaps. Sometimes men are unfortunate in war. I must ask you to forget the matter once you leave this table. No conversation about Harrow. We have a journalist visiting the Pavilions. Possibly she does not understand the problems of China and she may imagine Senor Abe was murdered. You understand?"

All eyes shifted to the three empty places.

Nevada nodded. "You see Firth this afternoon?" he asked.

"No."

"He went to town, looking for you."

"The laddie was in a wee bit of a hurry," McKay put in.

Mountain of Virtue raised her head calmly. "It is not unusual for Gimiendo's assistant to be going back and forth hurriedly.... He has many important things to do!" she said.

Mary Wier suddenly dropped her fork, making Tate start. Mary's face was flushed and angry.

"Why don't you say it out!" she cried bitterly. "Why not say it—" She turned, pointing an accusing finger at Mignon Chauvet. "And you, why don't you say it? You drove him to it. You hated Abe Harrow!"

Mignon turned pale, her eyes flashing hatred as she stared at Mary. Then, without a word, she rose and left.

"Mary!" Papa Wier's smooth hand drew the girl into her chair.

"It's awful!" Mary's lips trembled emotionally.

John Tate sat there nervously. He blushed as if he were sitting in on a personal problem. He watched Wang the banker leave the table with a curt bow. Then McKay nudged him. There was a saturnine expression on the doctor's face.

"She's trying to say Clive killed Harrow. *Of course he did! It was necessary!*"

An icy silence cut through the talk at the table. Not a fork dropped, barely a breath had been taken. In the sudden silence McKay's words stood out, bold and naked. Abruptly, McKay sucked in his breath and stared toward the doorway.

Clive Firth stood there, quietly surveying the terrace. His eyes, as they shot toward the Wiers, then at McKay, revealed an intellectual force that could be felt at once.

"So I killed Harrow!" he said flatly.

Doc McKay coughed harshly. He looked as though he were enjoying this.

"What is this—a conspiracy?" snapped Firth. "I haven't seen Harrow since this morning. The fact is, I didn't know he was dead until Sun told me, and that after I returned from town!"

Something in Firth's voice and in his way of looking straight into and through each person at the table left them with the feeling that the man was speaking the truth. He hadn't killed Harrow!

CHAPTER 5
Eleven-Eighteen to Eleven-Fifty

GIMIENDO QUINTO looked particularly upset for a man of his size and stability. He was, for his authority at the Pavilions had been seriously undermined. His smudgy black eyes quickly dropped upon each person at the table for a piercing instant.

"*No me gusta*, I don't like it," he said. "A dangerous precedent, very dangerous, murder without Gimiendo knowing the arrangements. I am *responsable* here, is that understood?"

There was an uneasy silence. The cricket, chirping in its cage, sounded like an off-key symphony. Quinto waited for a moment, fingers drumming on the table. "Well, who is *responsable* for. . . ah . . .Senor Harrow?" he finally demanded.

"You ought to be relieved that Harrow is dead and forget it," said McKay.

"I saw him start up the mountain this morning," Clive Firth put in, "but I said I didn't kill him! God knows, there were enough grounds for him facing a firing squad, but I didn't do it!"

Papa Wier looked up from across the table.

"Perhaps we're jumping at conclusions," he said in an even tone. "I doubt he was murdered. Mountains are dangerous and it could have been an accident after all."

Lieutenant Chi glanced at the missionary in an odd manner. "Funny accident," he murmured.

"Mountains are damn dangerous. Particularly when there were a couple of people up there besides Harrow who are hoping I won't mention the fact," Firth said bitingly.

"Others on the mountain?" McKay looked around quizzically. "Hmm, sportsmen around here."

Quinto stood up, his hands on the table.

"We begin immediately," he said. "I am going to find who killed Harrow by midnight if I have to keep everyone out of bed!"

John Tate had been listening to the developments with avid interest. He turned to McKay, asking:

"Do the Lingtung police come in?"

"Quinto *is* the police. This is a war. He's the commander here and it's his party, though I see no reason for so much fuss over Harrow. And if he throws Firth out, who's he going to suspect? Everyone around here had a motive—no one liked Harrow!"

Mountain of Virtue shook her head tolerantly and favored the doctor with a reproving glance.

"But Doctor McKay," she said, "since everyone knew, or thought Clive Firth would . . . execute . . . Mr. Harrow, why would they bother with such a business? It seems that they might have had some other reason for wanting Mr. Harrow murdered, and they might have wanted quicker action than the Chinese Army might furnish."

"We will discuss this later," Quinto interrupted. "*Ahora*, I have other work before we begin an investigation. Senor Tate, you can do me a favor . . ."

Tate's round face glowed, pleased at being taken into the Mexican's confidence so readily.

"First," Quinto went on, "this whisky-drinking Senorita Woodford is a writer. Writers are not to be trusted. I believe she had better leave Lingtung for a day or so. This for my own peace of mind. Take her to Sianfu. A fast car, no?"

"Sianfu?" Tate looked doubtful.

"It's only twelve miles. You will do it immediately. Virtue will telephone reservations at the Guest House. One of the guerrilleros can drive you. Now, let's see." Quinto turned to McKay. "Did the lady see Harrow's body when it was brought in?"

McKay shook his head.

"Hardly," said the doctor. "She heard Sun fuss about him being dead and she fainted on the spot."

"Good! Senor Tate, you tell her a mistake was made. It was not Harrow, but one of the guerrilleros who was brought in dead. Let her know that Abe Harrow is in Sianfu at the Guest House. She will go readily. In fact, she'll no longer be sick."

Lieutenant Chi was sent with Tate to drive out the Guerrilla School's official car, a Studebaker sedan which had been captured by error from a friendly General Staff on the other side of Sianfu. Meanwhile, Virtue went off to telephone Sianfu. Now Quinto, going with Firth and McKay into the billiard room, suddenly spoke in a lower voice.

"Who were the two on the mountain?" he asked Firth. "Besides Harrow."

"Who? Oh! Well, Papa Wier for one. The other fellow I've never seen and I didn't get a good look at him. A chap in a yellow trench-coat."

"Chinese?"

"That I don't know. They weren't on the top of the mountain, really. They were waiting in Chiang's cave, halfway up the trail."

"Did you speak with them?"

"No. They didn't see me. I tried spying on them but they just waited there a bit, then came down."

"Yes," said Quinto, thoughtfully, "waiting, perhaps waiting for Harrow!" He frowned for a moment while unpacking some tobacco and rolling himself a cigarette. "Ah, Firth, you had better run across the garden to Harrow's villa. See that no one enters until I come."

McKay and Quinto went through the library adjoining the billiard room into the doctor's surgery. It was a small, bare room fitted out with a table, a bench, a few shelves loaded with medicines. McKay himself lived in a small villa across the garden, which he shared with Lieutenant Chi.

"It's a hailsome sight to be looking at a corpse not peppered by shrapnel, bullets and the like," said the doctor.

Harrow's rigid body rested on the floor of the surgery in a blanket, exactly as it had been left by the peasants who had brought him to the villas. Quinto stooped over it, his fingers feeling through the dead man's pockets.

"No papers," he observed. "That's not right. Senor Harrow always carried official papers." He glanced at McKay questioningly.

"Didn't search him," said McKay. "Only looked to his hurts. There's plenty of them."

"No wounds?"

"Bullet or knife, you mean? Nay. There's not a thing wrong with him, but a broken neck, smashed third vertebrae, compound fracture right arm, hard bruises on the body. I think Clive simply gave him a hefty push off that cliff."

"What else?"

"Probably died instantly or a very few minutes after. Probably in very sharp but short pain."

Still kneeling beside the body, Quinto looked at it grimly. Suddenly he brushed Harrow's matted hair back over his brow and straightened the man's necktie. Then, as though not satisfied, he straightened the torn shirt and trousers. This time he stood up, shaking his head.

"*Yes*," he said, "There is something wrong with Harrow. He's not himself. Harrow was always very neat; his boots, his creased trousers, his tie and coat." Quinto stopped. "Yes, where is Harrow's coat?"

McKay didn't answer.

"He wore one, as usual?" said Quinto.

"I suppose so. Harrow never went without a coat."

"So . . . Why would anyone want it?"

"It was a good one. The peasants could have kept it."

Quinto's brows knitted together. Outside, in the night, an automobile engine roared. Tate taking the Englishwoman to Sianfu. The sound of the engine faded in the distance and the Mexican sighed, a weight relieved from his mind. He looked at the body again.

"When did he die?"

"Simple," said McKay, pointing at Harrow's arms. There were two watches strapped to his right wrist, one on his left. "The three of them stopped the minute he crashed among the rocks. But you figure it out."

Quinto knelt again, turning Harrow's stiff wrists with difficulty. Rigor mortis had already set in. "*Muy curiosa,*" he murmured at length. "The one watch reads 11:18, this morning naturally. The second says 11:30 and the third watch contradicts with an 11:50. So—it was very thoughtful of Senor Harrow. He died at three distinct times."

"Well, you've something to work with, man. That is, if you think someone else did it. I'm still in favor of crediting Clive. Give him a medal and let the fool business slide."

Quinto thrust up his shoulders dubiously. "It's like saying he died daylight-saving time, standard time and war time," he observed whimsically. "So, if it was an accident . . . But then there were people on the mountain?"

"Mountain climbing is a mania in China," McKay cut in dryly. "Probably find there were a dozen people up there."

"Yes, so I think," Quinto nodded wisely. "We'll check with Sergeant Sun and find who left the gardens this morning. Which reminds me. Where were you before you met me in Lingtung?"

"Me? Hah, right here. Had a case."

"Who? One of my guerrilleros?"

"Yes. Young Liang. He had a bad case of tri-motors—trench lice."

Quinto smiled complacently.

"Let's go see Sun. *Vamos.*"

As they left the *yamen* pavilion they came upon Virtue, who was watching a group of the Chinese guerrilleros surround the building, stationing themselves at the various doorways, windows and cracks. The students were preparing to lay a barrage of fireworks to keep evil spirits away from the body in McKay's surgery.

Seeing the girl, Quinto brightened up considerably, a tendency most men yielded to upon viewing her.

"Mr. Tate and the lady are gone," she said, smiling in amusement.

"Miss Woodford insisted upon driving herself. She wouldn't take Lieutenant Chi."

"Where is Firth?"

"You sent him to Harrow's villa."

"Ah, yes. Then let us visit the *sargento*."

"I have, already," Virtue smiled again.

"So?"

Virtue prefaced her words with a pretty tilting of her head to the right. "Sun speaks with exactness worthy of China," she said. "Mr. Harrow departed from the gardens at ten-thirty this morning, wearing his usual uniform, cross belts and a walking stick."

"Swagger stick," said McKay.

"Mr. Harrow was in no haste," she continued. "Shortly before that he was seen speaking with Papa Wier. Later, but before going up the mountain, he lingered beyond the North Gate conversing with a stranger in a yellow coat. He spoke with Mr. Yellow Coat for a moment, then they parted."

"Mr. Yellow Coat," said Quinto. "Is he Chinese?"

"No. Occidental."

"Where did this Yellow Coat go then?"

"Sun does not know."

Quinto, with Virtue anchored lightly to his arm, and the doctor walked through the starlit garden, making a small round before returning to the pavilion. Quinto rolled an inevitable cigarette.

"Nevada was at the guardhouse also," said Virtue. "And he climbed Running Wind Mountain this morning."

Quinto looked at her without surprise. "Did he tell you that?" he asked.

"No. He tried hiding it. It is my deduction."

"So, what have you found?"

"Nevada is hardly eloquent."

"Some deduction," McKay said.

"But I know what Nevada is hiding," Virtue went on calmly. "You know what? He was on the mountain, certainly. He was gathering flowers for Miss Wier. A beautiful, tender gesture, isn't it ? The handsome, silent American choosing flowers for a mere child of a woman."

"Cap'n G.H.Q.—" A Chinese soldier, wearing a red band on his sleeve to indicate that he was the Officer of the Night, appeared out of the garden shadows and saluted Quinto stiffly. "Sianfu telephone," he said.

Quinto smiled at the boy, one of his best guerrilleros. "*Mei yu fa tze*, not now," he said.

The officer insisted. "Won't let go wire."

Quinto looked annoyed, but he followed the boy into the *yamen*. He picked up the cradle French phone which had puzzled the Chinese for years and with a nod dismissed the boy. "*Lai*, who is it?" he shouted.

"Quinto?" replied the agitated phone voice.

"Yes, yes, Senor Tate. Oh yes."

Tate's voice returned with a frantic rise. "Hello, Quinto," he said, "we're in Sianfu. We've been, but can't we return?"

"*Madre! No!*" Quinto exploded. "You've hardly been there."

"Well, listen, Quinto, I'm just at my wit's end with what to do with Miss Woodford. I showed her the Chinese opera here. It's the second day and the theater had a beastly stench and you know how the English are about things like that. Have you settled the Harrow trouble so we can return?"

"No. But where are you now?"

"At the Guest House bar. Has anything new come up?"

"All right," said Quinto. "Drink the Senorita under a table or take her to a cinema next. There's an American one in Sianfu. But do not return until I call you."

The Mexican dropped the phone on its cradle.

"If she did not have such a ridiculous nose, she could stand the opera," he muttered disgustedly. "*Que vieja desgraciada hija de la guayava!*"*

*The author does not advise the reader to repeat this phrase to anyone who might understand it, and assumes no responsibility for damages resulting from its use.

CHAPTER 6
Deposit for Harrow

LIEUTENANT CHI was a patriot and a billiard player of no mean ability. He came from Hunanese stock, the South-of-the-Lake province where antimony is the chief wealth, people are soft spoken, red pepper is the principal diet, the manufacture of fireworks and enjoyment of revolution are the most common occupations. Hunan and Hupei are the Balkans of China.

Armed with such a background, plus a year laundrying in Brooklyn, U.S.A., Chi was prepared to revamp China in his inimitable modern manner. He introduced Y.M.C.A. exercises in the Fourth Route Army. So great was his admiration for Occidental habits that he scrubbed his teeth ruthlessly four times a day, wore golf togs when not in uniform, and sported fancy mechanical pencils for which he had no lead. The tables in his room sagged under the weight of numerous alarm clocks, for he admired the Western mania of exactitude.... A stitch in time saves . . .

In addition to billiards, Chi was an inveterate Brooklyn Dodger fan, but his judgment in this matter wasn't as good as his eye for a balkline shot, particularly the tricky reverse-English shot he had just made on the Pavilions' billiard table.

'You see that?" he called to Quinto. The latter had just stepped from his office to the billiard room and was muttering some deep and rather unintelligible things about telephones and Yorkshire noses.

"Spot you twenty-five, Captain," Chi added eagerly. 'Make it easy, straight-rail."

Quinto paused, his dark eyes moving over the warped billiard table. He selected a cue.

"Thirty," he said.

Chi bowed politely. "Twenty-six," he countered.

"Thirty," Quinto answered firmly.

A smile crossed the lieutenant's expressive face. "All right, I'll give you twenty-eight points and beat you anyway," he said, running around blocking the snooker holes at the corners and setting three chipped concrete balls on the table.

Quinto made the break and watched the balls wobble over the worn green cloth, bump sidewise over a patched area and settle sluggishly in perfect position for his opponent. He made a mental note that if ever, on one of his raids into Japanese territory, he should run across a billiard table with ivory balls he would bring back the balls.

"Did you dig out anything new on Harrow?" asked Chi as he addressed the table.

"Little things," replied Quinto. "Nothing important."

"Would my being on the mountain this morning help?"

"You were there too?"

"Right. My exercise."

"It was very interesting, no? Red sunrise, many people to watch?" Quinto's question followed the usual polite pattern of starting from the East and gradually approaching a problem from the Southwest.

The lieutenant was silent. His eyes eagerly followed a run of shots. Finally the run broke and he chalked up nine billiards for himself.

"If all my guerrilleros could only shoot as you play billiards!" Quinto complimented him.

"Did I mention I was on the mountain?" Chi suddenly asked.

"I'm not positive," Quinto murmured. Meanwhile he studied the balls intently and waited for Chi to perform an intricate Chinese mental maneuver, namely, the method of indirect accusation.

"Perhaps someone with a sharp eye whispered that I climb mountains," Chi spoke in a tone suggesting that everything he said was highly hypothetical. "Interesting goings-on on mountains," he continued. "My people revere them. The old emperors built roads to the tops of the best mountains and paid respect to many sunrises. Is it that someone has seen Lieutenant Chi paying such respect?"

"Doubtlessly," Quinto answered patiently.

"Was it Papa Wier or Wang or a stranger in a yellow coat?"

Quinto's cue slipped, gouging a furrow in the green billiard cloth. "Wang?" he asked.

"Oh, yes."

Quinto took a roll of adhesive tape from his pocket and carefully repaired the damage his cue had done to the cloth. "So Wang, Papa Wier and Mr. Yellow Coat were on the mountain. Hmm, and Nevada and Firth also. Did you see Nevada and Firth?"

"Firth, yes."

"Who else?"

"Harrow. No, I didn't see Harrow. That's sad, isn't it?"

Quinto deposited his cue upon the museum case containing the Generalissimo's teeth and patiently watched the lieutenant nurse the three billiard balls along the rail, then in a corner, carrying the run to where it would pass his own handicap. Suddenly Chi apologized for his high score.

"The balls are crooked," he said. "They come together with an unnatural affinity and I have no power to halt them."

"*Bueno*," said Quinto. "We'll pause and think about Harrow. When did you see the others on the mountain?"

"Standard time or war time?"

"Standard! "

"Well, then, about noon. Yes, noon exact. I recall having heard the Lunghai Express whistle as it rounded the curve. It was almost on time today."

"*Sigue adelante*—go on."

Chi contemplated the billiard score for a moment. "They were watching each other," he said. "A short time before noon I saw Wang. He passed Chiang's cave and went on up the trail. Then Papa Wier and Mr. Yellow Coat met in the cave at noon. They were apparently waiting for something. Mr. Firth crouched behind a rock watching them, that is, Wier and the Coat. Then these two returned toward Lingtung and Firth followed at a respectable distance. It was exactly then that Wang returned."

"So, what happened?"

"Wang saw Firth spying on the others, so he spied on Firth without Firth knowing it. So I spied on all of them and no one knew it."

Quinto thought this over for a moment.

"And only Wang went up the cliff trail?" he asked.

Chi nodded. "Perhaps he didn't like Harrow and wanted to erase him off. I regret, but I cannot believe in this theory of accident. In China there are only two sources of accident—flood and famine. If one does not die of these he eventually dies of old age or murder. Mr. Harrow hadn't much old age."

Quinto glanced toward the doorway and saw Mountain of Virtue step daintily around the spirit screen.

"Mr. Firth wishes you at Harrow's villa," she said. "He found something very extraordinary. A bank book!"

Quinto raised his brows interestedly.

"*Por Dios*," he murmured. "Did you see it?"

"Certainly, and it read very well. You will be pleasantly surprised."

Harrow's villa lay across the gardens, a hundred yards from the main pavilion and against the northwest wall. It was a small, low building designed in the Southern style. It had formerly been one of the private sleeping pavilions attached to the hotel. The place gave evidence of having absorbed some of Harrow's elaborate primness. Its two small rooms, a sitting room and sleeping quarters, were neatly arranged and furnished with lightweight rattan tables and chairs. In the bedroom, combs were placed just so upon a table. Boots and shoes were lined under the bed-edge like an army prepared to pass inspection.

In the larger sitting room the books, papers and a number of expensive pigskin valises were in greater disorder, mainly as a result of Clive Firth's investigation. Firth had emptied the contents of the cases on the floor, revealing Harrow's antiquarian leanings. There were dozens of silver pencils, cigarette cases, Chinese seal stones, a few excellent specimens of Han bronzes, a bronze kettle of the Chou Dynasty and a wider variety of jade objects.

Quinto suddenly reached down, his fingers closing upon a familiar jade fish. "So," he muttered. "Harrow even collected from me!"

"He was an expert collector," said Virtue and she exhibited a small statuette of a tiger cut in fine white jade sprinkled with green. "This tiger is beautiful. He has just had dinner. It is January and the sun is only beginning to warm the earth. He is not sure whether he smells the artist sculpting him or an odor of hyacinth. Do you know what this tiger is, Gimiendo?"

"Look here, Quinto," Firth interrupted. "I made out my report a week ago, Harrow stealing things. This is the proof. But God only knows, for some of this he must have robbed a museum!"

"Gimiendo, do you recognize this tiger?" Virtue asked again. "It is cut in what we call the *hua shueh tai tsao* jade, the moss entangled in melting snow. It is very very valuable. A Ming period piece. You will be able to trace it, I am sure."

Quinto took the tiger and, wrapping it in a wad of cotton, thrust it into his pocket. "Where is the bank book?" he said. "We'll let the jade stand until Tate returns. He knows such things."

Firth handed him a personal savings book issued by the Banque du Chine Central, a private French bank located in the foreign concession at Hankow. Harrow's name was typed upon the cover.

"He should have been shot the day he entered the army," said Firth.

Quinto waved his hand impatiently. As he flipped the pages of the bank book, his eyes grew larger and larger.

"Sixty-five thousand francs deposited in the last eight months," he said unbelievingly.

"Harrow didn't make that soldiering, I'll say that for him," Firth put in.

A folded slip of paper fell from the book. Quinto caught it in midair, and upon opening it, he simmered audibly. It was a military pass giving Captain Abe Harrow full permission to travel to Hankow and back and begging the railway officials to extend full military courtesy. It was written in English and signed by Gimiendo Quinto. In addition, it carried the official chop of the Guerrilla School.

"A forgery," said Quinto. "I made no pass for Harrow. Now another mystery. How did he get it? Look! Even the English is not in Harrow's handwriting!"

"But it's your handwriting, Gimiendo," said Virtue as she glanced at the pass. "Your hand is very distinctive."

"*Por Dios!* Mine. That's right," Quinto said vexedly. "But I didn't write it."

"It is likely," Virtue remarked, "as events complicate themselves, they become clearer. Mr. Harrow had sixty-five thousand francs in the bank. It would not be strange if he had more money to deposit, so he secures a pass to Hankow. But whoever helps him forge the pass suspects he has money—and murders him for it."

Virtue glanced idly at Quinto and Firth. "Did you know Papa Wier once practiced forgery?"

"Wier—a forger. Not the old man?" Clive Firth looked absolutely startled.

"But long ago," said Virtue. "Before New Zealand."

"It's not possible," cried Firth.

"But it is. I know."

"Where'd you hear it, *chica*?" asked Quinto.

Mountain of Virtue smiled enigmatically and the mere winsome parting of her lips worried Quinto more than the amazing fact that the straitlaced missionary had a background worth investigating.

"Teng Fa told me," said Virtue. Her lids drooped for a second, black lashes sweeping her cheeks with an air of indolent mystery.

CHAPTER 7
The Virtue of Virtue

QUINTO leaned over and looked at Virtue's tiny watch. It was 10 P.M., Harrow was still dead, and, as yet, no one was attached to the murder.

"Now it's my move," Quinto spoke with sudden decision. "My dear Virtue, between now and midnight you must see that Wang the banker has no desire to enter his villa. You begin instantly." He nodded to Firth. "Senor Clive, you come with me to the *yamen*."

With a new blush of rose on her cheeks and a certain artful smile made famous by Chinese artists for centuries, Mountain of Virtue departed. A moment later Quinto and Firth shut the door of Harrow's villa.

"You're going to search Wier's place too?" Firth asked as they crossed the gardens.

"Later," said Quinto. "Right now, I want what you call alibis. You will check where everyone was this morning between 11:18 and 11:50. Find where they went, why and when. Lieutenant Chi can give you the guerrillero roll call. Sun can also help you."

"Righto."

"I'll come to your villa later tonight for the list. Remain there," said Quinto as they entered the *yamen* where McKay and Nevada were playing billiards.

Quinto nodded at the men and stepped into his office and shut the door. He went to the phone.

"Connect me with Sianfu. Guest House. Suite 31." He waited a long two minutes, listening while the Chinese male operator in Lingtung convinced the Sianfu exchange that it was the Guest House and not Military Headquarters that was wanted. Finally there came a responsive click.

"Teng Fa?" said Quinto. "Yes. It is G.H.Q."

There was an appreciative answer in Chinese.

"*Mira*, Teng," said Quinto. "I want a favor. For China, yes. Please write me a complete biography of three people. Mr. Wang, the banker. James Wier. Yes, Wier, the former Shansi missionary. No, Shansi, not Shensi. Also a biography of Captain Harrow."

49

Teng Fa repeated the names.

"You might track down a man wearing a yellow trench coat. A raincoat," added Quinto.

"Chinese?" asked Teng Fa.

"No. I don't think so."

"Is that all?"

"Well, drop in at Lingtung Pavilions. How's your end of the war going?"

"Oh, fine."

Quinto set the phone down with a sigh of satisfaction for Teng Fa would not only furnish complete details on Senores Wier, Wang and Harrow, but he would even include family history up to the third generation back.

For the next ten minutes he busied himself shelling peanuts and stowing the empty shells in his pocket along with a small flashlight. Then he left the office, and upon coming down the steps of the building to the garden, he found Virtue already at work. She leaned, in the moonlight, against a scarlet pillar and was surrounded by an admiring crowd consisting of Wang, McKay, Nevada, Lieutenant Chi, Papa Wier, a few guerrilleros and a frail scholarly old Chinese named Mr. Ho.*

She had changed her dress and was now wearing a jacket of lake silk gauze with ivory buttons, a pair of teardrop earrings and, instead of a skirt, the traditional Chinese trousers of cream silk. Poised in the light of a late rising golden moon, she was like the liquid women portrayed in old silk water colors.

Mr. Ho, the old scholar, looked at her and almost swooned. With delirious roguishness he murmured the untranslatable of untranslatable Chinese words meaning woman of exquisite beauty:

"*Ayi, chia, jen . . . gulp . . . yuwan.*"

Virtue barely opened her lips, yet words fell forth like the strumming of lovely and exotic zithers. She recited the *Jade Staircase* of Li Fu:

> *Her jade white staircase is cold with dew,*
> *Her silk soles are moist, she lingered so long—*
> *Behind her closed casement, why does she wait,*
> *Watching through crystal panes the autumn moon?*

The men gathered around, sighed and stirred. Chi gazed at her in rapture, thinking of the poor princess waiting on a staircase until the dew descended, yet her loved one failed to come. Nevada stood by,

---

*Mr. Ho, pronounced *hoe.*

open-mouthed. Wang watched with subtle wolfishness.

With each recited verse, Mountain of Virtue changed her pose, always returning between numbers to the favorite pose of the ancient Chinese beauty, Princess Hsishih, who is usually pictured as an exquisite woman suffering from a toothache and showing her tiny but eloquent brows knitted. Such a pose hits even the most insensitive Chinese between the eyes with as much ease as *Mother Machree* in tenor reduces an Irishman to putty.

Quinto took one satisfied look at the scene and sailed past the group like a majestic battleship. On the gravel walk a dozen yards beyond, he saw Mignon Chauvet pacing up and down, glaring at Virtue and her admiring swains. He halted for a moment.

"You like poetry?" he asked. "*Es bonito, eh?*"

"I abhor it," Mignon snapped bitterly.

Quinto walked a few steps with her.

"You were very upset at dinner by the missionary *chica?*" he suddenly asked.

Mignon stopped abruptly and glared at him.

"Her," she cried. "I detest the little flirt." There was almost savage fury showing in her dark, excitable eyes.

Quinto raised his hand in a gesture of pacification. For a moment he stared around the side of the Pavilion where some four Chinese guerrilleros were setting off firecrackers at regular intervals to keep the spirits from McKay's surgery.

"Were you here around noon?" he finally asked.

"But yes."

"It is all I wish to know."

Quinto bowed informally and excused himself. He hurried around the east wing of the big Pavilion, across a small bridge that spanned the winding canal, past the Little Garden Theater where the guerrilleros were barracked, to Wang's private villa.

It was built much on the same pattern as Harrow's but had four rooms and an inner court. It was well hidden from the rest of the garden by a fence of thick bushes. Quinto scouted about cautiously, making sure Wang's two personal servants, who came each day from Lingtung, were not within. Then, almost painstakingly, he emptied his pocket, making little mounds of broken peanut shells upon the doorstep before entering.

Ignoring the bedroom and two sitting rooms that were furnished in a flamboyant Pekin style, polished hardwoods and gilded knickknacks, he went directly to Wang's personal office, a long L-shaped room on the south. He flashed his light around so that it took in the modern steel desk, a steel four-drawer filing cabinet, a table set with flowers, and a swivel chair imported by Wang from Shanghai.

Quinto went through the desk, examining the papers efficiently and carefully. They were almost all in Chinese, save one weather-stained, typed letter which instantly won the Mexican's undivided and puzzled attention. It was like nothing he had ever seen before and just as unintelligible:

3-15-38

SURFK	DLQUH	PLVHU	HFHWW	HVQXP	HURVH	1940D	5602V
HUD28	PDUVP	DLVRQ	WDQJS	DQWDR	SDLHP	HQWSR	XUVRO
GHGHW	RXWFR	PSWHV	XUGHU	QLHUS	DTXHW	GRLWH	WUHHU
QGXQR	WUHDJ	HQWPH	PHWHP	SFROQ	RKXUL	XVYXH	YVXHY

He did not attempt to make sense of the cipher, as it plainly appeared to be. It went into his pocket. He turned to the file cabinet, which produced more involved and uninteresting banking papers in the first two drawers and an assortment of shoes in the bottom two.

His searchlight flashed now toward three modern-style ledgers together on the table. They were thin and one was titled, "Wei jen," or "Dwarfmen," meaning Japanese. The second bore the Chinese character for foreigners and the third was untitled. Quinto opened number two book, then, as he read the pages, he sucked his breath in with a sibilant hiss. There was a page marked for Harrow, another for Wier, another with the name DuPont and perhaps a dozen more pages with unfamiliar foreign names. Under each name there were complicated entries dating back as far as ten months. Quinto studied the narrow page, reading:

> *Harrow*
> *February 10. Twelve chits numbered.*
> *February 30. Thirty-one chits numbered.*
> *March 20.   Eleven chits numbered.*
> *April 3.*

He got no further, for loud crackling of peanut shells on the outside door warned him of approaching footsteps. He flicked off his lamp and opening the tissue window shade let himself noiselessly over the sill into the garden brush outside.

There he listened, his huge body crouched in the shadows for a minute. From the *yamen* came the sound of exploding firecrackers. The peanut shells crackled again, then he heard a soft tapping. Moving stealthily, he crept through the brush, keeping out of the moonlight until he was in position to see Wang's doorway.

Suddenly a perplexed sound formed in his throat. He saw Mary Wier. She wore a black silk scarf over her head, partially hiding her face from the moon's rays, but her doll-like figure was easily recognizable. She raised her hand as though to knock on Wang's door again, then withdrew it and glanced nervously across the gardens toward the *yamen* where the firecrackers were bursting spasmodically. A few seconds passed and finally she hurried off, skirting around the rear of the *yamen* toward the villa she and her father occupied at the far side of the gardens.

"*Que pasa?*" Quinto murmured to himself. He hesitated a moment, then reentered Wang's office, took the three ledgers, and after a careful last look left. He returned to the main pavilion and entered the back way, unobserved. In his own office he shoved the ledgers under the bed and turned again to the phone.

"Sianfu. Guest House," he demanded.

Both operators, in Lingtung and Sianfu, were asleep. It took a few minutes to straighten them out. Finally the connection came through.

"Guest House. The room of Mr. Tate. American," said Quinto. "In the bar? Good. Give me the bar."

Tate's voice came over the phone:

"Hello, Captain Quinto. I'm following orders. I'm drinking her into immobility. It's very difficult. What did you want?"

"How good a calligraphist are you?" Quinto asked. "Do you know anything about ciphers?"

"A little," Tate replied. "But I'm a calligraphist. However, I had some cipher experience with the Press Bureau. What is it?"

"I have a cipher for you. Tomorrow return to Lingtung. Do not say anything. If possible, make Senorita Woodford remain in Sianfu. Perhaps she'll remain if you introduce her to my friend Ku Chu-tung, the Military Governor of Sianfu. He lives in the Guest House."

"I'll try."

"Don't drink too much. The woman is a dangerous drinker, I can tell."

"All right. I'll see you tomorrow. But I'll have to find someone to drive me back if I don't bring Miss Woodford. My arm, you know."

This time the phone clicked off at the Sianfu end.

Quinto busied himself about the room for a short while. He placed the jade tiger, found in Harrow's villa, along with the bank book in a small iron safe which had once been a prized possession of a neighboring warlord. He changed Wang's ledgers to a new hiding place under his mattress, the safe not being large enough. Then he ran through the personal columns of *Kiang County Daily News*, better known as the *Hsiang*

Kiang Erh Pao, hoping by some chance there might be another cipher there.

At quarter of twelve he set out, again by way of the Pavilion's back door, toward Firth's sleeping pavilion situated at the rear of the gardens near the South Gate which, according to Chinese custom, is opened only on rare occasions, such as to eject an inconstant wife.

He had to cross two small bridges, for the canal curved in a horseshoe at this point. To the right of Firth's pavilion was the darkened armory. Approaching his secretary's quarters, he suddenly heard voices and slowed his step.

Mignon Chauvet's voice came out, sharp and clear.

"*Mais oui!* I am not afraid to do it—if I must!"

"Quiet, Mignon! You speak too loud. There are others living in the gardens, you know." The latter voice was Clive Firth's.

Quinto stopped and listened, but the voices dwindled to a broken murmur and the firecrackers from the far end of the gardens caused an incessant din. Only once again did the voices increase in tone, and he caught a single phrase of Mignon's . . . "We will leave China then . . ."

Without having seen Firth, Quinto returned to the main pavilion, looking for Virtue. He found the girl still surrounded by ardent admirers and running through parts of the famous Chinese opera, *Liling Pei*. Quinto looked on, annoyed, for *Liling Pei*, at its shortest, was a three-day opera.

He yawned and peered at the raw outline of the Running Wind Mountain, its dark mass looming against the carbon-blue sky and pinhole stars. He resolved to see what the mountain had to say for itself in the morning. Then he glanced at his watch. It was midnight. Remembering his threat to uncover Harrow's murderer at this hour, he sighed meditatively.

"Tomorrow at midnight then. What is one midnight more or less?"

CHAPTER 8
Double the Dead

A HANDFUL of guerrilleros were shooting firecrackers under the surgery window at 6 A.M. At 6:30 a tinny bugle blew reveille, mostly as a formality, for everyone at the Lingtung Pavilions had been up for more than an hour. Throughout the early morning hours between reveille and sunrise, a steady crackle of rifles and the intermittent stutter of a machine-gun had accompanied the crowing of various sturdy roosters up and down the breadth of the garden-like Wei Ho Valley.

At eight o'clock Nevada and Gimiendo Quinto returned from the rifle range behind the gardens followed by fifty boisterous guerrilleros (ten others being on firecracker duty), who had dusted off some thirty sawdust-filled Japanese generals before breakfast. As they entered the *yamen*, Nevada set his light machine-gun, a Russian Dickteroff, upon the billiard table and headed directly for the student dining room.

"How about chow?" he called to Quinto.

"Later. I am expecting a visitor."

The easygoing Mexican entered his office and in confirmation of his very words, there was a visitor—Mr. Wang the banker. He stood in the exact center of the room, his face somber, his eyes glaring at Quinto with diamond hardness.

"You came early," remarked Quinto as he shut the door.

Wang stared venomously. His complexion was almost saffron color and his eyes bulged slightly. He was wearing the customary long black gown and the toes of his highly polished, pointed black military boots showed beneath the hem like the heads of diamond rattlers. A French Mauser automatic swung from a colored silk cord about his neck.

"My quarters were searched!" He spoke with an abrupt flatness and disregard for polite formalities. A sign that he was very angry.

"So?" Quinto asked blandly.

"Did you order it?" snapped Wang.

Quinto rolled his head negatively.

"Valuable papers were taken," said Wang. His eyes swept about the room, searching.

"I think you were robbed," Quinto answered cheerfully.

"I've never been robbed!"

Quinto hunched his shoulders and his face took on the bland immobility of the upper-class Oriental making a political deal. "It must have been the Japanese," he said. "I'll question *Sargento* Sun whether Japanese were about last night."

"You will return my papers immediately."

Quinto stepped to his map table, taking a bottle of Pedro Domecq and two cups. He calmly peeled the hard red shell from a pomegranate and broke its glossy fruit seeds into the cups. He then poured in the Domecq and mashed the seeds with a spoon.

"Will you take breakfast with me?" he said, waving a hand toward one of the cups.

"No. I breakfast alone," replied Wang.

With his cup, Quinto walked to the window. He looked out across the sunny garden as he spoke.

"I am very curious," he murmured. "I am not at all anxious to ask you why you went to the mountain yesterday. But it would be interesting to know who writes Wang messages in cipher? Eh?"

There was a strange silence. Sensing danger, Quinto spun around.

"I wouldn't do that!" he warned.

Wang stood there, his eyes flashing malevolence, the Mauser clutched in his hand, leveled at Quinto.

"The papers!" he snapped.

Suddenly the door opened behind the banker and Mountain of Virtue entered. Her mouth fell open a trifle, but only for an instant. She slipped into the room, shut the door partially and stared at Quinto with a speculative look that held something of a wistful tenderness.

"Good morning," she said, softly and liltingly.

Quinto sighed, for she looked particularly *hsiaochieh* with her creamy lids and their dark fringe of lashes sweeping over her eyes. Wang, on the other hand, shot her a disturbed glance. The malevolent glare in his eyes turned sort of wishy-washy. Thirty centuries of Chinese tradition had conditioned him for women like Virtue.

She merely extended her slim hand and Wang meekly handed her the Mauser. Another glance and she moved toward the door. Wang followed her obediently, gaining only enough composure as he went out to glare at Quinto with impotent malevolence.

As the door closed, leaving him alone, Quinto pursed his lips in a worried whistle.

"*Mi Padre!*" he murmured aggrievedly.

He was still simmering with a quiet kind of rage when the door opened a moment later and Mignon Chauvet entered. Mignon was in her hospital uniform and it made her body look very flat and sexless. She looked at Quinto, horrified. She was pale and trembling, leaning heavily against the door frame for support.

"Clive is dead—" she faltered.

CHAPTER 9
Firth

THE CORPSE of Clive Firth sat erect in a heavy reed chair. The chair faced the window diagonally, as though the young man had been looking out toward the South Gate. Clive's features were perfectly normal and he appeared to have accepted death calmly and willingly, in fact, hardly giving a thought to it.

Quinto frowned at the body. It was as if he didn't believe it. A suspicion of tears welled in the big man's eyes, making them incredibly soft and tender. He had loved Firth as one soldier loves another. Firth had been loyal—loyal to Quinto and to China. The Mexican brushed his hand over his face morosely, for he had not felt so deeply about anything for many years; not since the day, long ago, when they murdered Pancho.

"It's too bad, Quinto. But what do you make of it?" It was McKay. He was examining the bullet hole in Firth's chest.

Quinto ran his eyes thoughtfully around. Alertness returned to them. He saw the open window, facing the garden wall. The belongings in the room, a day-bed, a table, a file cabinet, a battered typewriter and a wardrobe had been hastily ransacked. Even the ribbon had been pulled out of the typewriter. There were papers scattered on the floor and clothes heaped in a bunch. The mattress of the bed had been ripped apart.

He turned to Mignon Chauvet, who sat on a stool, her back to the body. Her shoulders trembled emotionally. "You were here with Clive last night," he said.

Mignon shivered.

"Yes, but I went shortly after midnight."

"You were angry when you left?"

Mignon hesitated.

"*Venga*, senorita," Quinto spoke impatiently. "You argued. I heard you."

The Frenchwoman drew a sharp breath. "But yes, it was nothing, nothing at all," she cried.

"So you left Senor Clive dead?"

58

The girl's eyes and mouth showed sudden horror.

"*Non! Non!*" she cried bitterly. "He was alive when I left him! We had an argument, yes. That is all. I returned this morning because I was sorry for being angry and I found him . . ."

Quinto's smoky eyes were riveted across the room on a spot beneath the table. He went over and picked up a small capsule made of aluminum. Unscrewing the top, he tipped the object and shook it. A powdery, white crystalline substance fell into his palm—heroin! "*Muy interesante*," he murmured, refilling the capsule and slipping it into his pocket.

He turned again to Mignon, who had been watching him.

"The argument, what was it?" he asked.

"It wasn't important," replied the girl. "It had nothing to do with this, I swear."

"Then you were angry because he showed an interest in Mary Wier?"

Mignon nodded her head slowly.

"Last night you said, '*I am not afraid to do it, if I must*.' Do what—kill him?" Quinto asked.

The girl's lips froze.

Suddenly, without expecting an answer from her, Quinto turned to McKay. "Are you through yet?"

"Another minute," said the doctor.

Quinto turned his back on Mignon and went to the low tea table standing beside Firth's chair. He sniffed the contents of the two glasses on the table. Both contained whisky and both were half empty. He stooped rather quickly, and wetting his thumb, pressed it to the floor near Firth's left shoe; and then he took the corner of a carbon sheet and stamped his thumb against it. A minute bit of loosely woven burnt cloth transferred from the thumb to the carbon paper. Again he stooped, this time picking up a curved bit of dried reddish clay.

"Someone has been very careless," he observed.

"What's that?" McKay grunted.

"Careless," repeated Quinto. He slipped the clay and bit of carbon in separate envelopes, put them in his pocket.

McKay stood up and stretched. He took the whisky glasses from the table and finished both.

"Well, the laddie died quick," he said deliberately. "Bullet through the heart." He offered Quinto a dark-stained, twisted bit of lead.

"A .41 short. Eh, a very odd size," Quinto identified it.

"It hit him pretty hard," McKay went on professionally. "Smashed the sternum and cut through the pericardial septum and on into the tip of the heart. Then it came out at a ten-degree angle. He probably sat just as he is."

Quinto walked to the window again, measuring the angle and distance from the wall outside to Firth's body. "The wall isn't high back here," he said. "The shot could have come from the other side. Were there powder burns?"

"No sign of any."

Quinto took out the envelope with the burned shreds of cloth. "It's like cloth from a loosely woven shirt. A poor grade one."

"It's not Firth's," said McKay interestedly. "Do you suppose he was shot from inside?"

"What time did you say he died, Senor Mac?"

"I didn't. You can't set a time now. The best I can do is between eleven last night and two or three this morning."

"Twelve, midnight, I heard Clive and Senorita Chauvet myself at that hour. He died afterward. It's my word—*yo lo dicho*."

"Whatever you say, Quinto."

"Where were you last night?"

McKay grinned.

"Listening to Virtue. The party didn't break up until one o'clock. Then Chi and I turned in."

Quinto gathered up Firth's papers and paged through them rapidly. At length he nodded his head with a thoughtful slowness.

"Certain points become clear now," he said. "I ordered Firth to make me a list of where everyone was yesterday. It's not here."

He picked up a sheet of carbon paper and scrutinized the type impressions on it. It was impossible to read, for carbon paper in Lingtung during the war was carbonized on both sides and was very cheaply made.

"If Firth had made me the list, he would have made a copy also. But naturally that is gone too. He could have been shot from beyond the wall with a silenced gun. The firecrackers last night would also cut down the sound. The murderer could then come over the wall, search the room, and perhaps take this paper."

"It doesn't make sense," McKay interrupted. "What if Clive did discover that someone was on the mountain you didn't know about? How did the person know Clive was putting it down on a list? He would have had to see it before he murdered Clive."

"So he was searching for something else—but what?" Quinto asked rhetorically.

A knock on the door interrupted them. Sergeant Sun entered, carrying his enormous Japanese rifle. He grinningly saluted the three in the room, then seeing the corpse, sobered. "Velly bad," he said. "Good fighter him."

"What is it, Sun?" Quinto asked. "*Quibo pues, quate?*"

"Mista White Suit and foreign missy back ten minutes."

"Woodford?"

"Yessum drive whizz bang through gate ten minute."

"All right, Sun. Forget the lady. Tell me, what time did the guard make the rounds last night?"

"Each piece hour."

"Who?"

Sun beamed patriotically.

"Sun make 'cm."

"Did you see anyone outside the walls? Near the South Gate?"

The Sergeant thought for a moment, then he nodded his head positively.

"Yessum. Eleventy hour see same Mr. Yellow Coat. Go by South Gate I lose him. Wear fine Yellow Coat brass buckles. Look Doc Meeki exact."

Quinto swiveled his eyes toward the doctor and the latter stared at Sun in a funny manner.

"A coat like McKay's?" asked Quinto.

"No. Look like doc but youngerish gotta lot hair on him head black. Gotta big scar him on right face like Turk sword."

"A scar!" It was Mignon Chauvet. "It can't be!" she cried. Her voice was sharp and terrified.

Both Quinto and McKay stared at her.

"Senorita, what are you saying?"

"*Non, non!* It's too impossible—he's dead," Mignon's voice scaled hysterically.

"Who's dead?" Quinto interrupted, taking her hands firmly in his.

The girl abruptly fought to control herself. Her complexion was ghost white. She stood up stiffly and bit her lip. "I'm all right now," she murmured.

"But who did you say was dead?" Quinto persisted.

Mignon stared at him, then her eyes wandered around the room strangely. Her lips parted and she said:

"Clive—"

CHAPTER 10
Running Wind Mountain

JOHN TATE looked as if a herd of Szechwan sheep had camped along his extremities. He was dusty. His white Palm Beach was wrinkled and creased in a dozen places. He peered at Quinto with worried bloodshot eyes.

"I never expected she'd drink me right under the table," he said despondently. "After losing her that once when you called me to the phone, where does she appear but in my room, in my bed. She told the Guest House manager to rent her room, she wasn't using it, if you know what I mean!"

Tate paused, looking at the Mexican to see what he would say, then he went on.

"So I sat guard in the corridor. I didn't trust her. She might have gone back to Lingtung if I hadn't. I fell asleep, only to be trampled on by squads of Manchurian officers who kept hurrying in and out of rooms along the corridor as if they took turns sleeping there in half hour shifts...."

"In the morning, Miss Woodford began drinking all over again—" a despairing note crept into the calligraphist's voice—"I couldn't. Not that much! Then I tried shunting her off to the Military Governor as you advised, but before I knew it, we were in the car rocketing back here at a hundred *li* an hour. She drives like a maniac!"

"How much did she drink?" asked Quinto. "*Mucho?*"

Tate searched his pockets, bringing forth a small notebook. "I kept tab. Mostly for the expense account I shall turn in at Hankow." He calculated from the book. "Last night she drank thirty-two Shanghai Sherries at sixty Hankow *fen* each. Quite expensive. This morning she turned to whisky. She paid for those."

"Thirty-two sherries!" Quinto was impressed. "Doctor McKay will be most interested."

"Now, Quinto, I've about had enough of Miss Woodford. Send her back to Hankow, will you?"

Quinto pursed his lips, disagreeing.

"Send her away again and she'll grow suspicious," he explained.

"Then she writes articles charging that foreigners are being murdered in China. You see my logic. Next the British Ambassador, a very dear friend of mine, will have trouble on his hands. His government, though it does not mind Englishmen being killed by the Japanese in the war, frowns upon those same subjects being murdered by Chinese. Senorita Woodford doesn't know Firth was murdered, but no doubt she will. It is better to clear the case than have her go off suspicious."

"Firth murdered?" Tate cried, startled. "Why, I saw him at supper last night!"

"It happened after midnight."

"That's really a crime . . . . Do you know?"

Quinto shook his head, then he briefly explained what had occurred from the time Tate had gone to Sianfu to the present. Finally he returned to the subject of Mildred Woodford.

"She'll remain as long as she cares, but we'll keep her occupied. *Comprende?*"

"Mind you, I think it's unwise," Tate objected. "She's a journalist. She'll give China a black eye if you give her too much rope. Her sympathies are with the invader, you realize."

"We'll employ military tactics on her," smiled Quinto. "The tactic of strategic diversion, yes?"

"On Miss Woodford?"

Quinto patiently rolled himself a cigarette and lit it. He said:

"When Chiang Kai-shek once pressed after the great Guerrilla Route Army which is now known as the Eighth Route Army, this tactic was used with great success on Chiang's forces. It is rule number one of my own guerrilleros. When pursued, think of your enemy and leave him something to pursue. Thus, the Eighth Route Army enticed Chiang northward with a small rearguard column while the main army went west. Chiang was happy going northward—until he discovered he pursued nothing. The same applies to Senorita Woodford."

Tate looked mildly puzzled, for he envisioned the Englishwoman hounding an invisible army across the great Gobi desert. He looked doubtfully at Quinto, who was smiling expansively, evidently pleased with his own strategy.

"Senor Doc McKay has already informed the lady that Nevada is a remarkable hero," said Quinto. "He captured five hundred enemy machine-guns single-handed. That will please her. By now she is chasing poor Nevada."

"Did he capture that many?"

"No. Only fifteen."

"Well, I hope it works."

"Meanwhile," said Quinto, glancing at the calligraphist through a curling feather of cigarette smoke, "you have an assignment also. You must remain in Lingtung. Clive Firth was my major domo here. He was a secretary and political director and he watched after the internationals. Since you speak many languages, you'll be the cultural director of the school. Your duty is to see that the internationals do not interfere with the routine of my guerrilleros. I'll inform military headquarters in Sianfu. They'll communicate with your superiors in Hankow."

Tate was suddenly blushing.

"I hardly think I can handle the position," he said somewhat bewildered.

"I have every confidence," replied Quinto.

Tate reddened even more. His albino eyes wandered toward the various scrolls and mottos on the walls of Quinto's office. One in particular caught his eye. It was a single fuzzily drawn character in the *ts'ao* or free style. It translated,

"Going forward smoothly, step by step."

Scrawled beneath it, in Quinto's bold hand, were the words,

"Lesson for the Lunghai Express."

"Now," said Quinto. He handed him the cipher note that had been found in Wang's quarters. "See what you can do with it. Take it to your room, lock the door and work quickly. I am going up the mountain. I'll be back at noon or little after."

As Tate departed, Quinto called the Officer of the Day, stationed outside his door.

"Call in Mr. Ho and tell Lieutenant Chi to stand by," he said.

Mr. Ho bowed his way into the office. He was a frail old man with a wisp of a white beard and a bald head poised forward on his long neck with great natural dignity and grace.

Ho came from the densely populated coastal Kiangsu province, where wine is fragrant, women are pretty and men are mostly lawyers or scholars. Mr. Ho was a scholar of the old school. He held such academic degrees as *Kungsheng, Chugen* and *Chinshih* and to make sure people would recognize this fact, he often wore the red-tasseled, crystal-topped cap and the official navy-blue gown of the scholar. His gown was now a little faded, in keeping with the decline of old-time scholarship in China.

"May I trouble your chariot?" Quinto said, greeting the old man in the most formal of polite Chinese.

"My chariot is untroubled," answered Mr. Ho.

"Your honorable health is good?" asked Quinto.

Mr. Ho shook hands with himself, keeping his delicately tapered fingers well within his long loose sleeves. He glanced questioningly at Quinto. Generally he hated foreigners, but he had a certain respect for this huge Mexican ever since the day Quinto had rescued him from the plight of being a Japanese prisoner and had said that a scholar would add dignity to the Lingtung Gardens.

Quinto bowed. "Pray take an honored chair," he murmured.

Mr. Ho bowed, a shade lower than the Mexican.

"I am totally unworthy," he answered.

"The unworthiness is mine," said Quinto.

The old man waited politely until chairs were arranged: one facing the door, the other with its back to the door. Then both men bowed again and sat down. They stared at each other and both were ready now to drop a slight margin of formality and get down to business. Quinto took the tiny heroin capsule from his pocket and, handing it to Mr. Ho, watched his face closely.

"Would it honor you to recognize this miserable object?" he asked.

The old man opened the capsule and looked inside. "The drug— heroin," he said.

"Do you use heroin?" asked Quinto.

"It is not a worthy drug," said Mr. Ho.

"Where were you last night—after listening to Virtue?"

"Sleeping."

"All night?"

"I dreamed part of the night," said Mr. Ho as he bowed again.

"Are you sure you didn't have occasion to leave your pavilion?"

Quinto picked up a small chart, a map of the gardens. Mr. Ho's pavilion was marked as a small one, on the edge of a little lagoon, not far from Firth's.

"Your villa is near Senor Clive's," Quinto continued. "Did you hear a gunshot last night?"

"None."

"Are you positive?"

Mr. Ho looked hurt. "Truth can never be proven. It is merely suggested," he said. "I was asleep."

"It depends who suggests it," said Quinto.

Mr. Ho looked about wisely. His slim fingers came through his sleeves, revealing a small leather pocketbook from which he poured a half dozen tarrish pellets into his palm.

"Opium!" grunted Quinto.

"Yes, opium. With opium one sleeps well, and dreams. It is an old truth."

Quinto's heavy brows knitted.

"You don't use heroin, then?" he asked.

The old man smiled. "This unworthy person is above heroin," he said. "Heroin is unpatriotic. It is a Japanese import unworthy of a Chinese. The poppy, on the other hand—" Mr. Ho waved his slim hand in an expressive graceful gesture.

"Very good," said Quinto. "You are a patriot and a scholar, Mr. Ho. But one more question . . . . You are aware that two foreigners were murdered yesterday? What is your opinion?"

The scholar fingered his beard gently.

"So, so, very happy they are dead," he murmured. "China is not suitable for foreigners, with your exception, of course."

The effect of Mr. Ho's decisive opinion was lost at the moment, for the office door opened abruptly. Sergeant Sun poked his head in and grinned excitedly.

"Cap'n," he cried, "see Mista Yellow Coats run up mountain right chop chop."

"If we are quick, we may catch our mysterious friend, Senor Yellow Coat," said Quinto as he hurried through the North Gate and along the path which eventually wound up the side of Running Wind Mountain.

Lieutenant Chi had been unable to change to more suitable clothing on such short notice. He tagged alongside Quinto in his golf togs.

"Do we arrest or shoot him?" he asked.

"Find him first," answered Quinto.

The two men climbed steadily, thanks to the engineering of a certain Chinese emperor who had seen to it that the grade of the mountain trail was hardly noticeable. The lieutenant, however, had minor difficulties, for the rubber in his plus-fours was loose and the pants continually slipped to his ankles.

Thirty minutes brought them to a large cavern midway up the mountain. At its entrance there stood a huge granite rock on which red characters had been painted—the story of how, on December 12, 1936, a certain Generalissimo Chiang Kai-shek had been kidnaped from the Lingtung Pavilions; but before being caught, he had fled in the dead of night, wearing only a nightshirt, up this very mountain path to hide in the cave.

Lieutenant Chi halted in front of the entrance, reverently.

"China's history turned here," he said. "It's also the spot where I saw Firth spying on Mr. Yellow Coat and Papa Wier."

Quinto hastily examined the cold and gloomy cavern. Near the entrance there was a scattering of cigarette butts on the floor. "Mr. Yellow Coat's," Quinto observed. "Wier doesn't smoke. The cavern was a meeting place, *seguro*. They were waiting for Harrow, I imagine. But why does Yellow Coat return today?"

"Maybe he's farther up the mountain," suggested Chi.

Quinto took notice of the time on his watch. "We'll go on," he said.

The trail from the cavern to the mountain crest was narrower and steeper. The pines ended and the mountain shrubbery turned to scrub oak and brush. Following a series of hairpin twists, the trail ran along the mountain crest to its northern tip, where a magnificent view of the Wei Ho River and the town of Lingtung could be had.

"Well, we've lost Yellow Coat," puffed Chi as they came to the cliff edge where Harrow had died.

Quinto studied the cliff edge. Suddenly he dropped on hands and knees and went crawling along the perilous ledge, paying scant heed to the two-hundred-foot fall below him. At last he stopped and dug his nails into the reddish clay covering the escarpment top.

"Look, Chi," he called. "Harrow stood here on the edge. These are his foot prints. *Si, hombre*, and here are the other marks I had expected. This clay is the same texture as the bit I found in Senor Clive's room."

He indicated a set of heel prints, cut deeper in the clay than the marks made by Harrow's cordovan boots. The heel pits were narrow and sharply defined.

"The shoe a woman wears for sport, no? *Mira*. It has a higher heel than Harrow's. Now, from the position of Senor Abe's footprints, he was looking down toward the village. Perhaps he didn't hear the second person come up from behind. It was a little windy yesterday. A slight push, even by a woman, could have done it!"

CHAPTER 11
Sincerely, Colonel Nohuri

QUINTO PULLED out his watch, an old-fashioned Ingersoll with hands as enormous and articulate as his own. It was 11:50 A.M., exactly twenty-four hours since Harrow had died for the third time, according to the dead man's three watches.

"It takes one hour and a half to walk up here," said Quinto. "Going down, it may take fifty minutes at the most. Whoever cannot account for himself between nine o'clock yesterday morning and a half hour after noon may be suspected of murdering Abe Harrow."

"Me too?" said Lieutenant Chi.

"Yes, you." Quinto stood up and, brushing the reddish clay from his knees, glanced down the dizzy distance toward Lingtung. To the east, toward Hwayin Hsing, the Wei Ho river bent slightly. The lonely whistle of the Lunghai Express could be heard from that direction.

"To reach Lingtung proper it would take longer," Quinto continued. "Therefore Mr. Ho didn't kill Harrow. He was in town at noon. I saw him myself. Doc McKay, Virtue and myself cannot be considered suspects for similar reasons. Virtue was coming in on the Express, which arrived at noon or shortly after. McKay was at the station with me.

"Now, let's narrow the time, the moment of suspicion. *I am certain Mr. Harrow died at 11:50.* His other two watches were wrong. Do you see how I come to this conclusion, Chi?"

Lieutenant Chi shook his head and listened attentively.

"Senor Abe's watches stopped at 11:18, 11:30 and 11:50," said Quinto. "Obviously the first two are wrong. *Sargento* Sun saw him conversing with Mr. Yellow Coat near the North Gate between ten o'clock and fifteen minutes thereafter. Possibly Harrow did not walk directly to the cliff, so he arrived here at best around 11:40 or later. That is a good hour and a half climb. Now, I said it takes fifty minutes to go down. . . ."

Quinto took Chi by the arm and the two men, Chinese and Mexican, hurried back along the down-trail.

"Fifty minutes," remarked Quinto again. "It would be 12:30 before the murderer returned to the Pavilions or passed them."

"Alibis?" questioned Chi.

"We'll have them, but they are not important," mused Quinto. "Somehow, I prefer the ways of your Chinese police who think little of criminal alibis. A cunning mind is capable of framing any alibi. Your Chinese police prefer to study emotions and instincts. They deal with fundamentals rather than superficials, no?"

They passed the cave of Chiang Kai-shek, then after walking another few hundred yards, Quinto suddenly halted. Something crashed through the brush and trees to the right of the trail. The sound increased and a moment later Nevada appeared. He was thoroughly scratched and his lean face was in a sweat from the strenuous off-trail climb.

"*Ole, charro*," Quinto called.

Nevada leaped over a boulder to the trail.

"That damn reporter woman," he growled. "You must have been behind it, Quinto. Been a-pestering me all over the place. Been asking me if I was married. I got riled and come up the mountain for some peace and quiet."

Quinto smiled reprovingly.

"She is beautiful and rich, no?"

"Her," said Nevada. "She's a coyote if I ever seen one!"

"Have you been climbing long?"

"A spell."

"Did you see anyone? A man in a Yellow Coat?"

Nevada nodded slowly.

"Yeah, I seen him. He was coming down. Kind of funny, because he was off the trail."

A glow of keen interest flashed in Quinto's eyes. "Was he American?" he asked.

"French," Nevada drawled. "Maybe he is, I don't know. Used a lot of 'zees' and 'zoes' when he talked."

"And he spoke with you?"

"Asked me if Harrow was still around."

John Tate sat very rigidly, despite the mellow sun that clothed the gardens. He stared in curious fascination at Mountain of Virtue, who calmly munched lotus seeds, then delicately spat them at the white ducks in the canal below.

"You should eat them as I do," Virtue instructed him. "The seeds are so mild that when eaten raw from the pod you must think of nothing, absolutely nothing, to enjoy their tender fragrance. Now you try it."

Tate smiled timidly. That smile was nothing new to Virtue. It was the kind of smile men show when secretly wishing they could have a woman like herself. But even now, rather than meet her startling frank gaze, Tate let his eyes fall to the sheaf of paper on his knees—the solved cipher.

"You should see Gimiendo eat lotus," Virtue's lilting voice went on. "Sometimes he concentrates so thoroughly on the mildness that his mind is blank for half an hour at a time."

"My mind just isn't in condition for that," Tate murmured.

"Ah, the cipher—it bothers you?"

"I'm excited."

"May I see it?"

Tate looked a little worried.

"G.H.Q. ordered me not to let anyone see it until he did," he apologized.

Virtue leaned toward him, her delicate, slender shoulder passing his cheek. The fragrance of her perfume made him strangely dizzy. Then her lids lowered—the *hsiaochieh* look. It did things to him. Little, warm Christmas-tree bulbs broke inside his stomach, p-pop! pop! pop! He began to blush a great deal and he handed her the solved ciphers.

As Virtue studied the original, her brow knitted. Finally, she read the second page, Tate's solution:

Prochain remise recettes numerote 1940 a 5620 sera 28 Mars Maison Tang Pan Tao paiement pour solde de tout compte sur dernier paquet doit etre rendu notre agent meme temp—Col. Nohuri.

She glanced up at Tate questioningly. "But this is in French?"

"The cipher is in French," said Tate, gradually though not completely recovering from his encounter with Virtue's fatal charms. "It's a rather simple one. At first I suspected it was made in *pai hua*, the new alphabetical Chinese, but it didn't make sense. I tried frequency tests again in German, English and Russian. No luck. Finally I had an inspiration. I noticed the date on the cipher. Arabic numerals—3-15-38, in other words, March fifteenth. Do you know what happened that day?"

"No," Virtue answered solemnly.

"Caesar was murdered!"

"Caesar?"

"Yes. March fifteenth, the Ides of March."

"But this is China," Virtue protested.

"Oh, the date had nothing to do with the cipher, at least Caesar's date, but it gave me an idea. I puzzled with the cipher in Latin for a while, then I remembered—Julius Caesar used ciphers for Roman military dispatches. There is a certain cipher form bearing his name. An extension type in which you extend the alphabet backward or forward from the letters in the cipher. This one is a four-letter cipher. Look at my third page, the work sheet. The top line is the solution, the bottom line is the code. The alphabet was just extended four times to make a code, then the words were broken into five-letter units to cause confusion. Ten extra, meaningless letters were thrown in at the end for the same reason."

Virtue took the sheet indicated, reading the first part of Tate's method of solution:

Proch	*ainre*	*miser*	*ecett*	*esnum*	*erote*	*1940a*
qspdi	bjos					
rtqej	ckpt					
SURFK	DLQUH	PLVHU	HFHVV	HVQXP	HURVH	1940D

"It seems the code writers had difficulty extending numerals so they were left as is. It added to the confusion. Now the only trouble is, the thing still doesn't make sense," said Tate.

Virtue looked up. "You don't make sense of it?" she asked.

"Do you? I can read it, but then what? It says that the next delivery of receipts numbered 1,940 to 5,620 will be delivered at the house of Tang in Pan Tao and that payment in full account on the last delivery should be turned over to their agent at the same time. It's signed by Colonel Nohuri. Who is Nohuri? What are the receipts? Why is the cipher in French? Who is Tang? And isn't Pan Tao within our lines?"

Virtue creased her penciled brows prettily.

"Gimiendo will know," she said.

"You boarded the Lunghai Express in Pan Tao day before yesterday, didn't you?" Tate asked with sudden suspicion.

Mountain of Virtue smiled without answering. She gazed across the garden to where Quinto approached on his return from the mountain.

"The house of Tang," said Quinto, "is a tea house. Very good sherry there."

"And Colonel Nohuri?" asked Tate.

"A Japanese colonel with headquarters across the Yellow River."

Quinto's sunny expression swiftly changed to one of irritation as he mentioned the colonel's name. The cipher meant added complications in an already perplexing situation, and anything that took the big man from his work as a guerrillero instructor upset him.

"So this invader colonel has learned to write in French," he growled. "That is the only trouble with culture. It gets into bad hands." He glanced from the cipher translation to Tate's ruddy face. "Senor Tate, you must type out a military order for my guerrilleros with proper passes for crossing and reentering the lines. Ten guerrilleros will enter Japanese territory near Pan Tao and capture Colonel Nohuri. We'll find why he writes in French and what these receipts are."

Tate nodded, looking somewhat dazed by Quinto's unmilitary procedure.

"*Oiga*, Tate, you must also call military headquarters at Pan Tao. Inform them that my men will pass there."

"Gimiendo, the balls, remember!" said Virtue.

"Oh, yes. And Tate, in that order put in a reminder. My guerrilleros should remember to keep an eye out for new billiard balls. Ivory ones."

Quinto smiled gratefully at Virtue. He selected a lotus from the basket at her side, broke the pod expertly. For several minutes his features assumed a beatifically blank expression while he munched a few seeds. John Tate watched, engrossed. It was as if he had never seen a man stand, looking out over a sun-swept garden, beautiful with its winding canal and tile-roofed villas, and yet be so distant from it all.

At last the Mexican spat his seeds into the canal and sat down cross-legged upon the grassy bank.

"Where is the Senorita?" he asked lazily.

"Woodford? With Doctor McKay," said Tate.

Quinto nodded, satisfied. He spread his broad brown fingers upon his knees, rubbing creaseless cotton trousers. "I'm getting somewhere; slowly, step by step," he murmured. "A bit more light shed on Firth and Harrow may eventually show us who was so very interested in the two men."

"You suspect someone already?" Tate stood by interestedly.

"No. But if I fail to discover, by means of clues and inquiry, who pushed Harrow over the cliff, or who assassinated Senor Clive, I'll catch the criminal by other means: by dialectics. A good system, that. I'll take everything apart, searching into the lives of both men and all persons connected with the crimes. Somewhere, sometime, someone's path crossed the lives of these men. Perhaps five years ago, perhaps only yesterday . . ."

Quinto's eyes narrowed as he paused to roll himself a cigarette.

"The paths begin to cross," he said slowly. "We have Harrow, Papa Wier and Wang meeting secretly in Chiang's cave. The meeting time was noon yesterday, but Harrow was absent. However, a Mr. Yellow Coat appeared."

"Was it a fact they were to have a meeting?" Tate interrupted curiously.

"No. It's my suspicion. But the threads cross. Didn't we intercept a message in French to Wang? Aren't Harrow and Papa Wier in Wang's system of bookkeeping? It resembles a crossword puzzle, yet one thing stands out clearly."

Quinto lit his cigarette and calmly looked at Virtue and Tate through the billow of smoke he blew out.

"What?" Tate asked hesitantly.

"A piece of red clay was carried from the cliff where Harrow was murdered into Clive Firth's room. The heel that deposited that clay is the size of that on a woman's walking shoe. Did the person who murdered Senor Abe return to murder Clive?"

Virtue parted her lips as if to gasp, then her slender fingers went to her mouth and she belched delicately. Her gaze swept from man to man with a look of utter innocence in it. Tate's eyes shot toward Quinto. The Mexican was looking off in the distance. He hadn't seen Virtue's action.

"Most interesting at the moment," said Quinto, "is why Mignon Chauvet was shocked by the description of Mr. Yellow Coat. She became evasive. We also know she hated Harrow. Why? And she was very intimate with Clive Firth, though this arrangement has dimmed somewhat since Mary Wier and her father came to Lingtung. Senorita Chauvet argued with Firth last night. Was she the last to see him alive?"

Quinto posed his questions and let them stand.

"Naturally, if Miss Chauvet murdered," said Virtue, "she murdered one, not both."

"So?" Quinto looked up questioningly.

"The method," Virtue said softly. "Mignon is a woman. A Frenchwoman. When a woman murders, she makes plans only so far as the bare decision to murder. She doesn't plan. She kills in a burst of anger or jealousy with whatever weapon falls into her hand at the moment. I refuse to consider Mignon Chauvet murdering one man by throwing him over a cliff and the other with a gun. She would be too emotionally upset to kill a second man the same day."

"But why did she hate Harrow?" asked Tate.

"Mignon Chauvet is a very confused woman," said Virtue. "She has been jealous, and still is. She's jealous of Mary Wier because the little girl, for the short time she has been here, had much to say about Clive Firth. But. . . she had a stronger reason for hating Mr. Harrow."

Quinto looked up sharply.

"Miss Chauvet," said Virtue, "shot a man in Paris. She left France in great haste. Since then she has lived in Spanish Morocco. When war came to China, she came. She was a doctor. *Mr. Harrow knew of this!*"

Quinto sat up with a jerk.

CHAPTER 12
Air Raid

"HOW LONG has this situation existed?" asked the Mexican quickly.

"For some time," replied Virtue.

"Blackmail—" John Tate gasped. "Harrow blackmailed Miss Chauvet. That explains his bank deposits at Hankow. It's really rotten, taking advantage of a woman like that. I shan't blame her in the least if we find that she . . ."

"But what if Mr. Firth knew this also?" suggested Virtue.

"Did he?" asked Quinto.

Virtue pursed her roselike lips.

"Why, Gimiendo, how did you think I discovered Mignon had shot a man in Paris and that Harrow also knew this fact?" murmured the girl.

Tate's eyes widened in amazement. "You're almost saying Firth murdered Harrow to protect the French girl from blackmail," he cried. "Is that true? Then who killed Firth? Not Miss Chauvet?"

"Ah, the puzzles again." Quinto sighed once more as he relaxed upon the bank of the garden canal. "Who killed Senor Clive? Who? Wang . . . Wier . . . McKay . . . Chi . . . Mr. Ho . . . Senorita Chauvet? . . . Instinct tells me not to trust Wang. He spied on Clive Firth yesterday. Why? . . ."

He glanced searchingly at Virtue while a long wisp of cigarette smoke trailed through his lips and up his brown cheeks. "*Oye, chuela,*" he asked, "where was Wang last night?"

Virtue avoided the question.

"I hardly think Wang is guilty," she countered.

"Your poetry-reciting ended at one o'clock in the night, eh? Is it that Wang was alone after that?"

"I remained with Wang until two-thirty," Virtue answered demurely. "But Wang didn't kill Harrow or Firth. Wang is middle-class Chinese and no patriot. He does not murder. He hires others to do it."

Quinto stared at Virtue with eloquent suspicion and Virtue stared back—a portrait of innocence. This contrast between the huge, gentle-mannered adventurer and the lovely Eurasian girl could happen only in China. Even now, Virtue's mysterious way of knowing more than her eyes told, and of having gained her knowledge by methods which certain Boston missionaries would not have considered bona fide, shocked John Tate to a point where he said, "Good Lord!"

Suddenly, from the direction of Lingtung, distant bells began to toll. A second later, a bell in the gardens took up the clanging.

An annoyed expression clouded Quinto's features. "Air raid!" he said. "*Ai, vienen los aviones cobardes.*"

Tate turned pale.

"Here?"

"Perhaps," said Quinto. "It is usually the railway station, but sometimes they come here. Go to the *yamen*. See that no one stays in the building. It is most dangerous. The *refugio* or shelter is at the far end of the garden, a bit east of Senor Firth's pavilion."

The deep drone of bombers reverberated in the sky. Three planes rode high, looking like silver minnows flashing against the tile blue sky. The boom of an antiaircraft cannon echoed from Lingtung. The projectiles cut a hollow, ominous sound above the earth.

Tate leaped to his feet, trembling. He shot a worried glance at Quinto, who was stretched on his back the better to watch the planes. Virtue also stared upward while her delicately shaped fingers calmly broke lotus pods.

The drone of the planes, like the hum of angry bees, moved the earth to sudden action. In the gardens the Chinese guerrilleros scurried out of the Little Theater and the *yamen* to watch the sky.

"Under trees!" Quinto's voice suddenly roared.

Quinto's voice curbed Tate's headlong flight. The Mexican watched as the latter walked from tree to tree toward the air raid shelter, knees almost buckling from fright at each step.

Doc McKay and Mildred Woodford stood in the doorway of a peasant hut just beyond the West Gate of the gardens. Mildred ogled a half dozen cooing doves nesting under the eaves of the hut. An old Chinese woman with stringy black hair and worn features held another dove in her scrawny hand and stroked its head.

"I say, McKay old fruit, ask how much she'll sell them for," said Mildred.

The doctor translated the question for the Chinese woman and got an answer. "She says she'll begin at five *tael* apiece and bargain down to three *tael*."

"I'll take them," said Mildred.

"No, lassie. You've got to bargain a wee bit," McKay answered with a sly twinkle in his eyes. "Otherwise the price stays at five *tael*. That's the custom."

"Nonsense. Let's pay her the three and get it over with."

"Oh no. You must respect the custom."

"How long will it take?"

The doctor sucked on his dry pipe. "Perhaps a half hour," he said. "Spend an hour bargaining and you'll get the doves for a *tael* apiece."

"Well, what are they really worth?"

"They're a scrawny lot. Not much meat on them."

"Really? Well, I don't want them for meat," said Mildred. "Do they home?"

McKay looked puzzled, then he broke into a quiet laugh. "Homing pigeons," he snorted. "Trying to get past the censors? Well, you'll nay get a word out by these birds. First of all, some needful soldier would be eating them before they got to where you'd be sending them."

Mildred Woodford's Yorkshire nose crinkled angrily.

"Oh, so you're under Quinto's thumb too?" she charged harshly. "Now let me tell you something. I'm getting sick and tired of the whole business. You're not hiding anything. I know Mr. Harrow was murdered yesterday. Yes, and I know another man was murdered. An Englishman."

"A Scot," said McKay.

"Very well then, a Scot. And here's something else you can pass on to Quinto. You can tell him I'll get a story out of this and by the time I'm finished I'll have found out who murdered those two men before Quinto. I'm just waiting to see Quinto squirm."

"My bet is on G.H.Q.," said McKay.

Bells tolled in Lingtung, then in the Pavilion gardens. McKay managed to take the Englishwoman's arm, propelling her toward the West Gate.

"Come along," he said sharply. "We're going to the shelter. Air raid!"

"No, let's watch the thing."

"Come along!"

Bombs dropped upon Lingtung. They made a continuous, relentless sound like the rushing of air through a big funnel and finally banging into a hollow drum. SssssswwooommmmmMMBBBB! Geysers of yellow smoke shot up in the distance.

Flashing silver in the sunlight, the three bombers made a bowbend toward the Lingtung Pavilions, lacing bombs along the road as they came. The explosions broke closer and the sunlight seemed to rock and reverberate with each blast, as if the daylight were made of bricks and windows.

From the pink brick guardhouse came the sounds of rifle fire and boisterous laughter. Sergeant Sun and two Chinese guerrilleros danced upon the tile roof, firing at the planes with a shotgun, a rifle and a pistol, all the while enjoying themselves as much as at a first-rate duck hunt.

At the first warning of the bombers, Mary Wier and her father ran from their villa, leaving the door open. Papa Wier threw a fearful penetrating look at the sky and though he saw no planes, he raced across the garden, past the little lagoon to the air-raid shelter.

Mary hesitated in the path, then felt strong fingers take her arm, urging her forward. It was Nevada.

"Hurry!" The cowboy spoke in a quick tense voice. "They're going to drop here!"

Mary let him hold her around the waist. It was the first time she had ever done that.

"I'm afraid, Nevada," she whimpered.

"It's okay, kid. I'll take care of you."

In another few seconds they were at the shelter. "Okay, go in, Mary," said Nevada. "I'm staying out to watch."

The girl glanced at the *refugio*. It was a deep horseshoe tunnel with two entrances. It had been cut into rock. Mary shook her head and held Nevada's arm.

"I'll stay with you," she answered softly.

Mignon Chauvet hurried by and entered the gloomy tunnel. Then John Tate came. Nevada saw Mr. Ho standing a few feet within the second entrance complacently smoking his long clay pipe. Wang and two Chinese servants hurried in as the drone of the plane engines increased.

Nevada's lean face was tilted like a shoe box, his eyes glued to the three planes in the sky. He barely noticed McKay and the Englishwoman as they hurried to the tunnel. The planes let out a queer cackling sound, machine-gun signals. Suddenly Nevada pushed Mary to the ground and fell over her, his body a protective shield.

"Here it comes," he yelled. "Hold tight."

A dozen guerrilleros, standing in the shade of a nearby tree fell flat. The roar of the planes swelled and the earth shook with explosions. A bomb exploded with a burst of red flame. A pine tree rode the top of a dirt geyser. A second bomb followed, fifteen feet behind.

Nevada saw one of the Chinese students who was crouching in the open bounced into the air by the first concussion. The cowboy was on his knees in an instant. Abruptly, he felt a sharp blow against his ribs. The shock spun him around and threw him down.

He saw the bombers skate off across the sky. The dust of explosions hung over the gardens. Then he saw Mary kneeling at his side, pale and terrified.

"Nevada—" she cried. "You're hurt!"

Doc McKay appeared with Miss Woodford tagging behind him. The doctor lent a helping hand.

"On your feet, laddie," he said. "So the shrapnel caught you. Well, to the surgery. We'll dig it out."

Mary Wier was crying now.

Nevada sat on a stool in the surgery, his chest bare and his lips clamped together grimly while the doctor probed the wound in his side.

"Hold tight, laddie," murmured McKay. "You're lucky. The fourth rib deflected it. Just a minute now."

"Looks like I don't have to go to the front to get hit," Nevada grinned.

"That was very foolish, standing up in the bombing," said Quinto as he watched the operation.

"I thought one of the kids was hit," drawled Nevada. "Guess he weren't."

"Watch your grammar, laddie," said McKay.

The surgery door opened suddenly. Tate hastened in, red-faced and enthused. He was still a bit shaky from the air raid but his excitement overrode that.

"Look, Quinto—the gun!"

He dangled a small derringer model pistol by its trigger guard. The gun was of an old design, squat and no more than five inches long.

"Mignon Chauvet found it," said Tate animatedly. "Or she said she found it in the air raid shelter when the bombing ended. She stepped on it."

Quinto took the gun, examining it. McKay paused for a moment to stare at it as did Nevada. It was indeed a tiny gun. It had two stubby barrels, over-and-under type. The bullets could only be fired one at a time, being touched off by a single cap-striker which had to be adjusted separately for each barrel by a simple sliding catch. On its side the maker's name was engraved:

Comblain-Braendlin—1871

Quinto broke the barrels.

"Two shots fired," he observed, somewhat mystified. "Cartridges are still in, that is, the cases. Hmm, .41 caliber. This is the gun that murdered Senor Clive."

"I tried not to smudge any fingerprints," said Tate. "Miss Chauvet's are on there, but . . ."

"I care little for fingerprints," said Quinto. "If we had the laboratory of the Hankow or Shanghai police it might be different."

"Say, Quinto laddie—" There was a curious note in Doc McKay's dry voice. He held up a slippery, dark-crimsoned object, the cause of Nevada's wound. "This isn't shrapnel," he said slowly. "*It's a bullet.*"

Quinto snatched the bullet from his fingers. His face wore a forbidding expression as he wiped the pellet of blood and scrutinized it.

"Again .41 caliber, and from this gun," he said.

"You mean to say Nevada was shot at? It wasn't the bombs?" Tate gasped.

Quinto nodded impatiently.

"Where did you stand when you were hit?" he asked Nevada.

The cowboy thought for a moment and wet his drawn lips. "Near the west entrance of the tunnel," he said. "Me and Mary was there. I was facing Firth's villa just as I was clipped."

"That would put your left side to the tunnel. The side you were struck on," said Quinto.

"Yeah, that's right."

"You were shot by someone in that tunnel," Quinto spoke slowly. He turned toward Tate. "Senor Tate, I want you to make a list of all who were in the *refugio* and who stood near the two entrances. I think something very surprising will come of this."

CHAPTER 13
A Bridge Vanishes

AN HOUR after the air raid, Quinto led John Tate into town and then out along the Wei Ho River, following the track bed of the Lunghai railway.

"Guerrillero tactics," said Quinto.

The countryside was delightfully peaceful and sunny. The east- and westbound trains had already passed, as well as the Japanese bombers which had accounted for only two important military objectives—a water tank and a cow, both in Lingtung proper.

After the air raid and lunch, Quinto had called out his warlike students (all but the ten who had been dispatched to capture the Japanese Colonel Nohuri) and prepared to deploy them in their daily afternoon lesson.

"Today our objective is the railroad trestle which spans a small canal emptying into the Wei Ho where it curves by Running Wind Mountain," explained Quinto as he marched along, his clothes fluttering in the breeze. "We'll experiment with the *little-short-attack*."

Tate puffed along, listening interestedly, and wobbling with the rearguard motion of a heavy-set girl in a college gym. The floppy brim of his Panama shook before his eyes and his bandaged right arm bounced outward somewhat awkwardly with each step, making it look as though he had one wing and were about to take off.

His Mexican companion was in an expansive mood, particularly concerning partisan warfare.

"My guerrilleros, they are wonderful. The Chinese man is as good as a Mexican for this kind of fighting. If Doroteo Arango Pancho Villa could only see them, he would cry." Quinto threw his arm about Tate's shoulder in good fellowship. "I'll really show you how my men work. We are a special branch of the army, like nothing else. We never operate behind enemy lines in huge divisions as the excellent Eighth and Fourth Route Armies. My men are never more than one company. They are trained to capture trains, munition dumps, enemy generals, blow up roads and paralyze the invader without wishing to hold a position. An old Mexican trick, you will notice."

81

"The little-short-attack?" asked Tate.

"Ah," Quinto beamed, "the attack is a work of genius. Soldiers appear out of nowhere, attack the Japanese bridge, and disappear instantly. They approach singly, disperse as individuals. It makes pursuit impossible. I have many versions of the attack but today we'll use the Chu Teh style."

Tate stared about wonderingly. They had come to the railway trestle, a low wooden structure spanning an irrigation canal. All seemed too unusually peaceful. There were no signs of Quinto's fifty guerrilleros.

Below, on the left, the Wei Ho glistened and rippled in the afternoon sun. A fisherman poled a long, narrow boat through the rice grass along the bank. He fished with a tame cormorant which dove into the water, reappearing with a fish in its beak. A string wound about the bird's neck jerked tightly, a precaution to keep it from swallowing the catch. At the canal head, two peasants worked a water wheel and discussed the war. To the right of the tracks, in a small cultivated area that extended beneath the sheer cliff of Running Wind Mountain, some twenty peasants were noisily weeding and hoeing.

Quinto surveyed the bucolic scene with satisfaction. "Now the attack," he warned Tate.

The two men withdrew about twenty yards from the bridge. Quinto took out his watch and the little derringer pistol which had been found in the air raid shelter. Quinto had loaded the gun with two .38 cartridges, fitting the smaller-sized shells into the chambers by winding them with tissue paper—a trick he had learned in Old Mexico where bullets and guns did not always match.

He held the derringer overhead and fired. Tate jumped back in surprise, then astonishment.

The peace and quiet of the little valley suddenly blasted from its foundations. Firecrackers exploded in a dozen places. The peasants in the field dropped their hoes, seized guns and charged the bridge, uttering a wild series of war cries. The cormorant fisherman shoved his boat shoreward and scrambled up the bank. Three additional soldiers appeared out of the boat bottom.

"*Mis guerrilleros*, they disguise themselves well," said Quinto, his face glowing proudly.

"Disguise!" Tate gasped. "My God!"

Before his very eyes, the bridge just vanished. Guerrilleros swarmed all over it like a busy horde of locusts. The tracks were ripped up and hauled to one side. The wooden ties and planking were piled on the opposite bank of the canal. The guerrilleros shouted in unison as they labored—

"*He, ho, he, ho.*" With the last "*ho*" the bridge was no more.

Quinto raised his hand.

"The retreat!" he shouted in Chinese.

Before the echo of his voice had died, fifty destructive guerrilleros raced in various directions, crossing paths, dodging like football players through the field. Two of them suddenly remembered something, returned and put red lanterns at each end of where the bridge had been, then vanished with the rest. Within a minute all was peace and quiet in the Wei Ho Valley.

"It's utterly incredible," Tate murmured.

"Now," said Quinto, thoroughly satisfied, "we return to town. I must remember to have the station master send the track coolies to replace the bridge before the trains come tomorrow. You'll notice, Senor Tate, here it is simple. Track coolies repair the bridge immediately. For the Japanese it is far more difficult; Chinese coolies are unwilling to do repair work for them."

Still too astonished to say anything, Tate trudged along beside the Mexican. A short distance up the track he watched Quinto fasten a bit of paper to a stick and plant it between the ties. .

Quinto backed away from the paper, counting his steps until he had taken ten. Then he drew the derringer. He aimed carefully, fired point-blank, and missed.

"I never miss," he said, as if this were a plain statement of fact. To demonstrate, he now twirled forth his own service pistol. There came a thunderous roar as the gun kicked. Tate saw the bit of paper torn to shreds. "You see," he added, "the derringer gun makes a great difference in the murder of Senor Firth. It is inaccurate at a distance as short as twenty feet. Derringers are only for card players, for shooting across a table. Clive Firth was shot by someone inside his villa. Someone holding this gun. To shoot accurately into the heart, where else could one stand?"

"The criminal might have reached through the window," Tate suggested rather dubiously.

"Ah, no. Firth would have heard the sound. He sat almost facing the window. It was some person he knew. A friend who visited in his room. Senor Clive was relaxed in his chair. There were two glasses of liquor on the table. Men drink only with friends. It was someone he knew quite well."

Quinto waited, as if he wanted Tate to advance a possible suspect.

"Miss Chauvet?" the calligraphist hesitated. "Well, as for that, it might have been Wang, or Doctor McKay, or you or . . . Virtue."

"*Ai tu*, very good. But remember, Firth's eyes showed no fear, his face exhibited no surprise or shock. Now if I draw a gun, even a small one, and intend to shoot you, naturally you will react. You will attempt to save your life. Ah? Firth must have felt the visitor with the gun would not dare fire. He perhaps thought the person a coward or a bluff. Or, as you suggest, Senorita Chauvet. An angry woman threatens, but does not always shoot. Is it not so?"

"That's a point, because the gun is French."

"Ah, it means nothing. China is full of old guns, French, Spanish, German, English and American. When we have a country at war, a blockade against arms, men will use anything to fight with. Yet the gun has one very interesting point."

"Fingerprints?"

"No. The name. Comblain-Braendlin. It's a valuable gun. I believe I can get a good price for it. A collector's price. Perhaps one hundred and thirty dollars, American!"

"It was a very expensive murder—Firth's."

"Did you look into the arrangement of where the people stood in the *refugio* this morning or noon when Nevada was shot?"

Tate took out his note book. "Yes, here it is," he said. "The tunnel is horseshoe-shaped, with two entrances. Mr. Ho, the old Chinese, stood near the west entrance. Behind him were Wang, two of Wang's servants, and Papa Wier. In the east entrance the order is as follows: Mignon Chauvet, Doctor McKay, Miss Woodford and, I think, one of the Chinese boys. The entrances are so narrow that only the first or second person could have fired the shot at Nevada. Of course, there was so much concussion and dust during the actual bombing a gun shot couldn't be heard."

"And *mucho suerte* or luck for Nevada that the gun was a derringer. So inaccurate," murmured Quinto. He pursed his lips and walked on in thoughtful silence.

They came to the railroad station in town. A number of new windows had been shattered by a bomb which had exploded near by in the day's raid. The station water tank had also been hit. Its seams had burst and the water umbrellaed out. A coolie was now busily camouflaging it with branches and odd tatters of cloth.

Quinto stepped into the station building a moment to inform the master of the damage to his trestle. The railway man took the news complacently, for such things were not unusual in China. Why, a few years back, in 1876, the complete trackage of the first Chinese railway had to be torn up and the ties burned. Afterward, the railway had to be rerouted, because the line had been laid in a way which offended the *feng shui* or Wind and Water Spirits.

The *feng shui*, even now in the war, exerted a terrific influence on the Celestial Nation. They guide the Tiger and Dragon currents which run through the earth, hence, most life. The Chinese are not religious fanatics, but they do respect the supernatural. They practice what they call, "Politeness toward possibilities." It is this politeness which sometimes causes a railroad engineer to stop his train and wait for a few hours—suspecting *feng shui* of camping on his tracks. Even artillery men have been known to change their battery positions for similar reasons.

His duty performed, Quinto rejoined Tate and the two strolled through Lingtung, and then along the cypress-bordered road leading to the Pavilions. Tate was the first to resume conversation.

"What do you make of the derringer gun being found in the air raid shelter?" he asked.

"I don't know," Quinto murmured. "You?"

"It seems to fit almost too easily, doesn't it? Miss Chauvet found the gun beneath her foot. She says she found it. That doesn't mean she found it there or even found it. Maybe she had it all along."

"You suspect she fired at Nevada?"

"I don't know. I only thought . . ."

"If the gun was dropped," Quinto cut in, "it was sheer carelessness. A murderer wouldn't carry such incriminating evidence around for a full night and a morning. The gun was dropped in the *refugio* after Senor Clive was killed. The important fact is, the gun proves the murderer was in the room and Clive knew him well."

"Firth was a cool one?" asked Tate.

"Brave? . . . Yes . . . Like all Scots—the bravest soldiers on earth. And Senor Clive himself, *fue un chico valiente*."

"Must have been. I doubt if I could sit by calmly while someone waved a gun at me, even if it were my wife or mother."

"Firth was brave in more ways than you can imagine." Quinto spoke with the suggestion of a catch in his voice. "Senor Clive put aside his good position in England to fight beside the Chinese people."

"Position?" asked Tate. "Did he have a good job?"

Quinto smiled and dug a long, much-stamped envelope from his pocket and handed it to Tate. From the numerous changed addresses on it, the missive had probably wandered around China for months. The original post mark was *London, England*. It was addressed to Clive Firth.

Tate opened the letter, then raised his brows curiously. The letterhead was that of Simeon Shand, a well-known solicitor located at King's Row, London. "This is a curious thing to be wandering around China," he muttered.

"But read it," Quinto urged.
Tate read:

Dear Lord Firth:

It is my painful duty to inform you that your father, the late Lord Thomas Firth, died January fifteenth. Naturally you inherit his full title and such properties as are detailed in his last will. As family solicitor, I have been designated as executor of the said will, which, with the exception of six satisfactory legacies to family servants, places in your hands the entire Firth Estate in Scotland, the Firth Newspaper Enterprises and other assets in bank deposits and bonds valued at 50,000 pounds.

As your solicitor I beg to suggest it is advisable that you leave China and take up your inherited duties as head of the estate.

Sincerely,
Simeon B. Shand

Chapter 14
Teng Fa—Mostly a Memory

EIGHT HOURS after a certain bridge had disappeared in the Wei Ho Valley the Lingtung Pavilions had a distinguished visitor. He was a Chinese who had been born in Kwangtung, a province where people are impassioned, obstinate, fierce patriots and good cooks all at the same time. Save for the cooking part, the Cantonese are said to resemble the Irish, who carry a chip on each shoulder—one chip for the love of liberty, the other for the love of a good fight.

Although the evening visitor came unannounced, word got around among Quinto's guerrilla students, and they gathered in respectful, awed groups at the door of the office, waiting for a peep at their hero—Teng Fa.

"He wears *chung shan*, the uniform of a Kuomingtang official," whispered a farm lad from the South. "I know it's Teng Fa. He smiled broadly. He has the walk of a young tiger."

"Teng Fa," said another. "Last week I heard he was special guest of the enemy chief. It is his practice to live with the invader generals when spying on them. That is good protection. The best."

"Last week? No," murmured another student.

"And why, might I beg to ask?"

"Because last week he was in Tokyo itself. I have it on good account. And the Japanese little men thought Teng Fa was an ambassador from Thailand!"

"So—"

"This is all foolish woman talk," interrupted another student. "Teng Fa was at the Grand Canal Front last week. It was he who prepared it for the great battle of Tai-erh-chwang which goes on even now."

The majority of students nodded in agreement. Someone brought forth a mah jong box and a dozen of China's fiercest warriors sat upon the floor, playing until the time Teng Fa might appear.

Within the office, North China's lively young secret service chief paced the floor, puffed vehemently upon a cigarette, chewed sunflower seeds, sipped Pedro Domecq and scolded Quinto, who was lying on his bed, feet raised upon a pile of books. In his bright blue, knee-length Kuomingtang uniform, with a lethal-looking Luger automatic thrust in his belt, Teng Fa looked like a dangerous Gainsborough Blue Boy.

"My good Captain," he spoke in Chinese and shook a warning finger at Quinto, "in Sianfu no one minds your English friends drinking at the Guest House Bar, but please send no more of the same kind. The hotel manager begs you."

"*Si*, but I had reason, Teng."

"And so has the manager." Teng Fa flicked his cigarette through the window into the darkened garden. "The English," he said, "are always dropping what you call 'hygiene' down the drain, and a pair of scissors too. Guest House plumbing was stopped this entire day. Naturally, this is a blemish on the honorable name of Chinese bathrooms, which are as modern as their American and English sisters. But when they fail to work, they lose important face. China cannot afford to lose anything now."

His mind delivered of this delicate mission, Teng Fa unwrapped four books on Chinese calligraphy which he had brought to Lingtung. They were the Short Essentials, by Chang Yen Yuan.

"These I return to Mr. Tate," he said. "I borrowed them; there might be code within such ancient pages. I am suspicious of everyone. But I am so ashamed. They are indeed very good calligraphy. Mr. Tate is greatly honored to read them."

Quinto laughed and sat up.

"Did all this bring you here?" he asked.

"No. I want to see Mr. Harrow!"

"Harrow? Why?" Quinto's smoky eyes lighted.

"A matter of State."

"He's dead!"

The lively, boyish expression vanished from Teng Fa's face. His features took on a deadpan hardness.

"You shot him?" he asked.

"No. Furthermore, I don't know who murdered either Senor Harrow or Firth."

Teng Fa half opened his mouth, showed a set of remarkably even teeth which he abruptly clicked together like castanets.

"Mr. Clive, dead?" he murmured.

Quinto nodded quietly, then, briefly, he outlined the course of the past two days at Lingtung. While speaking he flipped over his mattress and brought forth the Wang ledgers and the Nohuri cipher. "Very important for matters of the State," he said, handing them to Teng.

The Chinese lad scrutinized the ledgers and the cipher. Finally he put them aside, saying:

"I suspicioned these would appear. I disliked Harrow traveling around China like a tourist. You understand. Teng Fa knows everything about everyone. It is very very important to know everything. Now I shall solve these murders."

"*Sentate.*" Quinto suddenly frowned. "These are my murders. I'll solve them."

"No. It is in my line of business."

"You can help, but it's my place to solve them."

Teng Fa bowed. "I give you a week."

"You brought the three dossiers I called for?" asked Quinto.

"The dossiers? Oh yes. I know everything. There is only one person in China who remains a mild mystery to Teng Fa. That is your beautiful companion, Mountain of Virtue. She is the blind spot in my files."

Quinto knitted his brows in irritation. "The dossiers of Wang, Wier and Harrow, where are they?" he demanded impatiently.

Teng Fa tapped his head. "Right here," he grinned. "Who first?"

"Harrow."

The young Chinese belched eloquently, then cleared his throat. "Mr. Harrow lived a short and unfortunate life," he began. "He was an American with noses for scandal. He worked for an American newspaper in Paris, making much money on American businessmen busy getting away from their wives. They did things. Harrow saw things. The businessmen paid well to have such information withdrawn from history.

"In 1930 Harrow came to Shanghai for the same purpose. But there was more money being economic adviser for little warlord Lin Chu Pi in Chekiang. Later, he found a better position with Chu Fang in middle Shansi. One day Chu Fang raided the Ping Yang foreign mission of James Wier. The daughter, Mary Wier, was kidnaped for a very high price. Wier was very angry. He threatened to kill Mr. Harrow if he ever saw him again."

"When was that?" Quinto interrupted.

"Four years ago, 1934."

"They had no other connections?"

"Yes, perhaps. A subtle connection." Teng Fa pointed to the Wang ledgers. "This . . ."

"What else? *Tenes algo mas importante*, something important?"

"Then Harrow joined the Chinese Service. He was a very bad soldier. He was under an official cloud—suspicion of robbing bodies at the front. This might explain the jades, watches and valuables you found in his room."

"Now about Wier."

Teng Fa paused, selecting a fresh cigarette from a little bamboo box he carried. He tapped the end a couple of times. Finally he continued with his recitation.

"James Wier," he said, "has been a missionary since he came to China from New Zealand twenty-two years ago. His character is that of a bitter man. He believes the Chinese were purposely created to make life difficult for him. He also disagrees with our fine art of kidnaping.

"Mr. Wier's woman died ten years ago. The daughter was born in China, but they are all American. Wier left America for New Zealand because he forged a check for someone, I think his brother."

"Brother?"

"Yes. The brother died in jail."

"*Que barbaridad, tal vez*, he was maybe a revolutionary, eh? In which prison did he die?"

"Joliet, U.S.A. You want the year? 1912."

"Now we'll take Wang," said Quinto.

Teng Fa nodded. "Wang is a Christian," he began in a tone implying that no sensible Chinese has a right to join upstart young Occidental sects which have only a mere nineteen hundred years to their credit. "Wang has always lived in Sianfu. His full name is Wang Chin Pi Liang and his Christian name is Benedict Wang. He has trouble with wives, which is why he lives in Lingtung now. He recently bought himself a *yima*, a number three wife. Number one and number two wife will not have the new one in the house and they argue, so Wang moved out to avoid the noise. . ."

"Tell me about Wang, not his *tsangtu*," Quinto cut in impatiently.

"Ah, Wang. I have many files on Wang. He is a crafty man. He is always interested in making deals. We suspect he would make a deal to sell our nation to the invader if there were some personal profit in it. In fact, he is such a banker at heart, he might even do it if the Bank of China could make some profit. You see, my file on Wang is most complete. I will give you his family history back to the Liang Dynasty."

"No. Just Wang himself," said Quinto. "Did Wang know Harrow, Wier or any of the internationals before coming to Lingtung Pavilions?"

"Oh, certainly. Wang banked for Harrow and Warlord Chu Fang. He negotiated the Wier girl's release. A fine deal, that. Wang negotiated for $10,000 Mexican, otherwise Mr. Wier might have only paid $5,000 Mexican. So it is to Wang's credit that he brought a lot more money into circulation."

Quinto thought this over carefully, recalling to mind the fact that Mary Wier had been seen knocking on Wang's door only twenty-four hours ago.

There came a rap upon the door. John Tate entered. He was puffing excitedly, while behind him a score of guerrilleros craned their necks to catch a glimpse of their hero. For an instant, Tate goggled in surprise at Teng Fa, then he abruptly stiffened and turned to the Mexican.

"Say, Quinto. There's been a theft," he said. "The museum case out in the hall. The Generalissimo's teeth are gone!"

CHAPTER 15
A Study in Teeth

THE TABLE on the garden terrace beyond the billiard room had been cleared. The oil lamps had been removed and in their place was a dazzling bright gasoline lamp which carved a big room of whiteness out of the jasmine-scented darkness. A rack of poker chips and two decks of well-worn cards stood on the table's oaken surface. Teng Fa fiddled with the cards while occasionally glancing from Tate to Quinto.

"I took the liberty of having Sergeant Sun invite a few guests," Teng explained. "We've searched one solid hour for the Generalissimo's teeth. I have still a few hours before I return to Sianfu. Poker is very invigorating. It brings out characteristics. One can study minds! Perhaps the teeth will show up in the poker game."

Quinto smiled, glancing at Tate. "You play poker?" he asked.

"Very little. I prefer bridge."

"Then watch your betting. Teng Fa plays like a sharp. There is no one better in China, naturally save myself."

Teng Fa grinned politely at the compliment. Tate stared at the two men worriedly. A moment later Nevada entered the terrace. His cold, hard eyes surveyed the cards and chips calmly and he sat down. Something in the way he looked at the cards indicated that the lean cowboy was also extremely proficient at poker.

Virtue came in, her gown rustling softly, her face an oval of beauty. She was all in blue, like Teng Fa. Then came Wang, who glanced at each person questioningly before taking his place beside the Eurasian girl. McKay hurried in, squeezing into an empty place between Tate and Quinto.

"Draw with table stakes," murmured Teng in a low, clipped, precise tone. He smiled ingratiatingly at each player in turn.

Chips were distributed. The cut for deal was made. Virtue bunched the cards, shuffled and dealt. Her playing style had the strange engrossing quality that might be called Asiatic. It was breathless to see. She sat perfectly poised, with a vague suggestion of a smile on her lips which never changed throughout the entire game. Her slender fingers flicked forth the cards expertly.

The first few hands passed sluggishly, then Tate opened on three jacks and filled his hand with two eights. He looked around cautiously. Apparently the faces of his opponents filled him with anxiety, for he hesitated. Nowhere in the world is poker played as blandly, intensely and ruthlessly as in China.

The expression on Teng Fa's face was enameled. Wang looked inscrutable. Quinto's eyes were smoky chunks of ice as he stared fixedly at the base of the lamp. Virtue's smile was taunting, while Nevada played a calm, relaxed game.

At last Tate pushed twenty dollars' worth of chips forward. He drummed the table with his fingers. McKay, on Tate's left, passed, while Teng Fa drew one card. Virtue tossed hers in. Wang drew two pasteboards.

The banker clutched his five cards up under his chin while his fingers spread the corners. His dark head tilted downward, staring wolfishly, not at the cards but upon the pool. Suddenly he threw his hand into the discard.

"Raise twenty-five," Nevada drawled.

Tate looked at the cowboy worriedly. Then Quinto met the bet. Again the calligraphist scrutinized his hand, three jacks and a pair. He peeped warily at the others and finally, taking a deep breath, shoved more chips to the center.

"A hundred," he whispered.

"Raise it twenty-five," said Teng Fa. A burning cigarette dangled from his lips with a long ash that stayed with peculiar tenacity.

Nevada met the bet and Quinto raised again. Sweat broke out on Tate's roly-poly brow. His cheeks flushed beneath Teng Fa's close, impersonal scrutiny.

The betting ran another round, then Tate called. He looked at the three-hundred-dollar pot hopefully while laying out his hand. His eyes brightened when Nevada threw his into the discard. Then Teng Fa flicked three queens on the table.

"Plunging is dangerous," murmured Quinto. He placed four tens on the table and slowly raked in the pot. "You see. I told you, Teng Fa and I are the best poker players in China."

Tate's lips compressed angrily. During the next half hour he bet more modestly, and finally dropped out of the game along with Doc McKay. The chips slowly drifted toward Mountain of Virtue's corner, and Tate watched with increasing amazement, for the girl won each time the deal came her way. And each time, she jockeyed the betting into a sizable pot before cleaning up.

Virtue became the center of serious suspicion. Teng Fa's bland eyes

studied Virtue's hands narrowly. Wang looked a little disturbed. Even
Nevada sat back in his chair when the girl dealt. His mouth fell open a
trifle while his eyes remained glued to the swift movement of her hands.

"Well, I'll be durned," he finally snorted. "I ain't never seen nothing like it. I'm sitting this hand out."

"It is very very strange," remarked Teng Fa. The cigarette barely
moved in his mouth as he spoke. "Two years ago in Shanghai I saw
Mountain of Virtue win five thousand dollars. She won it with three
queens and a pair. It was Shanghai, wasn't it, Virtue?"

Virtue smiled discreetly without taking her eyes from the cards.

"And you won again at poker after the embassy dinner in Nanking
last year," continued Teng Fa. "That was a few thousand dollars, I know.
And you won a British battleship from the Admiral in Hongkong. Remember?"

Virtue made a helpless little motion with her lashes.

"But the Admiral had nothing left to put up but his ship," she murmured reprovingly.

"You won a battleship?" Tate gasped.

Virtue nodded. "But I didn't take it," she sighed. "The admiral promised me something else instead."

Quinto frowned perceptibly, coughed, and smoldered pinkly at the
girl. She reached across the table and touched his hand reassuringly.
"It was nothing," she smiled. "The Admiral promised to help me rescue
three Chinese patriots who had been captured by the invader."

"Did he?" asked Tate.

"Oh, yes."

There was a lapse of silence. The poker game continued, paced
much faster than before. At length Wang threw down his cards and
with a curt bow left the terrace.

Teng Fa watched him go, then grinned at Quinto.

"Does Wang wear store teeth?"

Tate looked up interestedly. The fact that a pair of historically important false teeth had been mysteriously lifted from the museum case
apparently struck him as peculiarly ludicrous and yet sinister. Were the
teeth concerned in the murders?

"Maybe someone is wearing the teeth," he suggested.

Quinto leaned back in his chair and rolled his eyes at the
calligraphist as though the latter had committed a major heresy.

"The Generalissimo's teeth are a national memorial," he said. "Who
would wear them? They are the turning point in China's history, *comprende?*"

"Plus Chiang Kai-shek's," McKay put in tartly.

"You weren't in the Northwest when this thing happened, were you, Senor Tate? What occurred the eleventh of December, 1936, will be forever remembered as the immortal example of the strategy of *Ping Chien* or military persuasion which the outside world so rudely look upon as mere kidnaping.

"At that time the invader had taken Manchuria and was marching upon Pekin. The Generalissimo did nothing about resisting that invasion except to fly up to Sianfu in order to find out why Chang Hsueh-liang, the Young Marshal of Manchuria, and all his Tungpei troops were angry at him.

"Then a most interesting thing happened," Quinto nodded wisely. "Chiang Kai-shek drove to Lingtung Pavilions to sleep. Yes, *companeros*, he slept in this very building the night of December twelfth. Meanwhile at midnight, in Sianfu, his entire staff of blue-shirted guards and general staff were arrested at the Guest House. .

"The kidnaping," McKay interrupted.

"The *Ping Chien*," Quinto corrected him. "It was just the beginning. Also, at midnight, a captain of the Young Marshal's guards set out for Lingtung with three hundred Tungpei soldiers. Before dawn they drove into the garden here in lorries . . . ."

Teng Fa grinned. "Fine fight!"

"The Tungpei were challenged and fired upon," said Quinto. "You still see the bullet scars in the scarlet pillars outside the door. In the confusion and darkness, Chiang Kai-shek leaped out of bed. He was wearing a night shirt. Quickly, he grabbed a robe, flung it over his shoulders and ran up the mountain in his bare feet. He left his teeth behind in a glass of water."

"What is more natural?" McKay smiled.

Quinto motioned for silence until he finished.

"The Generalissimo hid in the cave on the mountain. He was cold, shivering, his feet were cut by stones, and he was very upset. The destiny of China shivered in that cave. But the Young Marshal's captain pursued. He found Chiang and carried him down the mountain on his back and when they returned to the Pavilions, the teeth in the glass were gone.

"The Generalissimo was held a prisoner twelve days. He got new teeth which didn't fit well, and it was such a lesson, he agreed to fight the Japanese. That is how a man can lose a little thing like teeth and become a great figure."

"But how did you get the teeth for the museum case?" Tate asked.

"The Young Marshal presented them to me."

Quinto pushed his last red chip into the pot as he finished speaking. Teng Fa did likewise, but instead of listening to the Mexican, he watched Virtue's deft hands as she laid out her final spread—three Queens and a pair of fives.

Virtue calmly swept the chips to her corner, stacked the gains and looked at Quinto disarmingly. "The Generalissimo had very dirty feet upon coming down the mountain?" she asked casually.

"The lower trail isn't dirty. It's mostly stone," replied Quinto.

"No red clay?" asked Virtue.

"There's red clay only at the top and near the cliff where—" Suddenly Quinto paused. "Red clay, did you say?"

Virtue nodded. "Yes, Gimiendo. Like the bit you found in Mr. Firth's room."

"*Mas claro*, Virtue," Quinto spoke sharply.

"You will notice Wang's fine boots are clean today. I polished them this morning."

Quinto swung his chair down on all four legs.

"So! You found the same clay on Wang's boots!"

Tate swiveled his eyes around alertly. "There you are. Something at last," he said. "Wang in Firth's room last night. His heel prints on the cliff. I noticed it myself. His boot heels were quite narrow and high, like a woman's heel."

Suddenly it became clear that no one was listening to Tate. They were all staring at Virtue. This was a very ticklish situation and even Virtue blushed. Shoe-polishing in China is a most intimate act.

Finally Teng Fa pushed back his chair and hurried to the door. "I want Wang first," he snapped.

"No. I get him, then you," said Quinto.

Sergeant Sun's beaming face appeared from behind a pillar as Quinto, Teng Fa and Tate raced from the *yamen* toward Wang's villa. "No gottum look Wang no more," he said. "He gone chop chop."

"Gone?" bellowed Quinto. "*El cabron se pelo.*"

"Wang go Sianfu direction, much chop chop."

"How did he go, Sun? Feet or car?"

"Lingtung rickshaw. Half hour."

"We can overtake him in the car. Want me to?" Tate asked.

"I'll go after him," Teng Fa cut in. "I'll have Wang for you. Please come to Sianfu tomorrow morning. Everyone should come. Tomorrow is Weeping at the Graves Festival. There will be many people in the city."

Teng Fa turned to reenter the *yamen*. Virtue stood on the step, in the doorway.

"You wish the Wang ledgers and cipher?" she asked.

"Yes, please," said Teng.

"They are gone. Wang took them."

"*Hijo de la chingada!*" Quinto exploded. "This is going too far!"

"To be expected," murmured Teng. "The spider takes his web with him. A very very important web."

"Please," Virtue smiled charmingly. "Mr. Tate can reconstruct the cipher. You can, Mr. Tate?"

Tate's blush was visible even in the semidarkness of the pavilion steps. He agreed that he could reproduce the cipher.

"Very well then," said Virtue. "And as for the ledgers, this afternoon while Gimiendo was away, I made a copy of the important pages. Gimiendo is very careless. I knew this would happen."

She handed Teng Fa a sheaf of typed papers.

CHAPTER 16
Kidnaped in Sianfu

CHINA'S ANCIENT capital, Sianfu, was always a sea of mud following the heavy spring rains. Muck cluttered the wheels of rickshaws and military lorries alike. Mud plastered the forty miles of gigantic medieval wall surrounding the cramped, dwarfish houses of the city. It ran through doorways, was tracked into government buildings, through the old palace and the Sianfu temples. It was packed hardest under the four huge gates which had once greeted the invading Tartars and Mongols and Genghis Khan. Mire ran deepest around the delousing stations at the gates and in the Moslem refugee camps beyond the city walls.

Now the rain miraculously stopped for Ch'ingming Day. It always did, for Ch'ingming was a major festival. The generals and the important people came to town looking for the graves of their ancestors, drinking a little over them.

With the rains suspended, the ceaseless dust again blew down from the Gobi. The dust and the sun returned to Sianfu its old familiar odors—the stench of packed houses, of decay and growth, of murder and intrigue. It lurked in dark corners and medieval alleyways, ready to leap out at the unwary visitor.

"It's wonderful!" John Tate murmured.

Sianfu was beautiful and wonderful on this morning, if one had an eye for history, and a congested nose.

Genghis Khan walked here as though it were only yesterday. The ancient scholars practiced in the palace, their deft fingers making strokes with the brush. Their strokes rose, fell, swept, crouched and sprang— new strokes in the vocabulary of calligraphy. Here one invented the *li* style which is writing like a tiger walks. Another perfected the *lsing* stroke with its informal soft angles; a stroke fitted for the writing of poetry and woman-words.

John Tate looked the part of a scholar. He looked as if he had just walked out of this kind of history, for he was staring vacantly over the head of the Annamite who pulled his rickshaw along the rutted street.

An officer, standing in a puddle of dust-coated mud, saluted the vehicle primly. He saluted, not Tate, but Mountain of Virtue, who was riding beside the calligraphist. The salute might have even included Mildred Woodford, who sat on Tate's left.

The rickshaw joggled along. Its blue-covered hood was embroidered with great white flowers in an oddly Victorian style. More officers saluted. Tate beamed at them absentmindedly. Then he smiled at Virtue and frowned a little at Mildred Woodford. He had been ordered by Quinto to spend the day with Virtue and to take Woodford sight-seeing.

Throughout the morning Virtue had pointed out the splendors of Sianfu. She had shown them the walls and the Drum Tower, which was now used as an air raid observation post. And now she called the rickshaw to a halt at the Pei-lin, the Forest of Tablets Museum.

Virtue descended, daintily lifting her silk trousers to keep the mud from their scarlet cuffs.

"You'll enjoy Pei-lin," she announced. "It contains much old calligraphy and rubbings."

Mildred Woodford wrinkled her Yorkshire nose at the thought of calligraphy. "Did we come to town to look at relics?" she asked. "Let's go to a bar, I'm parched."

"Oh, come on," said Tate.

"Dammit, I'm parched."

"The Pei-lin first," said Virtue. "Then I'll show you how to drink." Her dark eyes twinkled.

Virtue went ahead. In the museum she walked slightly in front, moving through the forest of glass cases, touching a case here and there, explaining:

"Here are tablets with very fine writing. The events of the five dynasties ending with Chou . . . ." She paused a moment before pointing at a life-size portrait of an old man with roguish eyes and President McKinley sidewhiskers. "Confucius," she murmured.

She went on to explain the thirteen classics which were cut in stone, the writing of the Han dynasty and the Nestorian tablets with their double Chinese and Syric script which the Emperor Taitsung had introduced.

Tate's slightly albino eyes fumbled with the precious tablets. His look of awe, which had at first been entirely upon the historical exhibits, soon shifted to Virtue's person. The Eurasian girl talked of calligraphy and such things with an astonishingly rare familiarity. Somehow, her scholarship was like that of Doctor Hu Shih, China's mental giant who, after years of study, finally invented a workable alphabet for Chinese vernacular.

"Where'd you study calligraphy?" he asked her.

"My uncle, Meng T'ien," Virtue smiled.

"Meng T'ien!" Tate almost choked on the name. He looked at the

girl queerly while his mind performed some rather startling calcula-
tions. Meng T'ien was the celebrated general of the First Emperor—he
who had finished the last thousand *li* of the Great Wall. Meng himself
had invented the new method of Chinese writing—with the brush. Pre-
viously, people were old fashioned and used the bamboo stylus.

Mildred Woodford had been listening to the conversation halfheart-
edly. Now she spoke to Virtue and her voice was dry and condescend-
ing.

"I knew a Chinaman once, studying at Cambridge," she said. "I
don't recall his name. Ming or something sounding like that. Perhaps
he was your uncle. Do you think so?"

Virtue shrugged her well poised shoulders.

"Oh, no," she whispered radiantly. "Uncle Meng died in 209 B.C.,
that is, by your calendar."

The appreciative expression on Tate's round face suddenly vanished. His jaw sagged loosely as he peered behind the glass case on
which Virtue leaned her arm. A sullen Chinese face blinked at him
through the glass. Tate let his glance swivel around slowly. There was a
second face. A third. Five. One winked ogrishly at him. He sucked in
his breath.

"V-V-Virtue, l-look out!" he finally stuttered.

The warning came too late. A dozen Chinese men, all heavily armed,
leaped from behind the cases. The first two grabbed Virtue. Another
two yanked at both of Mildred Woodford's arms.

Mildred jerked one arm free for an instant and succeeded in slap-
ping one of the faces a resounding crack.

"I say, you can't do this! I'm a British subject," she cried angrily.

"Famous last words—unquote," murmured Virtue.

Tate stiffened, feeling a hard, unyielding object jabbed into the
small of his back. He envisioned nothing less than an antitank cannon
on the verge of blowing out his fifth rib.

The Guest House, in the center of Sianfu, is a most amazing hotel.
Built during a capricious moment by Chang Hsueh-liang, the Young
Marshal, it was designed in the severely modern Germanic style. Altogether, it blends with Sianfu about as intimately as a Hollywood cheese-
burger gets along in Boston.

Being somewhat practical, the Young Marshal saw to it that the Guest
House had private baths, running water, central heating, a barber shop,
swinging doors and a New York Bar.

The bar, done in chrome metal and blue tile, was a sort of League
of Nations for the North. Here, according to the menus printed in Chi-

nese, French and English, one could indulge in such delicacies as White Horses whiski, lemin pie, FFPotatos, chipped potato, ham-egg and hat cakes.

Here one saw the most beautiful girls in all China, handsomely dressed officers, and others less handsome but more efficient. There were old men with close-cropped hair, Japanese masquerading as Chinese, white Russians as red Russians.

On this particular Ch'ingming Day an American novelist, a British poet and a salesman for Caterpillar Tractors sat at one table in the bar. They argued about war and death as if such things came naturally in job lots. At a farther table sat the provincial Minister of Pacification, a tubby little man whose business it was to keep the Mint'uan* or local bandits in order. Next to him were the moody-eyed Civil Governor of Sianfu and General Kuchu-tung, the businesslike Military Governor. The two governors and the minister watched each other with polite animosity and when they weren't doing this, they gazed at Gimiendo Quinto and Teng Fa with envious respect. They admired Teng Fa because he was a hero, and Quinto because of the twelve empty sherry glasses lined up on the table in front of him.

Quinto rolled an ounce of the liquor in his mouth and puckered his lips, speaking to Teng Fa in Chinese.

"And so you lost Wang last night?" he asked.

"But for the moment," Teng replied with immense Celestial *shunp'o* or simplicity. "Wang stepped from the main road last night. He didn't enter Sianfu or the guards at the gates would have seen his papers."

"*Esta muy malo*," Quinto murmured his disgust in Spanish.

"But I shall find him," Teng quickly added. "You may be certain of that. China is not so big that a man can get lost in it."

Both the Civil and Military Governors nodded at Quinto, at the same time making appreciative little noises as if to personally guarantee Teng's promise.

Quinto nodded his satisfaction and ran his eyes thoughtfully around. The Guest House bar was extremely crowded, particularly with generals and self-made warlords who had joined forces with the regular Chinese army.

Each April (this year it was the fifth of the month) they came to Sianfu to take part in the traditional pilgrimage to the graves of the Jo Emperors just outside the city. It was the custom to pay homage to one's ancestors this day. Sianfu profited, because actually the Jo Emperors were not known to have been very prolific, yet there were thousands of homage-paying sons.

"Many of the warlords here today," explained the Minister of Pacification, "were once nothing but poor bandits without ancestors. Now they have ancestors. They bought themselves ancestors."

"You wish to buy an ancestor, a Jo Emperor perhaps?" the Civil Governor suggested to Quinto. "It will give you much face."

"Has Wang the banker such ancestors?" asked Quinto.

"Wang has two sets of ancestors," replied the governor, as though he himself were impressed. "Wang has his own family ancestors, the Liangs, and he bought into the Jo family."

"The Jo name is expensive, isn't it?"

"*Ayi!* Wang is rich. He pays."

Teng Pa lifted his glass and looked through it. "Would you be interested," he spoke blandly, "if Wang and Mr. Wier had private bank accounts in a French bank in Hankow?"

"Banque du Chine Central?" queried Quinto.

Teng's boyish face fell.

"You already know, so why should I tell you?"

"How much?"

"In new deposits, 750,000 francs."

"Each?"

"No. Both together, with Wang having the larger account."

"Were the deposits made in francs?"

"Chinese dollar."

Suddenly Quinto rose from his chair and towered above the table. His gaze leaped across the crowded barroom to where a man in a Yellow Trench Coat stood in the doorway. The man looked in at the bar, hesitated, then turned and retreated hastily through the hotel lobby.

Almost in the same instant, Quinto pushed through the crowded bar toward the door. On his way, he bumped into a civil official, bowled the man over, stepped on his stomach and rushed on into the lobby. A flash of yellow gabardine whisked behind a swinging door marked MEN.

In the lobby a swath of startled spectators marked Quinto's progress, which ended with a loud bang when he crashed into the men's-room door. He rushed into the lavender-tiled cubicle and there halted. The place was empty! Through an open window he caught the last glimpse of Mr. Yellow Coat disappearing in the crowded street outside.

"This can't go on," he fumed, returning to the lobby. "Everyone disappearing right under my nose.'

"Mista Qui'to—?"

A Shensi coolie stood in Quinto's way, bowing.

"Beg to tell honorable gentlesmens Qui'to two piece missy kidnaped," he sang.

Quinto grabbed for the coolie as the latter darted away.

He jerked the shivering messenger back and held him, squirming, a foot off the floor.

"Kidnaped! Which missy?" he demanded.

"Hsiaochieh missy, foreign missy," the coolie gulped.

"Virtue and Woodford! Who kidnaped them?"

"Min-t'uan!"

"And the funny little fat man who was with them? The American?" Quinto demanded.

John Tate lifted his head tentatively toward the museum case, then let it bump back upon the stone floor. The insides, particularly the back part of his skull, ached miserably. He felt as if someone had driven spikes through his head and poured liquid lead through the holes. The lead was now seeping into the crevices of his brain.

He wondered how long he had been unconscious. It could have been days, or only hours. He knew one thing at least. He was alone. Mountain of Virtue, Miss Woodford and the blinking bandit faces were gone . . . . But where?

Now his right arm hurt and it felt worse than his head, because it tickled instead of ached. He craned his neck at an angle and moaned at what he saw. His arms were crossed in front. Coils of heavy rope had been wound about his middle. Something tasting like a fistful of mud had been crammed into his mouth.

Tate considered his position, then for fifteen minutes he struggled. Gritting his teeth to hold back the pain in his right arm, he finally balanced himself upright against a museum case. With that, he tumbled flat on his back.

Someone came down the museum aisle.

Tate breathed a sigh of relief, mainly through his nose.

A Chinese, wearing a long black gown, approached cautiously. For a moment, the visitor stood stock still and stared at Tate intently.

"Gruoff.... Rumpf!" Tate cried through his gag.

The Chinese shrugged his frail shoulders doubtfully. On serving the Chinese trait of philosophically accepting events as they are, he went on, casually examining the museum cases.

A half hour passed before Tate again managed to get himself into an upright position. This time he shoved the case, overturning it with a clatter of broken glass. It produced the results he desired, for a museum guard came on the run.

When Tate finally arrived at the Guest House it was midafternoon and he was haggard and hungry. But now there was no time for food. He found Gimiendo Quinto in the street aboard a sturdy little Mongol pony. There were more ponies on the hotel steps, and most of Quinto's guerrilla students, who, it turned out later, had been summoned from Lingtung. Some of the students had white horses, which, after the Chinese fashion, were dyed green or clay-red for camouflage purposes.

"Quinto—Good God!" Tate plunged into an explanation of his adventures.

"Never mind, *companero*," replied the Mexican. "I know that the senoritas were kidnaped." He grasped Tate's good arm and hoisted him to a spare pony. Then his hand swept eloquently toward the broken line of big, savage mountains in the South. The Bandit Mountains. "We are going to chase the Min-t'uan. *Vayamos pronto.*"

CHAPTER 17
The Chase

QUINTO WAS very satisfied with everything in general. He and Tate and the little band of guerrilleros had ridden far into the dry, dusty Bandit Mountains. They had ridden a full afternoon, a part of the night and now this, the morning of the second day.

As they rode through a sun-baked canyon, passing beneath sheer precipices of tawny rock, Quinto glowed with good will and pleasure over his indulgence in physical action.

"I am much more at home in the saddle," he announced. "I hate this business of questioning people in the manner of an English detective. We've had enough for a few days. Now that we have action, we'll come quickly to a solution of our problems."

It was not hard to imagine the Mexican approaching a solution aboard his Mongol pony. Unlike Tate, he was equipped for any and every eventuality. He wore a crossed bandoleer of bullets across his barrel chest. There was a sinister two-edged ax and a coiled horsehair lariat on his saddle. Quinto himself wore an automatic and a saber. Beneath his cotton jacket a shirt of light steel mesh was visible.

"I wear the mail," Quinto explained, "because I am so large bullets always get in my way."

In contrast to Tate, he rode easily. He sat erect in his carved saddle, his body swaying in almost uncanny unity with the measured pace of his sturdy little mount. Sometimes he hummed as he rode. He was taking the loss of Virtue as he always took her—philosophically. Kidnaping was something not beyond his ability to repair.

He kept whirling a small length of twine, at the end of which was a miniature lasso, and at times, as he rode at the head of his guerrilleros, he stopped humming to lightly sing his favorite song—the campaign song of cousin Pancho.

> *La cucaracha, La cucaracha,*
> *Ya no puede caminar*
> *Si lo no tiene, si lo no tiene,*
> *Uno gusto pare luchar.*

John Tate rode with less assurance, although the Mongol ponies were easy to manage in the Shensi dialect. Upon leaving the Guest House the afternoon before, he had placed himself in Quinto's hands without reserve. Now he appeared a little doubtful. What could twenty guerrilleros and two foreigners do in the Bandit Mountains?

"Perhaps that farmer back at Lan-tien was lying?" he murmured for the tenth time.

"*Por que?*" asked Quinto. "Didn't he say the Min-t'uan men passed there with a foreign lady who complained bitterly about garlic in the food. Senorita Woodford, naturally."

"But was it the truth?" Tate protested weakly. "The information cost us only five *tael.*"

"Peasants never charge the Republic's guerrilleros tourist prices."

"I thought there were no bandits," said Tate.

"There aren't. Bandits are honest men making a living in a way not quite bona fide but often necessary. The Mint'uan aren't bandits. They're what you call 'goons' or, in my country, '*hidalgos.*' Sometimes they are rich men's sons who band together to suppress peasants. Sometimes they are only hired by rich men."

"Wang's, I suppose?"

Sergeant Ping of the guerrilleros reined his horse up beside Quinto. He pointed toward the canyon back-trail, where a cloud of yellowish dust bloomed.

"We're being followed," he announced.

"Good," answered Quinto. "You know the strategy."

"Perfectly."

Ping saluted and curbed his horse. Quinto stood in his stirrups and shouted, "Prepare for battle."

"Where?" asked Tate nervously.

There was a certain eagerness showing in Quinto's eyes as he stared at something in the canyon up ahead. The something caused Tate to draw his breath in sharply. He saw a wisp of smoke curling up the canyon wall.

"Surrounded!" Quinto observed calmly.

A detachment of men under Ping's command swerved off into a small box arroyo, while Quinto, Tate and seven remaining guerrilleros spurred on toward the smoke.

"What do we do now?" Tate asked.

"A little maneuvering, *nada mas.* You are about to see my own variation of Cousin Pancho Villa's feint attack. Mine is called, *On being led into a trap and turning tables.*"

"Will there be fighting?" Tate glanced at his useless right arm.

"Oh, nothing but a short formal fight."

Quinto spurred his pony forward at a faster clip. *La Cucaracha* rollicked on his lips, inaudible two yards away. Tate's own mount almost swept from under him as the guerrilleros raced after Quinto. They rode like a band of charging Moors, shouting and brandishing rifles overhead. Suddenly the entire company plunged into a hollow where Min-t'uan men poked guns out from behind a dozen rocks. Almost instantly, another band of mounted Min-t'uan riders spurred up from behind, surrounding the guerrilleros. Tate managed to cling to his saddle while rifles and pistols spat at him from all sides. A bullet zzzinged past his ear, flicking off a tuft of hair. Riders, Min-t'uan and guerrilleros criss-crossed on every side. The din of battle grew terrific as well as heroic.

At this point something became strangely noticeable. For all the bullets and noise, not one man fell off his horse. Not a single horse whinnied in pain or fright. There were no gasps and screams from wounded men, only shrilly shouted war-cries and the calling out of popular Chinese propaganda slogans. All at once it became clear . . . . The guerrilleros and the Min-t'uan men were firing madly into the sky! Everyone was having a wonderful time. It was a sham battle.

Then, strangely, Quinto waved a white flag.

The shooting and noise abruptly subsided. A squat, swarthy-faced brigand with sympathetic eyes, obviously the leader of the Min-t'uan, rode up to the Mexican. Both men dismounted.

"We concede to a superior force," Quinto smiled.

The Min-t'uan chief saluted, then bowed.

"But we should be honored to concede victory to your superior cunning, generalship and bravery," he apologized.

Quinto lifted a deprecating hand. "But the honor is ours," he murmured.

"You are a great general!" The Min-t'uan chief bowed again, for it was seldom that a foreigner understood the subtleties of the traditional Chinese battle in which no one gets hurt and the army making the most noise or display of force is granted victory.

He turned to his brigands and gave out orders in a soft, sibilant voice.

"The foreigner we will release. The others will concede to becoming our prisoners." Then he glanced appraisingly at Quinto's guerrilleros. Something made him amend his plan. "On second thought," he said, glancing at Quinto, "the soldiers appear to have small value. Perhaps I will keep only the little pink-eyed man with the wrapped-up arm. Has he value?"

"Much value," Quinto answered. "Senor Tate is my second most valued treasure."

"Good then, I'll keep him. You may do us the honor of being go-between for the kidnap reward?"

Quinto nodded in affirmation.

Tate shot Quinto a baleful, protesting glance. His eyes grew alternately wide and small, like those of a squid.

"You're not going to leave me here with these bandits?" he cried. "But Quinto—"

Quinto smiled warmly and said nothing. He calmly studied the hands of his noisy Ingersoll watch. After a few minutes' silence the watch went back in his pocket and he suddenly clapped both hands. The sound came like a rifle report, echoing in the canyon hollow.

The signal brought dismay among the Min-t'uan men, for from behind a dozen rocks and boulders Sergeant Ping and the contingent of guerrilleros who had hidden in a box canyon until Quinto's group were surrounded, now stepped forth with leveled rifles. There came a businesslike click of bolts jamming cartridges into breeches. Ping's men displayed superb efficiency in surrounding and disarming the Min-t'uan, whose leader, meanwhile, flashed Quinto a hurt look. This, indeed, was no Chinese tactic.

Quinto bowed apologetically, murmuring:

"I am so sorry, but now, suddenly, I appear to have the superior force."

He calmly fished in his pocket for some loose shreds of tobacco, rolled a cigarette, and stuck it between his smiling lips. "Very simple," he added, still speaking to the Mint'uan chief. "We capture you by turning tables. Now you must lead us to the hideout where the beautiful Shan Te* and Senorita Woodford are being held. I am clever, no?"

The Min-t'uan chief shook his head.

"I am miserably sorry, but you can't do it," he said. "I admire your tactics, yet they are entirely impossible. You must release us at once."

"Release you—bandits!" Tate cut in, his courage having returned along with Sergeant Ping. "Are you mad?"

Quinto stepped between Tate and the chieftain.

"*Ai quates!* Less vehemence, please. We must observe the rules and strategy of political compromise."

"That's right," said the Min-tuan leader. "The rules of *yu shih wu ming.*"

"I propose an honorable deal in order to increase your face among your brethren," said Quinto.

The chieftain bowed. He waited attentively.

"First," continued Quinto, "you lead us to Mountain of Virtue, whom you might know as Shan Te. Also, there is an English woman. Then we'll release you. There'll be a reward, of course. The reward is for Mountain of Virtue."

"One does not quite see the direction," murmured the chieftain.

Quinto's hand dug into his pocket and he brought out a fistful of Chinese money. He carried it loose and crumpled, like handkerchiefs.

"May I improve your sight?" he suggested blandly. "Sun Yat Sen dollars. Very good."

*Mountain of Virtue's native name, pronounced, *Sharn-ter.*

The chieftain shook his head sadly.

"This is a most delicate question," he explained. "If I take you to the beautiful lady there will undoubtedly be great fighting over her. This cannot be risked. Mountain of Virtue might be harmed and she is far too beautiful to have tragedy befall to. A *hsiaochieh* woman is rare in China today!"

Quinto beamed appreciatively through the film of smoke curling from his lips. He nodded slowly, acknowledging the delicacy and understanding of the Min-t'uan chieftain.

"Careless of me," he muttered. "*Fui pendejo,* a real dope."

"You must allow yourself to be recaptured and returned to Ling-tung," insisted the chieftain. "I give personal guarantee comfort and service will be rendered the beautiful lady." The chieftain paused, thoughtfully. "And another thing," he said. "To make the deal more worthy and just, I beg one service of you?"

"Granted," said Quinto. "What?"

"For good measure, I'll throw in the long-nosed foreign woman. She is much too difficult for us to manage. She requires the iron hand of a foreign male. You will do this?"

"It's asking much," Quinto countered.

"I'll pay you. Five hundred dollars, Chinese," the chieftain spoke hastily.

"Very well."

Quinto accepted the money offered, this time by the Min-t'uan. He stuffed it into his jacket pocket. Meanwhile, the chieftain, his face now glowing with relief and good fellowship, ordered one of his men to cart Mildred Woodford from a nearby cave where she was being held.

"It won't do to search for Mountain of Virtue in the same cave. She is not there," he told Quinto.

"But where is she?"

"Right now, my mind is blank."

"Could it be enlightened?"

"Possibly."

"And the conditions?"

"Another deal," suggested the chieftain. "You, honorable Captain, the pink-eyed man and the long-nosed woman must concede to recapture. My men will escort you to Lingtung. When you agree, I am in a mood to be enlightened."

"It's a deal," replied Quinto. "How much enlightenment?"

"Five hundred dollars."

"Chinese?"

"Good enough," shrugged the chieftain.

Quinto took the five hundred dollars which he had received a moment earlier and returned it to the Min-t'uan leader. He realized, with satisfaction, that the negotiations had been quite inexpensive as a whole.

"Now, the whereabouts of Virtue?" he demanded.

"The village of Honan in the Loess regions."

For the first time during the negotiations, the adventurous Mexican seemed to lose some of his self-assurance. The big man's features clouded and his dismay was nothing less than eloquent. "Virtue, in Honan?" he asked unbelievingly.

The chieftain nodded.

"Yes, in the Loess Lands to the east. After the kidnaping in the Pei-Lin, our party split. I carried the long-nosed foreigner here. Others, moving by fast automobile, took the beautiful lady to Honan."

The clatter of unshod pony hoofs echoed among the rocks. The Min-t'uan man who had been sent after Mildred Woodford rode into sight. Mildred rode on a second pony. Her hands were tied behind her back and there was a rope coiled about her neck. The Min-t'uan rider held the other end.

Mildred was not a particularly pretty sight, for her mouth and lips were pinched as though she had sucked a dozen lemons. Though her face was beet-red with anger, she appeared absolutely incapable of speech.

"Her mouth will improve in a few days," the Min-t'uan chieftain explained. "She made me so much trouble I had to gag her with an unripe persimmon. It is a most effective gag."

Quinto mounted his pony and, taking the noose from Woodford's neck, prepared to depart. "*Vamos*," he cried. "Tell Wang I shall have his ears for the taking of Virtue," he added, waving cheerfully at the chieftain.

The band of twenty Lingtung guerrilleros rode ahead, escorted by three Min-t'uan guards. Quinto followed beside Tate. Mildred Woodford bumped along ahead. She was still unable to speak coherently, much to everyone's relief.

After a little while, Tate observed that the party of guerrilleros had mysteriously dwindled to seventeen. Ping and two men had disappeared. The guards were gone too!

"It's strange," he said. "I could swear I saw Ping riding off with us?"

Quinto smiled confidentially.

"Ping and the two *chicos* joined the Min-t'uan," he explained. "Very efficient, no? Not a sound. They overcame the guards at the last turn in the canyon. They are now wearing Min-t'uan clothes. It's part of our strategy. They'll find Virtue and bring me word whether she desires to be rescued."

"I don't see why you didn't arrest all the Min-t'uan and have it done with?"

"That wouldn't be *hanyan*."

"Why?"

"Well, you understand. The essence of good Chinese strategy is *hanyan*. When you see two enemy generals ride together as friends, that is *hanyan*. It is the art of not pressing your enemy to the wall, or not taking too much advantage. Thus the enemy, through knowing you better, is eventually impressed by your superior cunning."

Nevada looked steadily at Mary Wier as she stood in the sunlight near the scarlet pillars of the Lingtung Pavilions. The girl's transparent skin seemed to pale, and her eyes avoided his even before he spoke.

"Mary—" Nevada hesitated.

"What?"

The cowboy scraped the toe of his boot in the gravel path.

"Mary, after the funeral for Harrow and Firth, I'm leaving Lingtung. This afternoon. I'm going to the front."

A surprised, hurt look came into the girl's eyes. For a second she was very forlorn.

"Why, Nevada?"

"I can't stay here. I'm getting too mixed up.'

"I don't want you to go."

"You don't?"

Nevada grinned delightedly.

"No. Don't go," Mary repeated softly.

"Mary—will you marry me?"

For an instant the girl turned away. Two small tears quivered from her eyes. There was a moment of silence. Suddenly she was in his arms, her body relaxed against his and his lips fumbling upon her cheek, then her lips.

"Say yes, Mary."

The girl clung to him desperately. "I do love you," she cried softly. "I do, really. But I told you, I can't marry you. I can't . . . that's all."

Nevada's arms relaxed. His lips set in a thin line. "I don't get it," he said slowly.

"I can't marry you, the way things are here."

"What things?"

"Oh, don't ask me. If you knew you wouldn't ask me to marry you. Don't look at me that way, please!"

Nevada's eyes narrowed and grew hard. There came a vivid flash in his memory. The picture of Mary in the garden the afternoon Harrow had been murdered. The uneasy suspicion which he had put aside now festered in his mind. In spite of himself, he had to yield to its insistence.

"Mary! What was there between you and Firth?"

"There was nothing!"

"You're lying."

"Nevada, please."

"What was it? Did you—?"

The girl's eyes widened with terror and her hand went to her lips as though to stop her voice. "I didn't! Really, I didn't! He was dead when I went to his room! Believe me!" she screamed hysterically.

"You went to his room? That night?" Nevada gasped.

His fingers clenched and unclenched spasmodically as he stared at her.

"You don't understand, Nevada. I'll explain it all. Please let me."

Abruptly there was a crack. Mary's doll-like head snapped to one side. Her blond hair shook out loosely. Then she crumbled to the garden path—knocked out. She lay there, all in a heap, her fluffy pale-green dress ruffled; her face white and innocent looking.

Nevada stared at her, fascinated and bewildered. He had never struck a woman before. His girl. Suddenly he turned away.

"I'm a damn fool," he muttered.

CHAPTER 18
Something Big, Something Little

EARLY in the morning of the day following Mildred Woodford's rescue, Tate was sent in search of Mary Wier. He found her and Sergeant Sun admiring a young dwarf plum tree that had just flowered. A flavor of powdery pollen filled the little brick guardhouse and Sun was inordinately proud.

"I make him grow since him baby," he crowed.

Surreptitiously, Tate glanced at Mary's jaw, for he had already heard of the affair with Nevada. Mary's face was turned enough to reveal the slight swelling and the bluish bruise. He felt suddenly sorry for her.

"Miss Wier—" he called.

Mary looked around. She was very forlorn.

"G.H.Q. is back," Tate told her. "He wants to see you in the office."

"Now?"

"Yes. He's waiting."

A few minutes later Tate opened the door of the *yamen* and let Mary go ahead. His pinkish eyes still held her in half pitying, half curious scrutiny as she sank into a chair Quinto offered her.

"A drink! Can I get you a drink?"

"No thank you, Mr. Tate."

The girl's somber eyes looked inquiringly at Quinto, who had seated himself on a stool directly opposite her. Tate watched the entire business intently.

Quinto's start was somewhat disappointing.

"Senorita," he spoke gently, "I want you to answer a few questions. No. Don't be frightened. You must not imagine me as big and terrible. You know, once I was very small. I weighed only eight pounds. It was the day I was born. All the bigness I have today, I got since I have been alive. Think of me as eight pounds and don't be frightened."

Mary drew back startled.

"What do you want?" she asked.

"Some answers. Some truth. You understand, eh?"

"But what?"

Quinto favored her with a friendly smile.

113

"Senor Nevada is my friend," he began. "I want you to tell me why he struck you. You wouldn't say he made a habit of hitting girls, eh?"

A tiny thread of terror flamed in Mary's eyes. She shook her head.

"You make me feel like a beast—*pareco un bruto*," said Quinto and he patted her hand. "Now, Nevada loves you, doesn't he? Your eyes show something of the same feeling for him. Am I right?"

Mary's glance fell to her lap, where her fingers nervously folded the pleats of her skirt.

"Certainly. You are in love," Quinto added affirmatively.

"It's all over. He's gone," said Mary.

"Yes, he has gone. You're afraid he won't return. You want him back. You imagine it's too late now. Why do you think he'll never come back? What did you say to him?"

"Please—" Mary cried.

"Did you suspect Nevada murdered Senor Firth? Is that why?"

"No . . . no . . . not Nevada."

"Why did he hit you? Tell me, like I am your *padre*, eh?"

Mary's gaze went forth, helpless and pleading. Again, Quinto pressed her hand, reassuringly.

"You must tell me," he murmured. "There must be nothing hidden. *Absolutamente nada.*"

"I-I-I told him . . ."

"Yes, I'm listening? *Sigue.*"

The girl bit her lower lip and a little drop of blood oozed upon it. Finally the dam within released a torrent of confession.

"Nevada didn't mean to strike me," she cried. "I made him do it. Yes, I made him. I said I was in Clive's room the night . . ."

"The night he was murdered!" Tate cut in. He had pounced upon the word like an animal stalking its prey.

"You were in the room!" said Quinto. "At which hour? I am listening very closely now, *chiquita.*"

"I don't know," replied Mary.

"Try and remember."

"It was after midnight. It was between twelve-thirty and one o'clock. It was so terrible I didn't think of the time."

"And Senor Clive was dead?"

"Yes. In the chair.'

Quinto sat back, resuming his former placidity, which he had dropped for a moment. He took time to roll himself a cigarette and light it.

"Now," he continued. "Something very important. Tell me exactly what you saw. You went there after twelve-thirty. Senor Clive was dead?

He was sitting in the chair opposite the window? No. I am wrong. He was on the floor, eh?"

"He was in the chair," Mary spoke slowly. "I thought he was sleeping, he was so still. His back was to the door. Then I faced him and saw the blood on his shirt. I was terrified."

"And what did you do?"

"I ran out."

"Did you shut the door?"

"I . . . I think I left it open. But really, I'm not sure. I was so dazed. It was all so horrible."

"*Dime*—tell me how you saw the room. Were there papers on the floor? Is it that some *machuteno* searched there?"

"No. It was as neat as usual. Clive was very orderly. He was too orderly."

Quinto puckered his brows thoughtfully.

"*Chiquita*, you are telling me the room was *as neat as usual!*" Quinto emphasized the last four words by punctuating each with a little puff of smoke as he said them. "So, you've been in Senor Clive's room before?"

The girl's eyes widened. "Yes, I've been there."

"Midnight is a strange time to visit a single man, isn't it?"

"I had to see him."

"After midnight?"

"Yes . . . ." Mary hesitated. "Clive was a very close friend."

"*Pues*, why the visit?"

The girl's lips tightened. There came a moment or two of silence, very uneasy silence. Quinto waited patiently, his gaze pausing upon a popular slogan tacked to his wall—*Give as back our mountains and rivers.*

Suddenly his voice clipped forth with unusual sharpness. It caught Tate unaware and it made Mary turn deathly pale.

"Did your visit with Firth have something to do with a visit you perhaps paid Wang the night of the murder?"

Mary shook her head quickly. "I went to see Wang because he was bothering my father," she said.

"*Bueno*, this is something. Why was he bothering?"

"I don't know. Honestly."

"This brings me to the last question," said Quinto. "Now, perhaps you thought Senor Clive killed Harrow. At supper, exactly five days ago, the evening of the murder, you learned it wasn't so. Clive said he hadn't killed Harrow. After that, whom did you suspect? Whom do you suspect now?"

Mary's eyes scaled down to her lap again.

"No one. I haven't even thought about what happened then," she said. Her fingers were rigid.

Quinto stared at Mary, then at Tate as the latter endeavored a mild cough. He wondered if the calligraphist had the same impression as himself—that the girl was lying!

When Mary Wier had gone, Quinto summoned the officer of the day and sent him in search of Lieutenant Chi. Then he faced Tate, asking:

"Now, what do you think?"

"About Mary? Well, if you ask me, she's trying to protect someone," Tate replied thoughtfully.

Quinto listened indifferently. He gargled noisily with a mouthful of Domecq, spat it out the window, and began eating a solid triangular gob of gelatinous rice stuffed with ham and pork—a dish poetically entitled *tsun-gtse*.

"I wouldn't know whom she's protecting," Tate continued. "Perhaps her father. Perhaps Nevada. It's interesting, the fact that he knocked her out, then left Lingtung without even an army pass. Had he something to do with the murders?"

The door opened and Lieutenant Chi entered. He tapped his bandaged head in a smart salute. His two-tone shoes were brightly polished, his plus-fours were neatly creased along the seams, and he wore a golfer's suede jacket.

"Japanese Colonel Nohuri has been captured," said Chi. "The guerrilleros put the finger on him in his staff headquarters across the river."

"Very good," Quinto murmured. "What does the old *chalate* say?"

Chi clicked his heels and handed him a large coil of gold braid; at least a dozen yards of the stuff generals drape themselves with.

"Gold braid from Colonel Nohuri's Sunday uniform," he explained. "The guerrilleros sent it back because it might be valuable to China."

"When does Nohuri come?" Tate put in.

Chi's eyes twinkled. "Our men captured Nohuri in enemy territory. They also captured Colonel Nohuri's staff headquarters. He is being held prisoner there. The Colonel will naturally feel more at home in his headquarters and will feel freer to speak on the cipher messages than if he were brought to Lingtung."

"*Ai tu*," said Quinto, mainly for Tate's benefit. "You see. My guerrilleros think things out. They observe the finer distinctions."

"It's fantastic," Tate murmured.

Quinto ignored the remark and turned again to Lieutenant Chi. "*Teniente*," he said. "Today I want a thorough search made of Running

Wind Mountain. Fine-comb it, especially the lower escarpment where Senor Abe was murdered. I expect you to bring something back."

"Something big or something little?" asked Chi.

"Look for both. Something is still missing from the Harrow picture."

After the lieutenant had gone, Quinto moved toward the window and stared reflectively at the cypress beyond the frame.

"Senor Tate, you've been in Lingtung five days. You already know the people, yet you can look at them as an outsider. What do you think of the case?"

Tate looked up, somewhat pleased to have his opinion asked for. "Well, I think it's a muddle," he answered. "However, considering all that's happened and all we know, I suppose it's just one of those crimes you can't boil down to proofs. Wang was in touch with the Japanese. I think he was a spy and that Harrow worked under him. Firth discovered it and killed him. That threw a fright into Wang. If you ask me, Wang is Firth's murderer."

"Then why is Mignon Chauvet upset about Mr. Yellow Coat? Why is Mary Wier hiding something? Where are all the why's?" asked Quinto.

"I forgot about that."

"You see our trouble," Quinto observed pointedly, "The murders are surrounded by debris. It's time I begin clearing and straightening out our mysteries. *Primero*—we examine alibis connected with Senor Abe's death. The alibi is less important than character, remember, but here it may aid in the solution of the second murder. I can't begin on Firth's murder until I completely understand what happened on the mountain. I am a great one for wanting understanding, you see."

He suddenly stared down the shaft of the cigarette slanting from his lips and pointing at Tate like a gun. "Do you know how Harrow was murdered?" he asked.

Tate looked bewildered.

"Who? Me?"

"Forget it," Quinto smiled again. "Take your notebook. List the alibis as I give them."

Tate sat himself at the map table and poised a pencil expectantly. "Ready," he said.

"Ah . . . Mary Wier . . . . Where was she between 10:20 and 12:30, the morning and noon of the day Harrow died? *Sargento* Sun reports she was in the garden at noon. Obviously she wasn't on the mountain when Harrow died at 11:50 . . . .

"Mr. Ho. I saw him in Lingtung shortly before noon. McKay was in town with me. Virtue, Miss Woodford and yourself were on the Lunghai Express at 11:50 and didn't arrive until shortly after midday."

Quinto paused while Tate, in the role of secretary, scribbled out the time schedule.

"Whom have we left?" Quinto asked. "Wang—he was on the mountain. Where?" Quinto shrugged his shoulders eloquently. "We don't know. From Chi's description, Wang appeared near the cave sometime after midday, only a few minutes after Senor Clive Firth followed Papa Wier and Mr. Yellow Coat down the mountain . . . . *Bueno, pues.*

"Now, Nevada was climbing also, but Sun reports he returned to the garden by 12:30. Mignon Chauvet was at the Pavilions the entire day. However, we must take her word for this. The guerrilleros are all accounted for. They were on the firing range, except for one sick man and the Officer of the Day."

Quinto rubbed his jaw and went off on a new tangent. "Now consider motive," he said thoughtfully. "Papa Wier hated Harrow—the kidnaping incident at Ping Ying. Senorita Chauvet hated Harrow for possible blackmail. Nevada's dislike is in the same class as that of McKay, Firth, myself, Lieutenant Chi and Sun. We looked upon Senor Abe as a traitor to China. Mr. Ho cared little for Harrow because he was a foreigner. Wang the banker—I would like to know his motive. Had he one?"

"Was Abe Harrow double-crossing him?" Tate asked. "It was in Harrow's character."

Quinto took the list as Tate finished it and studied it carefully:

Abe Harrow—Died 11:50 A.M.

WHO	WHERE AT 11:50	MOTIVE	ALIBI
M. Weir	In garden	Ping Ying kidnapping	Sun
Mr. Ho	In Lingtung	Antiforeign	G.H.Q.
McKay	In Lingtung	Anti-Harrow	G.H.Q.
Virtue	Lunghai Express		G.H.Q.
Woodford	Lunghai Express		G.H.Q.
Tate	Lunghai Express		G.H.Q.
Wang	Mountain (hour-?)	Double-crossed (?)	Chi
Papa Wier	Mountain (noon)	Ping Ying incident	Chi & Firth
Mr. Y. Coat	Mountain (noon)		Chi & Firth
Nevada	Mountain, back in garden at 12:30		Sun

| Chauvet | Pavilions | Blackmail | ? |
| Sun | On duty | Anti-Harrow | ? |

Guerrilleros—have very little contact with the foreign residents of the Pavilions save through Quinto, McKay, Nevada and occasionally Miss Chauvet. All are accounted for.

"Very good," Quinto murmured as he placed the list among his papers. "There are still one or two considerations which might give rise to new motives. For example, did Senor Firth have some very important information we know nothing of?"

"About the meeting in the cave?" asked Tate.

"Possibly that he knew who killed Harrow!"

"But you talked with him after supper that evening?"

"*Ciertamente.* But after supper he was assigned to check up alibis as we've just done. Did he discover something we've missed?"

"What gives you that idea?"

"His room was searched, wasn't it? Why should someone ransack his quarters? Here's a motive without an owner. *The point to remember is, that the room was searched by someone who came after he was murdered!* First, there was the killer, then Mary Wier who observed that the place had not been searched, finally the searcher. The room was busy like a railroad station, eh?

"With this," Quinto continued, "I can establish the time of Senor Clive's death. It was between midnight and 12:30 or shortly after—if Senorita Wier told us the truth. If she didn't, it might mean she was also the searcher. It might also mean . . ."

"That she murdered Firth!" put in Tate.

CHAPTER 19
The Lady of Bath

THE PINCHED TASTE of unripe persimmons in Mildred Woodford's mouth slowly yielded to the cheerful flavor of Pedro Domecq loaned by Gimiendo Quinto. Miss Woodford felt definitely herself again as she polished off the last half of the bottle just for precaution. With a sigh of regret, she tossed the empty fifth behind the pink brick guardhouse. Then, arming herself with her saddlebag purse and leatherette notebook, she tackled the Sergeant of the Guard.

For almost five days she had grown frantic in an attempt to find the lay of the land. Success had not been altogether lacking. Her black notebook was crammed with dynamite. She, of all the people in Lingtung, knew who had murdered Clive Firth. Now she wanted details on Harrow. Such details, properly colored, would make a story, a scoop!

But in the case of Harrow all her requests were met by a wall of bland innocence. This time she hoped her strategy would work, for she now offered Sergeant Sun a sizeable bribe of one pound thrupence.

Sun immediately felt that one English pound was worth a lot more murders than Harrow alone so he promptly furnished Mildred with all the lurid details of the murder and quartering of 25,000 Manchus in Sianfu a dozen years back. For the extra thrupence he tossed in details on the three million souls killed by typhus during the 1921 Northwest famine.

Like a good journalist, whose bribes buy nothing but circumlocution, Mildred promptly stormed off to Lingtung, refilled on a half dozen local sherries at the teahouse, then appeared at the railway telegraph office with two prepared messages.

"I'm going to get this story out if I have to plot the rest of the details myself," she muttered defiantly as she handed in her two messages.

The station master, an old gray-headed rogue with yellowish eyes, studied the messages carefully for a full five minutes. He scanned first one, then the other, pursed his lips, scratched his head doubtfully, grinned a little and shrugged.

Finally, with crooked teeth showing through an insecure smile, he asked in tolerable English: "What speech these written in?"

"English," replied Mildred with proper British scorn for the illiterate.

The station master made a polite, bowing gesture.

"Gotta getum censor," he said.

"Censored!" yapped Mildred. "Say, this is the first time I've ever had birthday greetings censored."

"Birthday greetin gotta censor. . . funeral greetin gotta censor," replied the master in all simplicity.

"Really, now, don't you think you're carrying this a bit too far? You've my word. These telegrams are strictly okay." Mildred changed her tone, speaking cheerfully, almost inanely.

"Gotum censor."

"All right. Where's the censor?"

"Me callum."

"Well, then, do it quickly."

The station master had already picked up the phone. As usual, he was put in touch with Hankow and Kaifeng alternately, then he got the Lingtung number he wanted. What followed was in such rapid-fire Chinese that Mildred thought he was singing in the phone.

The old man hung up and turned toward Mildred pleasantly. "Come backee hour," he said. "Censor say he come chopping chop. Gotta eat. Gotta shave first. Me keep messages."

"Chop chop," Mildred repeated with profound British humor. "I hope he chops himself."

Mildred paraded about Lingtung for an hour, that is, from one cafe to another. She liked the sight of men in cafes, even though they were Chinese, and she fancied they liked her. She did indeed look rather well, for she wore a sleek, cream-colored sport dress instead of the usual B.E.F. tweeds. The dress had wowed Hankow when she wore it there. She figured it would have the same effect in Lingtung today.

The hour gone, she returned to the railway station, utterly confident that she could sway the censor if he had an eye for clothes at all. The censor, naturally, would be Chinese. Now, if Mildred had known that the Chinese seldom grow hair on their chins and consequently don't shave, her confidence would have been less secure.

It was only after she entered the station that her lobster-pink face fell in dismay. The familiar, picaresque figure of G.H.Q. loomed before her like a foreboding mountain. To one side, the station master blinked whimsically and pointed at the Mexican mountain.

"Him censor," he simpered.

"It's preposterous!" Mildred sputtered.

"It's a fact," Quinto grinned. "*Que pasa, chuela?*"

Mildred threw what hips she had about and stamped upon the floor angrily. "Now listen! This is going too far," she cried. "It's dictatorship. Every time I go places, you crowd in. Am I to be pinched now?"

Quinto armored himself with a pleasant smile.

"I'm so sorry," he murmured.

"You sorry! What am I supposed to feel—happy?"

"Your telegrams are very clever," Quinto mused, picking up the forms. "Do you always send birthday greetings to the New York and the London *Times*? It is a fine sentiment, eh?"

He held the cable addressed to the New York *Times* in his right hand. It read:

EDITORIAL
NEW YORK TIMES
NEW YORK U.S.A.

    ABE HARROW AMER OFFICER CHI ARMY MYSTERIOUSLY MURDERED HERE BEHIND LINES. C. FIRTH BRITISH DEAD SELF KIDNAPED WANT STORY CABLE RATES WORDS POSSIBLE WAVE OF MURDERS AMONG FOREIGNERS WOODFORD LINGTUNG

"Now, see here," Mildred blustered, pushing the cable aside, "if my messages are cut one word I'll see that the British Embassy and the Press Delegation in Hankow hear of it, really I shall!"

Quinto scratched himself and grinned.

"But my dear Senorita," he murmured, "I had every intention of passing your cables through. It was but my duty to read, not to stop your messages. I see nothing wrong in them, so *mira* . . . ." With a magnificent flourish, he handed the uncut messages to the station master. "Send them," he directed.

Mildred shot him a funny look and said, "Oh!"

"We must have a drink on that," Quinto observed as he gallantly took her arm.

Mildred glanced at him curiously, then smiled. "Well, I wouldn't mind a drink," she said.

A dozen drinks later, Mildred experienced a certain warm feeling in her heart for the huge, carelessly dressed Mexican. Her pink face glowed with cheerfulness, while her gaze meandered idly over the crimson furnishings of the tiny teahouse where they drank. The tinkling voice of a singsong girl ran an exotic scale to the accompaniment of a four-stringed moon guitar.

Her glance returned to the table and Quinto.

"Quinto! You drink like a gentleman," she gurgled in an intimate mood. "Not a bad sort, after all. Boy, how you do drink! "

"Ah. But you should see Virtue drink—like a queen."

"Really, Quinto, I had you all wrong. I apologize."

"So you did."

Mildred gazed upon her companion and sighed. At this moment Quinto appeared more like a parade of men, and parades were something which left Mildred limp with emotions of a vehement, irresponsible sort.

"Quinto," she said suddenly, "you look like a man who might be a match for me. What do you say? I'll bet you I can out-drink you, glass for glass."

"*No me quadra*—I don't agree," Quinto challenged back.

"Five pounds. Put up," said Mildred.

"*Entonces*," murmured Quinto. He deposited a crumpled Chinese banknote, the equivalent of five British pounds, upon the tile table. Mildred slipped her own money under a glass. At a signal from Quinto, the waiter rushed more metal teapots filled with liquor that tasted like Bols. Meanwhile, both the Englishwoman and the Mexican settled themselves comfortably, for it was seldom that either found anyone who could approach their respective saturation points.

By the fifteenth round the teahouse customers and the singsong girls sensed something unusual. They gatherer, around the table and watched eagerly. The drinking progressed professionally. As it passed the twenty-second and twenty-third glass each, the spectators hedged in closer. Here was a new kind of battle—dramatic and amazing. The Chinese men placed side bets.

For a while the wagering was heaviest on the foreign lady. She gained a good deal of face by tossing her whiskies off neat and without a shudder. Nearing the twenty-fifth glass, odds shifted heavily to Quinto. He distinguished himself by drinking slowly, methodically, all the while humming a hilarious little Mexican campaign song.

Two drinks later Mildred showed signs of sagging. She leaned her chin on the palm of one hand and ogled Quinto most affably. Quinto was momentarily shocked, for he realized that Mildred was trying her hardest to act like Mountain of Virtue.

"Quinto. Lemme call you darling," she murmured and shook her head so it fell from her palm. "You're jussh wonderful," she repeated, bringing her head up after some difficulty. "I feel wonderful, don't you?"

Quinto drew another glass, sipping it slowly while he frowned at Mildred's long shanks out beside the table. He was two drinks ahead and was just getting to the point where he felt like really drinking. He almost hoped she wouldn't give up now.

"Wonderful fella," crowed Mildred as she tipped her glass over. "You sent that cable, didn't you. I tricked you. I made you do it, old f-f-fruit. Tricked you. Ha . . . Ha . . . Ha . . . ."

Quinto's whimsical laughter matched her own.

"*Ai que chistoso*, so funny," he grinned radiantly. "The coincidence— I did not tell you. Ah, I forgot. The telegraph lines broke down just before I gave the station master your cables. That is very funny, no?"

Mildred giggled irrepressibly.

"L-L-Lines broke down," she laughed. "Wonderful . . . . Telephone poles tired, they fall down . . . Ha . . . Ha . . . Ha . . . ."

She swayed limply in her chair and worked desperately to fix her wandering blue eyes upon Quinto.

"Y'know what?" she whispered hoarsely.

"What?"

"Quinto, I see a bunch of you! And you know what else?"

"I am listening avidly."

"Quinto, darling . . . . I love you . . . . Are we alone? . . . Jussh you'n me. . . .

Mildred's voice tapered off in a long-drawn-out "swishhhh." She saw, somewhat vaguely, a dozen Quintos rise from the table. Oh so many Chinese moved aside. There was a singsong voice. She felt Quinto's firm arm about her waist. He was leading her away somewhere and she felt delightfully happy.

One hour later she came to her senses.

The awakening occurred, not rudely, but with a pleasant awareness of liquid warmth. At length a strong odor of garlic and onions, mixed with steam, assailed her nostrils. She felt strong arms holding her.

Forcing her eyes open, one at a time, she looked about aghast, for she was sitting waist-deep in water. Two grinning, naked peasant women were holding her upright and splashing water in her face.

"Amazons!" gasped Mildred. She promptly passed out again.

The Chinese women relaxed their grip but kept on laughing. Six or seven fat-bodied, noodle-eating Northern women and a few assorted male and female children splashed around in the pool, giggling in open amusement.

Mildred opened her eyes again. The pool and the women were still there. "Where am I?" she asked frantically.

The peasant woman on her right chuckled.

"Public bath . . . . Me boss," she replied.

"The public bath! Oh, this is horrible!" Mildred made a desperate, confused attempt to collect her thoughts. She also gained a modicum of control. "How the devil did I get here? It won't wash, dammit! Where are my clothes? Get me my things, will you!"

"No got clothes," replied one of the Amazons—the boss.

"What do you mean, no got?"

"Capn Qui-to take all clothes. Say you maybe like stay bath couple day. He come back Monday."

CHAPTER 20
One Murderer More or Less

GIMIENDO QUINTO returned to the Pavilions at about three in the afternoon. He was none the worse for some twenty-nine glasses of whisky. He entered his *yamen* and briskly set about transferring Mildred Woodford's cream sport dress, stockings and silk underthings to a hook behind the door. He surveyed the silks appreciatively, his mind momentarily thinking tender thoughts about Mountain of Virtue. Finally, with a deep sigh, he began examining the contents of Mildred's handbag.

Englishwomen were like most other women, he observed, as the collection of feminine knickknacks grew upon his map table. The purse produced a fund of lip rouge, face powder, a tube of camphor, mirrors, fountain pen, a wad of English banknotes big enough to choke a prime minister, a comb and hairpins.

Quinto glanced in her blue-covered passport and put it back. The picture was worse than usual.

Casually he paged through her leatherette notebook. It was filled out in diary form, interspersed with hastily drawn maps of unimportant military positions along the Chinese fronts. One page was devoted to bridge scores. Another to a sketch titled *Nevada*, but done in modern style and thoroughly unrecognizable. He felt a little hurt upon finding no picture of himself in the book.

He read through Mildred's record of the last six days and winced once or twice. The Englishwoman had very strong opinions. Suddenly his eyes paused, then raced through one passage:

April 5th. A.M.

Progress at last on my own investigation. Early this morning the Wiers were arguing in the garden and I was lucky enough to hear. I know who murdered Firth—"Papa" James Wier!

They argued it out. It seems Mary Wier walked into Firth's room the night of the murder and found her father holding the gun. She hid the pistol in the ARP shelter where Miss Chauvet found it later. The girl was trying to protect her father. The Wiers may attempt to leave Lingtung. Wouldn't be surprised if they're gone when we return from Sianfu. Quinto is a bit slower than he thinks. He'll be surprised.

Quinto's mouth gaped a trifle as he reread the passage and fumed a little over the last line. Then he snapped the book shut and called the Officer of the Day.

"Arrest Papa Wier. Bring him here," he ordered curtly.

A moment later John Tate breezed through the doorway. He looked like a minor version of Aeolus, the windy god. His cheeks puffed out ruddily, his white coattails fluttered, and his bandaged arm stuck out like a stubby white penguin's wing.

"I've traced Nevada," he said exultantly. "He went off toward Kaifeng on a transport truck. Should I phone the military police at headquarters there?"

"No," Quinto motioned calmly. "He will return alone."

Tate looked astonished.

"Sit down," Quinto murmured. "I'm expecting Papa Wier. I have a feeling it will be a stormy session."

Tate relaxed and looked around the room absentmindedly. His eyes came up with a start on Mildred Woodford's clothes neatly hung behind the door. "Say, what are you doing with Woodford's clothes? Where did she—" The questions died on his lips, for the door opened and Papa Wier entered.

Wier had changed a great deal in the last few days. He no longer had the appearance of a prim, chauvinistic Old China Hand. He had aged overnight. His eyes and brain grasped at things with the peculiar difficulty of a man broken by worry.

"*Buenas tardes,*" said Quinto as he waved a welcoming hand toward a chair. "Sit down, please."

Papa Wier fumbled with the chair back. He sat down and crossed his fingers nervously. He stared at Quinto, his eyes shifting nervously, worse than his hands.

"Senor Wier, something has told me you are planning to leave China?" Quinto began slowly.

Wier nodded.

"Why?" asked Quinto. "You are perhaps tired of China?"

The missionary spread his fingers in a helpless gesture. "Why shouldn't we? Nothing remains. The Japanese occupied our mission. Nothing remains."

Quinto walked around the man's chair while slowly rolling himself a cigarette. He placed the cigarette in his mouth where it hung, unlit.

"Do the two murders have anything to do with such plans that are in your mind?' he asked Wier.

Tate watched hawkishly. Wier stiffened and flashed the Mexican an agonized glance. While Quinto's back was turned, the missionary made an effort to control himself. He answered with forced brittleness:

"Mr. Quinto, I didn't come here to be insulted or to be dragged into a murder scandal. I don't know what happened. Nothing at all."

Quinto suddenly faced the missionary. He looked gigantic and challenging. Wier's eyes faltered.

"Senor," Quinto spoke with staccato force, words shooting forth like well-aimed bullets. "You . . . shot . . . Clive . . . Firth! Is it so?"

"No!"

Wier's voice came forth in a strangled gasp. His body froze.

"It's too late to deny it," Quinto continued. "You shot Senor Clive Firth. Your daughter Mary found you in the room, holding the gun. You shot him. You broke down. You were bewildered. Mary protected you. She hid the gun in the *refugio*. That much I know. Ah, yes, there is other proof. Do you recognize this?"

Quinto reached in a little box on his table and held up the heroin capsule found in Firth's room. Papa Wier glanced at it dully. He was huddled in his chair, his stiffness broken, his face drawn of color. He looked completely exhausted.

"I sometimes thought you used heroin," said Quinto. "One night I saw your daughter Mary go to visit Wang. She knew you used heroin. She also knew Wang supplied you with it. But this is not our business at the moment. What I want to know is why you murdered Firth?"

"I-I-I didn't shoot him," Wier muttered. The words slipped forth with no breath behind them.

"Then explain the gun," demanded Quinto. "Mary found you with it. *Digame*, do you carry such guns?"

"But I didn't," Wier protested despairingly. "Oh, it's no use. You won't believe me. Mary doesn't believe me. There's really nothing left. Even my daughter doubts me."

Quinto signaled to Tate, who quickly filled a glass with cognac and brought it to the missionary. Wier looked at it vacantly and shook his head.

"Never drink," he murmured.

"Every man to his own vice," Tate whispered almost inaudibly.

Now Quinto patted the missionary's drooping shoulder. "Bring yourself together, Senor," he said. "I've still a few questions. *No quiero ser duro*, no hard feelings, understand ?"

Wier shrugged. "What's the use?" he protested. "No one believes me. There's nothing left. Even Mary . . ."

"Where did you get the gun that killed Firth?" Quinto repeated. "It was an expensive gun. One doesn't find those anywhere. You are a collector, perhaps?"

"The gun?" Wier looked up blankly. "The gun? . . . I found it in the room, on the table."

"Which room?"

"Firth's."

"You're telling me you shot him with his own gun?"

"No! No! He was already dead. He was dead when I came in . . . . Oh, what's the use . . ."

Tate looked at Quinto dubiously.

"You found Firth dead. Then what did you do?" asked Quinto. "You held the gun like this, first. Then you shot—bang! bang! Then what did you do?"

"I can't remember what I did," Wier mumbled exasperatedly. "Perhaps I shot him. I don't know. No one will believe me, so let me alone, will you!"

Quinto maneuvered his questions, patiently, yet firmly.

"*Ai bueno*, perhaps Senor Clive asked you to his room at midnight or later? Why did you go?"

Papa Wier hesitated.

"Ah . . . because . . . because of my daughter."

"She shot him? Are you trying to cover her?"

A look of horror entered the man's eyes. "No! Not that," he pleaded. "I went because Mary had been visiting Firth. There was something between them. I can't say what. I don't know. But Mr. Firth wasn't the type of man for Mary. He was too hard, too ruthless."

"*Entonces*—then you found the room with great disorder?"

"I hardly remember."

"Was it ransacked?"

"No. I don't think so."

Quinto paused and studied the missionary thoughtfully. Then he lit the cigarette that danced between his lips.

"By any chance, did you have another reason for visiting Firth?" he asked. "Perhaps you wished to ask Senor Clive if he saw you on the mountain the same noon Harrow was murdered? Were you afraid of what he might have seen?"

"Harrow?" Wier murmured. "No. I had nothing to do with him"

"Nothing?" asked Quinto. His brow flicked up doubtfully. "Am I to think you left America under disagreeable circumstances many years back?"

Wier sighed bitterly.

"You know that too!"

"Naturally," said Quinto. "For the moment, I'm a detective. It's my business to know. I assure you, once we clear this case, I will forget everything. But now . . ."

Again Quinto reached into the shoebox on the table and brought forth the military pass which had been found in Harrow's room. He held the slip out and looked at Wier reprovingly. "After so many years you put your hand to practice again. You forged my name to this *salvo-conducto,* the form which Harrow stole from my room."

"No. I didn't, really," Wier denied it, but it was evident he was lying.

"Forgery is dangerous," Quinto went on blandly. "You must have been very friendly with Senor Abe?"

A loud blast from the exhaust of a motor car sounded from outside, drowning Wier's denial. Quinto stepped to the window, glanced out, and then returned to Wier.

"You were to meet Harrow in the mountain cave, weren't you?" he asked. "You were with a man in a yellow raincoat, no? What do you know of Mr. Yellow Coat?"

There was naked silence in the room. Papa Wier slumped in his chair, tired eyes gazing blankly at his long fingers as they twitched spasmodically upon his knees. He muttered something that neither Tate nor Quinto caught.

Quinto leaned close to his ear. He asked:

"Here are perhaps some names you know—Lin Tan, DuPont, Fu Tien, Harrow?"

Just then the door opened and Teng Fa entered, looking cheerful and very victorious. He was wearing the normal Chinese mufti with the exception of a white Mohammedan ceremonial fez, for he had just returned from a flying trip into the *Ma* country.

"*Hola, Teng!*" Quinto beamed pleasantly.

Teng Fa glanced at Wier, taking in the entire situation at once. "Business?" he asked.

"Come in," smiled Quinto. "*Que hubole*—how goes it?"

The young secret service ace turned toward the door and motioned for someone to enter, then he grinned at Quinto, saying:

"I arrested Mr. Yellow Coat! All this while he lived in the room adjoining my quarters at the Guest House. He was very clever. He seldom wore his coat. A fine camouflage so it took time to find him. Now . . . Mr. Yellow Coat . . . "

CHAPTER 21
Mr. Yellow Coat

TENG FA stepped aside.

A man of medium build, with dark eyes, brows, and smooth, pompadoured black hair entered the room. A long scar, curving thickly in the manner of a Turkish scimitar, extended from the lower lid of his right eye down to the base of his chin. He wore a yellowish gabardine trenchcoat into the pockets of which his hands were thrust.

Mr. Yellow Coat looked cool and composed. His eyes flitted indifferently from Wier to Tate to Quinto. For a second, one hand came out of his pocket, put a ready-made cigarette in his mouth. He lit it and puffed vigorously.

"His papers," said Teng Fa, handing Quinto a large leather wallet. "Nothing irregular. He belonged to the same unit of the Ambulance Corps as Harrow."

"A doctor?" asked Quinto, shifting his gaze toward the man. "You have the look of a medico, no?"

"*C'est ca,*" Yellow Coat grunted.

"I must go, Quinto," Teng Fa interrupted. "He's yours. I shall bring Wang, perhaps tomorrow, perhaps the next day. Good-by."

Teng saluted and left the room. A moment later the roar of his motor car rumbled through the gardens.

In the meantime, Quinto glanced through Mr. Yellow Coat's papers. "French, eh?" he murmured. Once or twice he arched his brows and again he voiced a birdlike little "tsk." Finally he stepped to the door and gave the attending officer instructions.

"And now," he began. He faced Mr. Yellow Coat and pulled himself to his full and rather overwhelming height, displaying most prominently his Order of the Blue Sky and White Sun. Then he introduced himself in rapid-fire French. "I am Gimiendo Hernandez Quinto!" It was like saying, "I am the president."

Mr. Yellow Coat stared back coldly.

"*Sans blague.* I know that," he said.

Quinto smiled. "You know then. Very good." He now produced the Comblain derringer and held it in the palm of his hand for Mr. Yellow

131

Coat to see. He watched the Frenchman's reactions closely.

"You recognize it?" he asked.

Mr. Yellow Coat blew a stream of smoke from his nostrils.

"*Non, pas du tout,*" he answered brittlely.

"Naturally," replied Quinto. "Knowing what occurred in Lingtung, you would not recognize the gun. Foolish of me to ask such a question, eh?"

"Quite," answered Mr. Yellow Coat.

"Senor Yellow Coat, you have another name. A pseudonym. On Wang's books you are known as DuPont. Isn't it so?"

The shot told, for the Frenchman flinched, though only for an instant.

"You shouldn't leave your pseudonym lying about in your wallet," Quinto smiled. "A kind of carelessness, eh?"

"Quite true," replied Mr. Yellow Coat.

"Do you receive or send codes in French?" Quinto asked abruptly.

"I speak French. Does that interest you?"

Quinto pointed toward Papa Wier, who still sagged in his chair, gazing blankly at the door.

"You met Papa Wier on the mountain five days ago. Why? Is it that you are both studying mountains."

"Which mountain?" The Frenchman curled his lips defiantly.

"Ah," Quinto murmured in admiration. "You are a cool one. Good. Let us begin earlier. What did Abe Harrow say to you the morning he was murdered?"

"Harrow?" Mr. Yellow Coat asked blankly.

Quinto shot him an exasperated glance. "Answer the questions," he commanded. The roll of his voice was heavy with annoyance. "Why were you on the mountain? Why did you return the second day? Why were you snooping near the garden walls the night Harrow was murdered? . . . Remain silent another instant and I'll return you to Teng Fa."

The Frenchman merely smiled and shrugged.

"You are very brave," Quinto observed, for the threat of being handed over to Teng Fa would, in ordinary cases, bring a man to his knees.

"That's my affair," replied the Frenchman. He turned his gaze toward the door as it opened. Suddenly he stiffened.

Mignon Chauvet stepped in. The instant she saw Mr. Yellow Coat, she stopped. Her hand reached back toward the door frame for support. Her eyes were saucer-wide and there was a look of terror deep within them, as if she saw a ghost.

"Michel—" she gasped.

She turned and tried to flee but Quinto quickly blocked the way.

"It's nothing, Senorita," he murmured reassuringly. *"It is nothing but your husband."*

Mignon rested on Quinto's bed. Her face was pale and drawn. She avoided her husband's eyes and looked appealingly at Quinto.

"Why is Michel here? How?" she asked weakly.

Mr. Yellow Coat gave his wife a cold, ironic stare.

"Eh bien," he said icily. "So you're surprised. Yes, surprised to see me alive!"

Quinto interrupted, imposing a certain amount of calm upon the electric atmosphere in the room.

"I'll explain," he said. "Through Virtue I learned that Senorita Chauvet had shot her husband in Paris. She fled the country, thinking she had killed him. Instead, he is with us now. In Lingtung, the Senorita fell deeply in love with Clive Firth. Senor Clive, she discovered with much bitterness, is interested first in China, then perhaps even other *chiquitas*.

"She had told Firth of her marriage to Chauvet; and their argument, just before Clive's death, was about her wanting to marry him. When I overheard her say, that midnight, *'I must do it,'* or, *'I am not afraid to do it,'* she referred to clearing herself in France. She had shot Mr. Yellow Coat in self-defense. Isn't it so?"

He glanced at Mignon for confirmation. The girl nodded her head.

"Very well," Quinto continued. "The morning Sun described your husband, you reacted violently. You couldn't believe it was the same man. Still, there was that possibility. On the other hand, Senor Chauvet had heard from Harrow that you were here. However, I don't think he cared. He was no longer interested in you. Of course, Harrow black-mailed you because Harrow couldn't even resist taking little money. He was like that.

"Now, how do I know that Senor Chauvet, alias Mr. Yellow Coat, alias DuPont, had no interest in his wife? Simple. Logical. He had another reason for being around Lingtung—the same which sent Wang into Firth's room. Yes, the same reason that was to draw Wang, Papa Wier, Harrow to the cave for a meeting which did not materialize."

Quinto stared straight at Mr. Yellow Coat.

"You *were* to have an important meeting on the mountain, no?" he demanded.

"C'est mon affaire!" the Frenchman snapped.

"You were not in Firth's room," continued Quinto. "I am very sure of that, perhaps. There is no evidence. Also, you were a stranger and

Firth's face was calm when he died. He died at the hand of a friend possibly."

"Well, what do you want then?" Mr. Chauvet demanded. "A confession?"

"Ah, no," murmured Quinto. "But at this very moment I'm much closer to recognizing who killed Harrow. The proof should be here any minute. Needless to say, you'll be held here under guard until that time."

Papa Wier suddenly stirred in his chair and looked at Quinto queerly.

"What did you say?" he asked.

"Quinto! Look out!" Tate's warning rang out hoarsely.

For all his bulk, Quinto spun around and faced Michel Chauvet. He found himself staring into the bore of his own service pistol. In the instant while he had looked toward Papa Wier, the Frenchman had leaped to where Quinto's holster hung on a wall peg and drawn the gun.

Mr. Yellow Coat waved the weapon warningly. There was a chilling, purposeful glint in his eyes. "Back! Over against the wall," he clipped out. "Don't attempt to stop me. I'll shoot."

Quinto held his ground in his usual unruffled manner. In fact, he brightened at the challenge.

"Ah, Senor Chauvet," he said. "The door is guarded. There's a guerrillero stationed outside. I think you'd better drop that gun. You are convinced, no?"

Chauvet's face changed for an instant, flashing a sort of cold desperation. The scimitar scar under his eye grew livid. The Frenchman took his eyes off those in the room for a bare second to glance toward the garden window.

Quinto closed in on him slowly. The cigarette in his mouth sent a curling line of smoke up toward eyes that failed to blink and were as cold as ice.

"Michel—!" Mignon had found her voice for a single cry of terror.

The Frenchman hooked one leg over the window sill. He balanced there and aimed the gun steadily at Quinto's head. "Back!" he snarled. His finger closed upon the trigger.

Suddenly there was a rifle report from outside. The Frenchman, already half out the window, jerked around. A foolish expression crossed his face for an instant, then his body tumbled out of sight.

"He was shot!" gasped Tate.

Both Quinto and the calligraphist leaped toward the window. They saw Doctor McKay appear from around the corner of the Pavilion. He was dragging a rifle along the ground. Arriving before the window, he nodded, then knelt in the earth beside Chauvet's motionless body.

"Bandits," he said. "Stone dead! I should have let him shoot you, Quinto laddie. Lost a good chance to get at that enormous liver of yours."

CHAPTER 22
One Alphabet Wanted

IT WAS late afternoon of the day following Mr. Yellow Coat's death. The atmosphere around the Pavilions was tenuous and crammed with suspense, for events seemed to be piling up like combers on a beach.

Mignon Chauvet was under McKay's care. She had suffered a nervous collapse, having been confronted by a husband she thought dead, then having him reappear only to be shot down before her eyes.

The remaining internationals at the Pavilions were on edge. It wasn't entirely due to the Yellow Coat incident. The developments following it were much more disturbing. McKay had suggested pinning both the murder of Harrow and Firth on the dead Frenchman and closing the case. He was convinced Quinto was still that far from a solution.

Instead, Quinto locked himself in his office and pored over his notes on the case throughout the night. Early this morning he had gone with Lieutenant Chi to the mountain. Added to this was the fact that Mildred Woodford had mysteriously disappeared and her clothes were on a hook behind Quinto's door. Where was she?

"Strange how a mystery, a murder, can get everyone down," murmured John Tate. "It was almost as if they had each been in on it. Partners in crime." His albino eyes swept through the window of his small room and across the flower-laden garden. Even the day contributed to the tension. The sky was overcast. It was going to rain. The trees outside had a dull, flat appearance.

Across the garden the stubby figure of Sergeant Sun could be seen standing on the roof of the guardhouse, gazing off toward Lingtung. In the path to the right, the gentle scholar, Mr. Ho, paced back and forth, deeply preoccupied. He carried his arms in front, hands hidden by long Chinese sleeves.

With an irritated sigh, Tate turned from the window. His attention rested momentarily on the twin portraits of Dr. Sun Yat Sen and Pancho Villa which had been hung over his narrow army cot. Finally he sat down at his desk and returned to the study of his books: Watter's *Essays on the Chinese Language* and the *Lexicon of Kang Hsi*, China's great standard dictionary. He frowned a little, for there was one problem which bothered his scholarly mind. Quinto had asked why Chinese and Japanese write ciphers in French.

Opening the dictionary at random, his eyes paused upon the character, *chiao*. *Chiao*—the word seemed to strike a responsive chord. Soon he was so busy referring to the official Ministry of Communications code book and crossing back to the dictionary that he completely overlooked the impending rains and the tension at the Pavilions.

When Quinto entered his room an hour later, the calligraphist beamed over his books like a proud archeologist about to take credit for the laying of a dinosaur egg. "You can recall the guerrilleros, Quinto," he crowed. "I've solved it. I see now why the Wang-Nohuri code was in French!"

Quinto smiled, satisfied himself.

"I knew you'd get it," he said. "Did he study in Paris, eh?"

"You can't cipher Chinese!"

"I didn't think of that. Are you sure."

"It's absolutely simple," Tate went on with authority and enthusiasm. "There's only one way to codify Chinese. For example, the telegraph company sends messages by numerals, then decodes them with reference to the Ministry of Communications code book. There are so many characters in the language, it's the only way. Imagine, forty thousand words. But number codes are easy to break down and it's dangerous, because both parties have to have code books.

"With ciphers it's different. You just transpose the letters in the words. Both parties need only to know the key. For Wang and Nohuri there was a catch. Chinese words aren't made up of letters. There's no alphabet. Each character is a word picture in itself, so Nohuri had to look for a language with an alphabet."

"But the new *pai hua* which the government teaches has an alphabet," Quinto interrupted. "So are you sure?"

"I thought of that," Tate protested. "They can't use *pai hua*. Sometimes a single word has a dozen meanings. You recognize the exact meaning by its connotation in the sentence, or by the four-tone system of inflection. In Canton, by the nine-tone system.

"Look." Tate wrote out the word *chiao*. "If this were ciphered without tonal keys thrown in there'd be no exactness. *Chiao* can mean—unite, reptile, dog, silk thread, cushion. It has eight meanings."

He paused for breath, wet his lips, glanced at the Mexican for approval, and concluded rapidly: "So naturally, when messages must be brief, hidden and concise as in cipher, you must use a language with an alphabet. French, of course, is the best. The diplomatic language."

Quinto thought this over for a moment. His brow knitted together.

"Very interesting," he murmured. "It furnishes one of the missing parts in our case. Very important, perhaps. But we must still search. Like a bloodhound with long ears."

"For what?" asked Tate.

"The remaining missing parts, naturally. We're getting nowhere until certain little factors bubble up. I am aware that there are some very substantial motives for the murders of Senores Firth and Harrow. However, it is a great repetition to say that no one liked Harrow. I look for something to put my teeth into. His connection with Wang and Papa Wier, yes.

"In the case of Senor Clive—well, I absolve Mr. Yellow Coat. It could have been, but I doubt it. It might have been Mignon Chauvet—jealousy. Wang because he was in the room. Mr. Ho since he had no alibi. Perhaps McKay, though he had Chi for an alibi."

"But Papa Wier practically confessed," said Tate.

"He's confused . . . A rooster with a lost head."

"And bitter enough to murder."

"You're too quick to condemn," murmured Quinto. "Tate, you have a great thickness of New England American ancestry. If you condemn Wier you have all sorts of little unanswered ends flying around. Can you answer why the Generalissimo's teeth are gone? Where is Harrow's coat? Why did four men wish to meet in the cave? Why was Firth's room ransacked?"

"Money in Firth's room?"

Quinto shook his head.

"He had little money in China. He drew only regular army pay."

Tate hesitated a moment, glancing at the Mexican cautiously and at the same time measuring his distance to the door.

"Have you thought about Virtue?" he asked.

"Ah, she's safe," said Quinto. "She's always safe."

"I don't mean that, exactly. I was thinking of Virtue and Wang. Why did Wang release Miss Woodford and not Virtue? Perhaps she is tied up with him?"

After a night and a full day in the communal baths at Lingtung, Mildred Woodford finally exhausted her entire repertoire of emotions—anger, disgust, belligerency, hate, despair and embarrassment.

This last emotion was something new to Mildred. She had experienced it during the few minutes while the Mayor of Lingtung and General Ku-Chu-Tung, the Military Governor of Sianfu, looked in at the baths with the view of converting them into a gasoline dump for the new transport station soon to be established in the town.

"The foreign maiden is very clean," the slightly roguish mayor had observed with an air of pride in the fact that Lingtung had such unusual attractions to exhibit.

Both he and the Military Governor eyed Mildred as though she were a valuable bit of statuary. Then the Governor passed comments to the effect that the British had a tendency to overdo things, particularly bathing, imperialism, exercise and drinking.

Mildred smoldered a deep pink. Then she blew up! Driving the peasant women (who had come in droves on this second day to see the English lady bathing) from the pool under an avalanche of postwar literary epithets and partially drowning the two male government officials, she splashed a good half of the water out of the pool.

Eight hours later, having eaten three unsavory meals while half immersed in hot water, Mildred's mood was one of profound desperation. It showed best in her face, which glowed with an unholy cleanliness.

Her interest gradually settled upon a turnscrew at the deep end of the pool. Slowly it dawned upon her that this was the water drain. An idea formed. Weakened though she was by the long imprisonment in steaming water, she succeeded in opening the valve. In a half hour the pool was empty.

Mildred set up a veritable row. She sang and screamed and shouted until the female bath attendant rushed in and gazed upon the major catastrophe.

"I say, now, will you let me go!" Mildred demanded. "I want my clothes. I'll freeze."

The bath attendant, who was under Quinto's strictest orders to keep the Englishwoman in water, painfully seized the dilemma by both horns. After some powerful thinking she tossed it. There was only one solution—to refill the pool, which would take a dozen hours by as many coolies carrying buckets of water, then replace the English lady in it. With a disapproving glance at Mildred, the bath attendant hurried out in search of coolies.

That was half the battle. Mildred wasted no time. She made a frantic search for her clothes, and finding none, she wrapped herself in a large cotton bath curtain. It was dark when she fared forth into the streets of Lingtung and it was beginning to rain.

Tate glanced up from where Quinto was packing the tiger-jade in a cotton-lined box and looked toward the office door as it swung inward. Then his jaw sagged! China was full of many strange sights but none as incredibly fantastic as this!

Lieutenant Chi swaggered into the room, his handsome face coppery with the bloom of good health. He wore a Tyrolean mountaineer's outfit—leather knee-length shorts, an embroidered silk shirt, leather suspenders and a sleeveless leather vest. His feet were shod with spiked mountain boots, while his muscular legs sported bright woolen bands about the calves.

Chi deposited an Alpinist pick and a coil of rope by the door and grinned at Tate. Doffing his Robin Hood green hat, in the band of which a chamois brush and two feathers had been thrust, he straightened his white head-bandage.

"Weather getting bad for mountain sports," he said. "I returned in the rain."

"Finish the mountain?" Quinto asked. He regarded Chi whimsically.

"With okay success," reported Chi.

He produced a tightly rolled, slightly damp bundle from under his arm and thrust it at Quinto. "Mr. Harrow's coat! Also his swagger stick and cross belt," he said.

Quinto took the bundle, unrolled it and threw it on his bed. The coat was weather-stained and faded from long exposure upon the mountain. The Mexican's stubby fingers carefully pressed out the wrinkles. For a minute or two he examined it for tears and blood stains. There were none.

"Where'd you find it, Chi?" he asked.

The Chinese lieutenant smoothed the crown of his hat and replaced it cockily upon his head—unChinese like.

"On the same side that Harrow fell," he replied. "I found it up the cliff, fifty feet above X-marks-the-spot place. A very difficult ascent, truly."

The office door opened again, so suddenly this time that it slammed into the small of Chi's back, pitching him against Tate.

"Good Lord—" Tate gasped.

"My pardon," murmured Chi.

"Not you. Look!" Tate pointed in amazement toward the doorway.

Mildred Woodford stood there, her lanky body wrapped toga-wise in a wet sheet. Her bare feet and shivering lips were blue with cold.

She glared at the three men in the room, but especially at Quinto.

"Where the devil are my clothes?" she demanded hoarsely. "And where's my notebook and my handbag? Keys to my villa are in that bag."

Quinto regarded her in his usual undisturbed manner.

"I am so sorry," he murmured. "You are not angry, are you, Senorita?"

"Angry! I'm burning up!"

"But how did you get here?" asked Quinto.

"Rickshaw."

Mildred snatched her clothes from the hook behind the door, wedged her purse precariously under one arm, swept up her shoes with the same hand while clutching her toga together.

"Where's my notebook?" she demanded.

"It's now State evidence. I must keep it for a while," Quinto explained.

Mildred started for the door but stopped abruptly. She darted a glance dripping with venom at Quinto.

"Mind you," she said, "what I'd like to know, Mr. Quinto, is exactly what happened between the time I passed out and the time you put me in the bath yesterday!"

CHAPTER 23
The Fortunes of Harrow

QUINTO chuckled reminiscently and made a polite bow as Mildred slammed the door.

"W-W-Where was she?" Tate asked, bewildered. "It sounds as though you and she . . ." He stopped when he saw Lieutenant Chi.

Chi was rubbing his back and favoring the Mexican with a look of untold admiration. It was obvious that Chi had his own ideas on what had happened between Quinto and Miss Woodford.

"An alarmist," Quinto said of Mildred. "*Una mitotera.*"

He gave the key in the door a twist and returned to the business of examining Abe Harrow's coat. During the next five minutes he methodically turned each pocket inside out, laying the contents in separate piles. At his request, Tate itemized the stuff.

There was a wallet containing 1200 Chinese dollars, the Sun Yat Sen variety . . . .

"More than any man but a paymaster or general should carry in this army," observed Quinto.

In another pocket a small assortment of change was found. Chinese, French, English and American coins. The breast pocket revealed Harrow's usual armament of four fountain pens which Chi eyed vexedly.

Having cleaned out the pockets, Quinto went on with the inspection. He ran his fingers along the lining and lapels. Suddenly, up behind the collar, he ripped out the lining.

"You are right, Chi—success," he murmured.

Tate and the Lieutenant leaned forward, watching silently and expectantly. They saw Quinto rip out an oil-silk, very thin pouch from the collar. When undone, it revealed a sheaf of uniform sized chits printed with Chinese characters.

As Quinto went through them, it became apparent that they were government issues. They were numbered, but not consecutively. The numbering ranged in wide gaps of thousands. Each chit had the chop or signature of an officer from the Central Bank of China or one of its many branches.

"Very bad!" Chi said excitedly.

"Bank receipts. Special type," said Quinto.

"Receipts!" Tate gasped.

"Bank of China chits," Quinto explained eagerly. "Because of bombings and police who are not entirely high class in some provinces, the Central Bank has allowed people to deposit not only their savings, but their personal jewels, jades, family heirlooms and such things in the bank for safekeeping. The government moves this property to safe territory whenever it is threatened. Sixty trucks moved such deposits when Nanking fell. These chits are receipts for goods deposited. One need only present the receipts to get one's goods back."

"But how did Harrow get them?" asked Tate.

"Don't be blind," replied Quinto. "Look. The lowest numbered chit in this group is numbered 1,940. The highest is numbered 5,620."

"Good Lord—the Nohuri cipher," Tate burst out.

"*Claro hombre*. The cipher spoke of receipts 1,940 to 5,620 to be delivered at Pan Tao. Harrow, of course went to Pan Tao to get these from a Japanese agent."

"It fits. No wonder Harrow had so much money banked."

Quinto nodded comprehendingly. "Yes, but even the answer raises two new questions," he muttered. "Where did the invader get these chits? And more puzzling, how did Harrow cash them? The chits aren't valid in the foreign or private banks; nor could he cash more than one in each branch of the Central Bank of China. A very dangerous procedure, to say the least."

"What about Wang?" Tate asked suddenly.

"*Ai!* You've hit the important point. Papa Wier and Wang! You see, the connection between them is slowly appearing. Our task now is to tie the chits, the cipher, Wang's bookkeeping and the murders together. *Esta mas claro, eh?*"

Quinto selected one of the chits from the group, creased it and handed it to Tate. "The remainder go to Teng Fa," he explained. "But you will take that sample chit along to Hankow."

"Hankow?" Tate asked in surprise.

"*Si, companero*. You and I must carry our investigation on in Hankow."

"But it'll take days to get there?"

"No. We leave tonight for Sianfu. Early tomorrow morning we'll take a military plane which Teng Fa will arrange for. *Teniente* Chi remains in charge here. He'll see that no one leaves the Pavilions."

The Guerrilla School's big car plunged through the funnel of its own headlights, which sucked up the road toward Sianfu. It roared over the straight twelve-mile road while the speedometer needle hovered around eighty. Tate watched it anxiously. He also watched the shaved head of the young Chinese chauffeur limned against the piercing lights. On each side of the road armies of huge camphor trees leaped out of the night like weird hordes.

In the darkness of the back seat, Quinto's heavy hand suddenly dropped upon Tate's knee.

"And now I will tell you something," said Quinto. "I don't think Senor Abe was murdered!"

Tate sat up with a jerk.

"You know?" he asked.

Quinto sighed. "In China, one never knows. The proverbs insist that one only thinks and suggests. Perhaps a wind killed Harrow."

"A wind?"

"Wind on the mountain. It was windy the day he died. On the mountain cliff it was probably very strong. Harrow stood close to the edge. A gust of wind could have blown him off balance. A wind, *quien sabe*—who knows."

"It's not very plausible," Tate countered. "People don't take chances like that."

"So," murmured Quinto, pursuing his logic. "If Harrow was actually murdered, we know the best motive is the receipts. But Harrow's murderer should have taken his coat, or at least he should have taken the receipts before throwing the coat after the body. It's not logical to kill a man for receipts and then not take them."

"Wang's heel marks were on the cliff, remember?"

"Those heels, ah, yes, those heels," Quinto murmured rather disappointedly. He fell into a profoundly thoughtful mood as the car raced toward the outskirts of Sianfu.

CHAPTER 24
The Ambassador Makes a Point

THE DISTANCE between Sianfu and Hankow is four hundred and thirty miles as the crow flies. For Tate and Quinto, flying in a battered American Douglas piloted by a Manchurian aviator, the distance ran a little more than six hundred miles, due to the pilot's enthusiasm for sacred mountains along the route. On four different occasions the plane described zigzags to the left and right, circling such peaks before arriving at Hankow from the southeast instead of the northwest.

"Fine trip," observed Pilot Lan upon landing at the military airport. "I cut off twenty miles this time."

Tate and Quinto taxied into the city proper, shouldering through the jammed streets, past the foreign consulates, the French concession, still active though surrounded by barbed wire, the public libraries, the book stalls and the shops maintained by White Russians who lived in China on Nassen passports and bitter memories.

The two men drank a preliminary brandy at Mary's Bar, then Tate was sent off alone toward the Chinese section of the city. Quinto had given him an assignment. It was to check up on Harrow and Wang.

First he visited the Ministry of War. A casual mention of Teng Fa's name miraculously opened a series of doors and lips. He soon discovered that Abe Harrow had actually been under official suspicion of robbing the bodies of wounded and dead men at the front. Then he procured a complete list of the cash deposits and dates from the accounts of Harrow, Wang and Wier at the various foreign banks in the city. Harrow hadn't deposited chits—only cash!

Tate now walked two streets from the War Department building. He came to a bookshop displaying a sign: *Propaganda Store*. Inside there were framed silk watercolors of ducks. He paused for a moment, purchasing volumes one and two of Ch'en Su's *Flowers in the Garden of Calligraphy*. "I must remember to buy the remaining eighteen volumes when I have time," he told the bookseller.

His next stop was a shop that boasted prosperity by having plate-glass windows instead of the usual lattice with paper-backed screens. The shop was squeezed between two barbershops and it was owned by China's wealthiest rare-object dealer, Mr. Kung.

Mr. Kung, a pleasant, esthetic-looking man, who could be shrewd if necessary, bowed as Tate entered the gloomy, knickknack-filled place.

"My shop is favored by your visit," he murmured.

"It is a poor man's delight," Tate replied formally.

Mr. Kung smiled. He was pleased that a foreigner should observe the customary openings. Most foreigners just bought things. "The shop shrinks in humble shame before your footsteps," he said.

Tate fumbled with a package he laid upon the counter. The Chinese helped him undo the string. When the cover was set back, the Chinese caught his breath at the sight of the jade tiger which gleamed in the gray light of the shop.

Tate immediately dropped all formality.

"You've seen the jade before?" he asked.

The Chinese speared him with a penetrating, suspicious glance. "I sold it," he replied. He, too, dropped his previous formality.

"When?" Tate asked excitedly.

"Five years ago."

"Do you recall who purchased it?"

Mr. Kung nodded. "A very rich man," he murmured. "It is a fine piece—*hua shueh tai tsao*. It is the most rare work of the Ming Dynasty."

"Who bought it? The name?"

"A Cantonese official—Mr. Li Tao."

Tate's brow creased with disappointment. "In Canton," he muttered.

"The honorable Li Tao is in Hankow now," said Mr. Kung. "He is the Minister of Justice. You bought this from him? He must favor you greatly?"

"No," said Tate as he wrapped the jade tiger with one hand. "I've got to find him."

The next stop was the Ministry of Justice, which was located near the War Office. The Minister of Justice was not in, but two small bribes and the use of Teng Fa's name again paved the trail to a nearby teahouse.

Tate dropped into a chair beside the surprised and rather oldish minister. Without wasting a moment, he unwrapped the jade tiger again.

"Is this yours?" he asked.

The minister turned pale. He looked sharply at Tate. "Who are you to have this piece?" he asked.

"I'm from the *hsien ping*—secret police," Tate replied.

The minister arched his brows. "That jade belonged to my son. Have you news?" he asked anxiously.

"News?"

"He gave you the tiger?"

"No." Tate explained briefly how he had gotten the tiger, but without giving too much information.

The spark of hope which, for a moment, had glowed in the old minister's eyes quickly faded. He caressed the snowy jade with tired fingers. "I gave this tiger to my son," he murmured. "Four years ago. But my son is dead. The jade was deposited with my son's personal property at the Central Bank. I do not understand?"

"Did your son have a chit for his deposit?"

The minister nodded.

"But my son had it. My son was a captain in the army. He was killed or captured by the invader. I cannot understand . . . the tiger . . ."

"Where was he killed?" Tate asked animatedly.

"Feng Yang! My son stood against the invader at Feng Yang," said the old man. "His body was never returned."

"Feng Yang?" Tate looked befuddled. "I'm sorry," he murmured.

For a minute, he sat back, utterly confused. The old minister continued petting the jade.

"The telephone," said Tate. At once he leaped to his feet and hurried to a public phone at the far end of the teahouse. He called a newspaper office, the number of which Quinto had given him. A moment later he had Quinto on the line.

"Hello, G.H.Q.," said Tate. "I've got everything we need on Harrow and I've traced the owner of the jade, the Minister of Justice. But listen. There's something wrong. Harrow was suspected of robbing bodies on the Kaifeng front. Was he ever on the Feng Yang battle front?"

"No," replied Quinto. "He was only at Kaifeng."

"Well, then," said Tate, "it doesn't make sense. The bank chit for that jade was captured by the invader at the Feng Yang front. Where does Harrow fit in?"

"*Si quate*, but it is nothing," replied Quinto. "Remember the Nohuri cipher. It said, *receipts for delivery*. Simple, eh? We have a Receipt Ring. It is something I have suspected, so I sent you to gather more information."

"A Receipt Ring?" Tate glowed excitedly.

"*Nada mas*—just that. Senor Harrow robbed bodies of their receipts at the front and behind Chinese lines, you see? The Japanese took receipts from the Chinese they captured. Sometimes Harrow, sometimes others, met these Japanese agents who delivered such chits. The visit to Pan Tao, no? My Yellow Coat was also in on it. And Wier— maybe he carried receipts from the invader and confused us by saying he had been driven from his mission.

"All receipts came to Wang. He is a Bank of China official. He could cash them on call and then divide the proceeds between his many agents and return a certain value in cash to the Japanese."

"A fine way to finance an invasion," Tate commented.

"*Bueno*," said Quinto. "You leave the jade tiger with the old minister and meet me at the airport later. You will make a report then. Now I must visit the ambassador."

Sir Oliver Quist, the British Ambassador, was a jolly hulk of a man with a sense of humor. He had bright pink cheeks, gray hair and a graying mustache. Although in his fifties and a Britisher, he liked informality and he liked the Chinese.

The Chinese, on their part, also admired the ambassador, for when he had moved the embassy from Nanking to Hankow, his household had included two robin's-egg blue Soochow bathtubs. The Hankow plumbers had been faced with quite a problem—two bathtubs in one house. After a decent amount of worry and consultation among each other, the plumbers installed the tubs side by side—one for hot water, the other for cold water. The news got around town and the ambassador gained much face because of his two tubs.

When Gimiendo Quinto arrived in Hankow, Sir Oliver knocked off work for the day. He was a great admirer of the Mexican ever since the two men had met a number of years before in Saigon.

Sir Oliver called in the headman from the famous Lao restaurant and for a half hour he discussed the setting of a banquet for two. He and the restaurant man argued vehemently over the temperature, the foods in season, foods available, the wines and the number of courses, which came in regulation numbers of either eight, twelve, sixteen or thirty-six courses. Sir Oliver glanced at Quinto and chose the thirty-six-course dinner.

"Now, then, G.H.Q. We'll begin with a dash of quince wine from Canton," he chuckled heartily. "Then shark's fin soup followed by eleven meat courses. Think that's enough, old chap? Eventually we'll work up to brandy at the Last Chance Bar or Mary's."

"*Magnifico, hombre*," Quinto looked affectionately at the ambassador. "But business first, remember?"

"Oh, bah, the business," growled Sir Oliver. "The Empire will hold! Mind you, G.H.Q., the Empire still owes you a debt for getting the Prince o' Wales out of that scrape in Saigon that time."

Quinto smiled reminiscently.

"But first the matter of Clive Firth," he said.

"Ah ha!" Sir Oliver Quist shook his head, "Lord Firth's lad. Very sad indeed, I must say. I heard from our friend Teng Fa that he died.

Air raid or something, wasn't it? But I say, no one to blame, no one at all. Gad! China lost a friend in your Firth, and England a hero."

"He was a hero," Quinto murmured.

"Come to think of it. How's his little wife taking it? She returned to England yet?"

"Wife!" Quinto sprang up.

Sir Oliver nodded wonderingly.

"Don't tell me you didn't know?" he said. "Well, perhaps you wouldn't. They were married in Nanking last summer. It's true, they separated two weeks after, but I was given to understand she and her father moved in on you at Lingtung. I fancy they patched it up, you know."

"Mary Wier?" Quinto asked abruptly.

"Right ho, that's the maiden name. Yes, that's odd. He called her that name in his will."

"His will!" Quinto murmured thoughtfully. "Yes, I knew Clive had received a letter from his solicitor suggesting he return to England. I didn't know he wrote a will, though."

"It came today," replied Sir Oliver. "Seems he posted it some two weeks ago. Your mails up North are dashed slow. Well, really, young Firth begged me to pass the thing on to his solicitors."

"Let me see it," said Quinto. "*Por favor.*"

"It's not quite ethical, you know." The ambassador grinned, and reaching across his desk, rang a small hand bell. Almost instantly a smooth, innocuous young man entered. The embassy secretary. "Howell, look in the files, will you?" said the ambassador. "Bring me the packet marked 'Firth.' "

Quinto let his eyes circle around the embassy once. It was a huge room with a desk in the center that looked like the landing deck on an airplane carrier. There was but one other bit of furniture in the room, a bookcase bulging with volumes in ten languages on the art of eating and cooking.

Presently Howell returned. Sir Oliver took the manila envelope, opened the clasp, and extracted two letters. One was from Clive Firth to the ambassador, asking the latter to forward his will to Simeon B. Shand of London. The other was the will.

"*Gracias,*" Quinto murmured as he took the second letter and read it:

March 26, 1938

Dear Simeon:
 I am deeply grieved to hear of my father, Lord Firth's death, and

more so since I was unable to be with him.

Now, in regard to my returning to England to assume responsibility as the sole heir of the estate, I'm afraid it is impossible. I intend remaining in China until the war is over. I trust you can manage the estate as you have done during my father's declining years.

In the event, or against the possibility of my dying here, I want the following to stand as my will and testament.

I will the Firth Estate in Scotland as well as the Newspaper Enterprises to my wife, Mary Wier, in China now. The deposits, other assets, bonds, etc., valued at 50,000 pounds be divided as follows: one half the total sum, upon liquidation, to be contributed in father's name to the Chinese Red Cross; 10,000 pounds to Sir Clive Blankfort; 5,000 pounds to Lady Goodwin; the remainder to be divided equally among the ffamily servants.

I trust you'll see that this is duly filed, Simeon.

Sincerely,
Clive Firth

"Who is Sir Clive Blankfort?" Quinto asked.

"Big-game hunter," the ambassador replied. "I believe he was young Clive's godfather."

"A relative?"

Sir Oliver Quist pondered this for a moment. "No, doubt if he is," he answered. "The Firth line was on its last lap. No grandchildren. Young Clive appeared to be the last one. Oh, yes, Lady Goodwin is a cousin. Painter. She gave up studying under Picasso to marry Lord Goodwin. Then she divorced him and married again. Quite a scandal, I dare say."

"Where is Blankfort now?"

"India, I fancy."

"This Lady Goodwin, who did she marry?"

Sir Oliver shrugged impatiently. "Oh, someone very respectable and ordinary. Never hear of them now . . . . Come Quinto, let's eat!"

Quinto raised a hand, begging for time. He hurriedly reread the will as well as Clive's letter to Sir Oliver. Finally he turned the will over, glancing at the back of the sheet. Suddenly his brow arched.

The back of the will was covered with typing but the letters were backward and the lines read from right to left.

"Have you got a mirror?" he asked.

Sir Oliver smoldered a little but produced a small pocket mirror. Quinto placed the glass so it reflected the typing on the back of the paper.

"It's the will again, a carbon copy, only backward," he said.

" 'Pears as though young Firth intended making a duplicate but he put the carbon paper in backward. Imprint took on the reverse of the original," said Sir Oliver. "But I say, Quinto, why such a dither?"

Quinto made a slight grimace. "It's very important," he said. "Clive Firth was murdered! You didn't know that."

"Murdered?" The ambassador looked shocked.

"Yes. Seven days ago," Quinto glanced toward the door thoughtfully. "This carbon on the reverse of the will is very important, *es verdad*. I know now who murdered Senor Clive. I need only one more bit of proof."

Even before he had finished speaking, Quinto grabbed the phone from the ambassador's desk. He jiggled the hook impatiently. "Sianfu... connect with Sianfu. . . .

Guest House," he barked into the mouthpiece.

"Who are you calling?" asked Sir Oliver.

"Teng Fa! "

Quinto, Tate and Sir Oliver Quist crossed from the administration building to the Douglas plane. Quinto carried a bundle of newspapers, *The St. Louis Baseball News*. He knew that Lieutenant Chi, the inveterate Brooklyn Dodgers fan, would be interested.

Tate had just finished his excited explanation of the Receipt Ring. "So you see," he said. "This ought to shut our case. It's Wang, with no doubt about it."

"Yes," Quinto replied. "We both come to the same conclusions at the same time."

They arrived at the plane. Pilot Lan was already warming her up. Tate went inside and took his seat, while Quinto squatted in the cabin door, conversing with the ambassador.

A saw-toothed wind ripped across the airport, tearing at the moored plane and raising swirls of yellow dust. In the southwest corner of the field ten prospective Chinese air students maneuvered through intricate squadron formations—on the ground.

The new students wore long black silk gowns which fluttered in the wind. The gowns made them delicate looking, for they kept their hands hidden in the sleeves. Little red buttons on their black skull caps blinked cheerfully at the world. The students zigzagged across the field on foot, elbows extended like wings and dipping from side to side.

In the backwash of the Douglas, Sir Oliver presented a most unambassador-like spectacle. He clutched a large, half-eaten turkey leg in one hand while clamping his recently dented bowler hat in place with the other. From time to time he let go his hold on the hat to reach a big fist in his coat pocket, which was stuffed with loose boiled rice. He munched the rice to sort of batten down the banquet he had already eaten.

"I say, G.H.Q., no bother about that smashed window at the Last Chance. I'll cover it. Damn glad to, old chap. When are you coming back?" His hale voice boomed above the roar of the plane and whipping wind.

Quinto leaned from the cabin doorway, face flushed from the vigors of a pleasant afternoon with the ambassador. "Remember, Oliver," he answered. "I want you to be in Lingtung tomorrow night. You'll see justice done. Actually, I need you. If you are not there I will be in a position *muy desperado*."

A sudden gust of wind twirled Sir Oliver's bowler across the field. The ambassador hurled the turkey drumstick after it but missed.

"See here, G.H.Q.," he roared. "You can count on me coming, but I want a return favor. I say, how about bringing your guerrilleros down here the following weekend and making a private raid on Nanking for me?"

Quinto's face lighted with amusement.

"So?" he asked. "You left something behind when the invader took Nanking?"

Sir Oliver Quist kissed his fingertips while his face glowed like that of an Italian chef.

"Girl!" he shouted. "I left a flower of a girl behind during the retreat."

Now Quinto's eyes softened. He had a feeling of tenderness toward big men like himself who are helplessly in love.

"*Bueno*, I'll make the raid," he shouted back. "What is the *muchacha's* name?"

"Mountain of Virtue—" Sir Oliver shouted.

Suddenly the plane kicked off in a swirl of dust and taxied across the field before the ambassador caught the surprised, aggrieved astonishment on Quinto's round face.

CHAPTER 25
Kidnaping the Lunghai Express

LAN, the Manchurian pilot, was no partisan of night flying. Deep down, he realized how the *feng shui* and other roving spirits might make a monkey of a man's compass and flying instruments. Then where would one be, particularly with China in a blackout?

Playing safe, he followed the railroad northward to Chengchow Junction, where he expected to make a left turn and pick up the Lunghai Express tracks. All in all, it added nothing more than an extra five hundred and eighty miles to the distance back to Sianfu.

But shortly before Chengchow, the plane's patched-up radial engine started sputtering. Streaks of oil splattered across the cabin windows. The motor coughed asthmatically. Lan Cut the throttle, wagged the wing-tips and glanced back at Tate and Quinto without alarm, saying, "*Feng Shui* in eng-line!"

A minute later he expertly landed the plane in the pitch dark.

"What do we do now?" Tate asked in disgust. It was just midnight by his watch.

"Sleep," replied Quinto. "We'll walk to Chengchow in the morning and catch the Lunghai Express. It leaves at noon."

"Fifteen miles!" Tate groaned.

He looked hopefully at Lan, who stood before the plane engine, staring at it in respectful silence. This was the "politeness toward possibilities tactic."

Quinto shook his head tolerantly. "Spirits," he said. "Might be three or four days before they agree to abandon the motor. Lan won't touch it. Only Eighth Route Army men will touch engines like that."

At noon the following day, Tate boarded the rear camouflaged car of the Lunghai Express. He appeared very unhappy as he settled down beside Quinto, who had found himself four Chinese fan tan players of passing ability.

He watched the game open and then stood at the window, looking out at Chengchow during the few minutes before the train pulled out.

Chengchow was still the same. The town was flat and dusty. The sun seemed to flatten across the stretch of railway yards flanked by the squat buildings of the town. Four charred railway trucks lay in a siding behind the station, the end product of a bombing raid. Soldiers and civilians hurried across the flats and swarmed over the Express like locusts.

A peasant woman hawked food outside. Tate drew a few coppers from his pocket and with one hand managed a difficult exchange, purchasing a boiled chicken which was varnished red with soya bean oil.

While munching the chicken, he followed Quinto's orders and surveyed the passengers boarding the train. Perhaps a certain split-lipped Chinese man who had spied upon Quinto during the entire morning in Chengchow would be lurking about. The man seemed to have vanished.

Suddenly a mournful wail from the Belgian locomotive reached back along the tracks. The train jerked slightly. The Lunghai Express moved forward slowly, brushing people off the tracks with casual and complete disregard for civil liberties.

"*Que hubole?*" Quinto grinned, seeing Tate suddenly shiver, chilling at the eerie sound of the train whistle. "You are afraid of the ride? Maybe the guns at Tung Kwan? It is nothing to worry about. My guerrilleros who captured Nohuri have made the invader cannons at Tung Kwan a little bit crooked. They shoot now and they think it is their aim which is bad."

Tate smiled weakly but his fright seemed to increase as the train wound through the weird Loess Lands just beyond Chengchow, for even in the sunlight the Loess country was like a page torn from a medieval fantasy. A strange landscape hurtled by the car window; the infinite variety of embattled shapes, hills like castles, rows of mammoth hummocks, others like rounded scones. It was as if those low hills had been ripped by some gigantic hand which left the imprints of angry fingers. Perhaps it was a land designed by a mad god.

Tate's glance shifted from the window into the compartment. Quinto, as usual, was winning at fan tan.

It was during that instant that the passengers in other compartments and those riding on the roof began shouting excitedly. Tate looked again through the window and blinked in surprise . . . . The train was riding backward at an impossible speed!

More cries from the roof: Chinese voices making bets as to when they'd jump the tracks and crash. Tate leaned out the open window. He pulled back as though he had been struck across the face. "Quinto, look!" he cried.

Quinto leaped to the window.

"Look," Tate repeated.

Up ahead, perhaps a half mile, the Belgian engine and seven cars chugged along serenely. The Express rounded a curve on the crest of a hill and disappeared. Meanwhile the eighth, the camouflaged car, in which they rode, slid backward, rolling swiftly on its own.

Excitement reached a fever pitch aboard the prodigal car. Men shouted while the less brave leaped off here and there. They could be seen rolling in the loess dust as they landed. Amidst the uproar, a cheerful Chinese man with a split lower lip retired from the front of the car where he had cut the coupling with an acetylene torch. Still carrying the blazing torch, he passed along the corridor to the rear platform where he calmly set it down and began turning the brake wheel.

Quinto's face clouded when he saw the torch wielder pass. It was the same man who had spied on him in Chengchow. "The Min-t'uan!" he snapped.

The compartment door slid opened and a thin, cold-faced Chinese entered. He wore Western mail-order clothes. In his hand he held an automatic which he leveled at Quinto and Tate.

"No move!" he hissed dangerously.

"*Que pasa desgraciado?*" Quinto snapped his annoyance. He glanced at the gun but did not move. He was unarmed himself.

"You prisoner," said the gunman. "Everything all right. We cut car from train with torch. You stay in compartment when train stop."

He waved the four frightened fan-tan-playing passengers from the compartment with the gun and stationed himself at the door.

Tate turned pale and even Quinto bit his lip, for upon looking from the gunman to the window, and feeling the car come to a halt, it was clear a group of armed desperados had surrounded the train. There were about twelve of them, half Japanese and half Chinese Min-t'uan. The fact that there were Japanese on Chinese-held territory disturbed Quinto. It was a bad sign.

Within a few minutes the desperados had herded the passengers from the train and marched them down the tracks toward Chengchow. "Now what are they going to do?" Tate asked worriedly. It didn't take long to find out . . . .

The compartment door slid back again and Wang the banker entered, followed by Virtue.

Quinto flashed the beautiful Eurasian girl a disturbed, hurt look. Virtue merely smiled in her dazzling way and calmly lit herself a cigarette.

A wisp of a smirk flavored Wang's thin lips as he bowed stiffly toward Quinto. There was a touch of mockery in that bow. He quoted from a popular proverb:

"Predestined enemies always meet in narrow alleyways."

Behind him, Mountain of Virtue coughed politely and murmured another proverb. "A rat gnaws at a tiger's tail, invites destruction."

Quinto looked relieved. Not to be outdone and since Chinese etiquette demands a proverb for a proverb, he added one from the Confucian *Analects*: he murmured, "A true hero never incurs present risk."

Wang bowed slightly, softened by Quinto's worthy choice. "You are very sensible," he spoke icily. "Cooperation and compromise are indeed hidden virtues thus far unknown in the foreigner." Suddenly his voice tightened. "You will hand me the chits!"

Quinto regarded the banker whimsically.

"Chits?" he inquired blandly.

Mr. Wang's pointed military boots edged out from beneath his black silk gown hem. They gleamed like black, sharp ferret-eyes, dangerous and lurking. Somehow, there was a certain incongruousness to the scene, remindful of a famous line from a Yuan drama:

> *Tip us the wink said Iron Staff Li*
> *Then I'll cheat you and you'll cheat me.*

"You are too Chinese," Wang answered Quinto. "I want the bank receipts, immediately. Before Mr. Harrow died he was in possession of certain bank chits belonging to me. After he died, his body was dispossessed of them. I've given you a week to find them. Where are they?"

"And if I refuse to tell you?" asked Quinto.

"You'll be shot!" said Wang. He glanced at Tate. "You too! "

Quinto waved the danger aside as if it were completely unimportant.

"*Bueno*, if I give the chits to you?" he asked.

Wang reflected for a moment.

"You'll be shot anyway. You know too much!" he answered.

"The chits are in good hands—Teng Fa's," said Quinto.

The barb told. Mr. Wang jerked back a step. His lips compressed into thin angry slits.

Virtue raised her lovely head and shook a warning finger at Quinto. "Gimiendo," she said softly. "Please return the chits. Wang must have them or the Japanese will be very angry with him. They threatened to chop his head off and hang it on a pole if he does not recover the chits."

"Hah," Tate spoke up. "The Receipt Ring. So that's why there are Japanese soldiers here with the Min-t'uan."

"Quiet!" snapped Wang.

Tate stared at the banker and suddenly his legs began to wobble. It was evident that he wasn't made for adventure. He seemed to realize that now, in looking at Wang. But Wang didn't realize it. The banker crossed his hands formally and turned to the guard at the door.

"Take them out. Shoot them!" he said.

"S-S-Shoot me?" Tate stuttered.

Wang favored him with a contemptuous glance.

"Come *companero*," Quinto cut in as he seized Tate's trembling arm and headed for the door. "It is not so bad as in some countries where they shoot you, then give you a fair trial and maybe find you not guilty. That is irony, eh?"

Tate eyed his huge companion unappreciatively. This was no time for humor. As he stumbled from the camouflaged car, the sun struck him in the face and it made him look even paler.

A Min-t'uan man nudged the two prisoners along the track bed with a bayonet, then halted them with a jerk. Tate glanced helplessly at Quinto and at the eight Japanese soldiers who had lined up at some twenty paces opposite the train . . . . The firing squad!

Virtue leaned against the compartment window sill for she had remained in the car. She spoke to Wang:

"You must do it with honors," she reminded him. "Gimiendo is a captain."

Wang thought this over for a minute. Though he appeared somewhat irritated by Virtue's words, he turned and issued hasty orders, having two graves dug—a large one for Quinto, a small one for Tate.

CHAPTER 26
Nevada Fires a Shot

NEVADA and four fully armed Chinese soldiers halted upon the crest of a scone-shaped hill to stare in the distance at the base of another dogbiscuit-like hill. The abandoned camouflaged car of the Lunghai express rested there.

"Express not very strong. Leave off train there. Maybe another some place else. Come back later, pick em up," suggested one of the Chinese boys.

Nevada shaded his eyes with the palm of his hand and squinted. "Looks deserted," he drawled.

"Maybe camouflage car get tired always ride in rear. Maybe she want ride up front. She go on strike," reasoned a second lad at Nevada's side.

The four soldiers waited patiently for the cowboy's answer. The tall American with the voice that walked on slow feet was technically their prisoner. At least, he had been until they left Chengchow Junction that morning. How he had become a prisoner would be very amazing, if it had not happened in China. Upon leaving Lingtung, Nevada managed to reach the Lanchow front. Then, when it was discovered that he had resumed his machine-gun post while still carrying wounds not completely healed, he had been arrested. The staff colonel at Lanchow ordered him back to Lingtung under a four-man guard. Instructions had also been sent back that Nevada should be tried and shot if he ever deserted to the front before getting a proper medical discharge. This was his fourth offense.

At Chengchow, an even stranger thing happened. Instead of boarding the Lunghai Express, Nevada and his four guards set off on a diagonal, toward the Loess Lands and the Yellow River. Somehow they had heard that there were bothersome machine-gun emplacements on the Japanese-held side of the river which needed raiding. Nevada and his companions decided to start work on the emplacement near Tsing Hwa. The idea offered endless prospects, because they could fight their way all the distance up the river and it would take weeks to reach Lingtung. By that time, Nevada figured, his wounds would be healed.

Now, for the moment, the invader machine-guns were forgotten. The cowboy's steady gaze remained fixed upon the distant railway coach. He made out the movement of human figures there. A group of men lining up, then some of them digging.

It was too distant to see plainly. The sunlight had an image shattering quality to it. He watched another few minutes until the men who were digging stopped. Again he saw the figures line up.

"What we do?" inquired one of the guards at his elbow.

Nevada shrugged.

"Should we mosey down and see what's happening, or do we go in and raid the Japs along the river?" he asked.

"The invaders," cried three of the guards.

"Tell you what. I'll toss a coin." He took out a copper coin while with his right hand he eased an old-fashioned Frontier Model Colt six-gun in its holster which was tied down hard to his lean flank. It was one of the guns he had brought from America. "If I hit heads, it's the river; if I clip the tails, it's the train."

He flicked the copper into the sunlight and seemed to hardly touch his right-hand gun. The explosion which followed delighted the four Chinese. Their expressions of delight changed swiftly to awe when they saw the coin flip off to one side, struck by the bullet.

All five men scrambled, searching for the coin. They didn't realize it was gone!

Wang's gravediggers completed their gruesome task and put aside the spades they had borrowed from the camouflaged car. Wang himself silently measured Tate and Quinto, then compared the measurements with the mounds of freshly turned earth. Finally he took out a pair of dark glasses and put them on, a precaution against Mountain of Virtue's beauty and charm which might interfere with his plans.

"We are ready!" he announced.

"Ah, no!" Quinto interrupted.

Wang looked at him coldly.

"I am never ready to die," said Quinto.

The banker glared at him and was on the point of answering when a pistol shot rang out over the Loess hills. The Chinese man jerked to attention while his mixed band of desperados hesitated, swinging their rifles in different directions.

Wang whirled on a dime, his dark eyes darting suspiciously at Mountain of Virtue, who stood complacently at the compartment window, a very dream of fragrance and loveliness, enough to put flowers to shame. He seemed a bit sorry that he had put dark glasses on.

"You are too hasty, Wang," she smiled disarmingly. "Slow preparations, step by step, are necessary for an assassination. You should post lookouts."

"Lookouts!" the banker snapped defiantly. He quickly detailed two Min-t'uan men to search the hills for the source of the gunshot.

Virtue smiled again and turned her gaze toward Tate and Quinto. The little calligraphist was growing weaker and weaker. He was losing his sense of perspective. The strain was too much. Virtue expected that of him. Quinto, on the other hand, was as she expected him—two hundred and twenty pounds of nobleness and bravery.

Suddenly she leaned forward, her lilting whisper carrying only to Quinto and Tate.

"One makes progress with slow delays, Gimiendo. If we persuade Wang to dig another grave . . . for me perhaps. . . . Only last night I sent Sergeant Ping and the guerrilleros who joined the Min-t'uan back to Lingtung for aid. Perhaps Ping returns."

Virtue smiled again, seeing the ramrod of courage that stiffened Tate's spine, only to splinter almost immediately.

"We go on with the execution!" Wang commanded.

There came another pistol shot, less distant. It was followed by a single sharp cry of pain.

"The shooting, quickly!" Wang snapped. "We must depart."

Tate choked back an involuntary sob. The Japanese rifle barrels pointed at him with a deadly finality. The bright air around them was bathed in a crystal sheen. A donkey brayed in the distance. Quinto's strong fingers gripped Tate's arm, supporting him.

"Put them guns down!" a voice drawled, close at hand, in English.

Tate raced his eyes around in astonishment.

At the far end of the coach stood the lean figure of Nevada. It was like a mirage. The cowboy's hands rested easily on the butts of holstered pistols. Ranged behind him were four grinning Chinese soldiers, arms piled high with hand-grenades.

A Min-t'uan man moved ever so slightly, raising his rifle barrel. Quinto sucked his breath in. He tried to shout out a warning.

A terrific blast thundered forth. Nevada's hands had been brown blurs as he palmed guns that thundered before they even left their holsters. His smooth, swift draw had been too fast for the eye to see. The Min-t'uan man's rifle kicked into the air while the man somersaulted backward.

Cornered, Wang grabbed for his own automatic. He hardly got his finger into the trigger guard when the gun spun off at a tangent. The crafty banker screamed with pain and doubled up, clutching a bleeding, shattered wrist to his stomach. Abruptly, the Min-t'uan and Japanese began firing indiscriminately at Nevada, at the camouflaged coach, at Quinto and at two innocent scone-shaped hills to the right. Virtue vanished below her window sill and reappeared with a dainty pearl-handled automatic. She fired methodically and gracefully at the Japanese. Tate crashed to the ground. Quinto landed at his side. A bullet ricocheted, whining off the iron wheel of the train, plunking into the earth between them.

"Grenades—" shouted Quinto. "Head down!"

Tate flattened himself. Suddenly there came a brilliant flare . . . an explosion. Weeds along the trackbed were swept flat by the concussion. Chunks of metal hissed a bare foot above the ground and peppered the side of the coach. One explosion followed another. Parts of the Japanese Min-t'uan firing squad flew in various directions. A battered, slightly gory arm with no body or shoulder attached to it slid past Tate and lodged against the railroad track. Tate gulped sickeningly.

Grenades were blowing up all over now—and unreasonably. Nevada's Chinese guards, having accounted for the majority of the Japanese with their first throws, thought it unwise to waste beautiful noises contained in their assorted grenades.

It was at least ten minutes before the noise subsided and the curtains of acrid powder smoke drifted aside. When this had occurred, it was revealed that there were only four Min-t'uan men, two in battered condition, and Wang left. The Japanese had been annihilated.

Nevada holstered his smoking guns and joined Quinto. "What are you doing here?" Quinto asked, thankfully.

"Prisoner," Nevada drawled. He explained his position briefly.

"That was wonderful, absolutely wonderful," Tate put in. He reached for the cowboy's hand, pumping it as though Nevada were a long-lost brother. Then he beamed at Quinto, saying, "Hah, we've got Wang now."

Quinto nodded and smiled appreciatively as Mountain of Virtue attached herself to his arm. "We'll turn the remaining Min-t'uan over to the nearest town constabulary. They'll readily accept the prisoners, hearing that Teng Fa will be glad to see them."

"And Wang?"

"He goes to Lingtung with us. Teng Fa wants him personally. He does not always get traitorous leaders of a receipt ring . . . ."

"And the murderer of Firth and Harrow," added Tate.

"No, not quite."

"What?" Tate looked surprised.

"Wang is not the murderer," murmured Quinto, resuming his usual placidity.

"But who? I don't understand?"

Quinto waved the question away. He turned toward Nevada and unexpectedly flipped the cowboy's two guns from their holsters. He slipped them into his own belt.

"I am sorry, Nevada," he said. "I'm putting you under arrest. I must make sure you return to Lingtung!"

CHAPTER 27
Tai Erh Chwang—A Victory

A MOUNTING nervous tension wavered in dissonant confusion and tightened upon the Lingtung Gardens. It was sensed, yet remained unseen in the brilliant sunlight which bathed the jasmine-heavy paths and gentle willows.

A great flow of noise permeated the gardens, forming a facade for the tension. Firecrackers exploded from morning until night, while drums and tambourines set up a constant din. The guerrilla students were celebrating the newly won victory of the Chinese Armies at Tai Erh Chwang on the Grand Canal Front.

The noise gathered toward evening: expanding, growing more and more intense, like summer heat swelling with electrical suspension before the breaking of a storm. The pattern of uneasiness wove through the nerves of each of the Internationals, linking the Wiers, Wang, Mignon Chauvet, McKay, Mr. Ho, Mildred Woodford, and Tate.

Early in the morning, after having spent a wild night riding in a borrowed military truck, the party from the Loess Lands had returned. Quinto had immediately locked himself in the *yamen* with Virtue. For three hours there had been a furious pounding at a typewriter. A few minutes later, Virtue went with a score of Chinese guerrilleros into the Little Garden Theatre. They remained locked up there.

In the afternoon, Quinto called Tate into the *yamen*.

"Events have arranged themselves nicely," Quinto announced. "Tonight all things come together and we will bury the ghosts of Senores Firth and Harrow."

Tate looked surprised, then curious. "Who is it?" he asked. "Nevada or Wang, or both?"

Quinto made a little motion with his hands, appealing for patience.

"In China, if one is to follow the philosophy of Mr. Ho," he said, "one never points out a truth. It is merely suggested. For a week now, our community of nerves have been on edge. Virtue and Miss Woodford were kidnaped. Three men were killed. You worked on a difficult assignment. It has been very hard . . . . *Ahora vamos a vacilar, eh?* .

"Tonight we'll be entertained. We'll rest. My guerrilleros will give a

163

play, directed by Virtue. It will serve to take the edge off our nerves . . . Then . . . I shall suggest who murdered Harrow and Firth. But at this moment I want your opinion. Very frankly. There may be the possibility that I've overlooked some angle."

"You mean you want me to sum up?" asked Tate.

"*Si, hombre*. You have been with me all this time. You have seen the hundred little things that make a crime. I'll be happy if you are only able to uncover one mystery—the strange disappearance of the Generalissimo's teeth which are still missing."

"Well," Tate began cautiously, "I don't know why you arrested Nevada. That rather upset all my theory."

"I arrested Nevada for a reason you yourself see but fail to recognize," murmured Quinto. "But go on."

"Well, I think the whole case rests on the Receipt Ring. Even Virtue added to our proof that Wang was head of the Chinese branch of the ring and he was desperate. Perhaps Harrow planned to double-cross him. Wang tried to get him on the cliff, but Harrow slipped out of his grasp, along with the coat and receipts."

"Very good," murmured Quinto. He rolled himself a cigarette and waited thoughtfully.

"Then," continued Tate, "you assigned Firth to guard Harrow's quarters. Naturally Wang imagined Firth took the receipts, so either he, or Papa Wier who was under his control because of the heroin habit, entered Firth's villa, murdering him and searching the room. Unsuccessful, Wang next kidnaped Virtue and Woodford to bring pressure on you as well as to have a club over your head because you were getting too close to the secret of the Receipt Ring. I believe that puts most of it together, don't you?"

Quinto nodded silently. He sucked deeply on his cigarette and blew out a ring of smoke.

"Anything else?" asked Tate.

"*Bueno*. Will you tell Sergeant Sun that no one is to leave the gardens? Especially Wang and both Wiers. Secondly, everyone must attend the Little Garden Theatre exactly at seven o'clock. *A las siete en punto*."

Immediately after his talk with Tate, Quinto drove off to Sianfu. He returned an hour later accompanied by Teng Fa, the Sianfu Civil Governor and the Military Governor. The four men promptly went to the villa, where Nevada had been placed under guard. Then Papa Wier and Mary were escorted there by Sergeant Sun. It was then five o'clock.

At six o'clock, a handful of guerrilleros made a triumphal entry into the gardens. They brought Japanese Colonel Nohuri, who was thoroughly tied up with gold braid ripped from his weekday uniform.

****

With nightfall, the tension in the gardens strained to its breaking point. It was inexplicable, for it seemed to vibrate with the feverish intensity of finely pitched tuning forks.

There was something wrong with the night. Sounds carried with a crystal-clear sharpness. The increased tempo of firecrackers and drums, the cooing of disturbed doves beneath the eaves of the pagoda-like roofs, gave the air a magnetic, irritating body.

At seven o'clock exactly, Tate went with Doc McKay to the tiny theater. Others had already arrived, so they were not the first. The calligraphist and the doctor sat down at a small table and a guerrilla student brought two pots of tea and a bowl of sunflower seeds. The little theater was being run in the Chinese style, where people sit at tables, eat, drink and talk while a play goes on.

At a table close to the stage sat the Governors of Sianfu—Civil and Military. With them were the Mayor of Lingtung and Mildred Woodford. Mildred chatted a mile a minute, in English. Mignon Chauvet, sallow-checked and weary from lack of sleep, occupied a table behind the Mayor. She sat almost rigidly. Farther behind and near the left wall of the theater were Papa Wier, Mary and Nevada. The old missionary was white and trembling. His eyes wandered around with a harried look. Although beside him, Mary was turned facing Nevada. The two were whispering.

Tate's eyes swiveled around until they rested on Mr. Ho, the scholar. The old man sat complacently. He rolled walnuts in his right hand to keep his fingers supple for writing characters. Behind Ho stood Teng Fa, respondent in an olive-green uniform with a couple of patches in the trouser seat. Lined up against the wall, tied to stools and deprived of tea and melon seeds, were Wang, four Min-t'uan prisoners and Colonel Nohuri, who was a short man with high cheek bones and very thick glasses.

"Looks like a quorum," McKay grinned.

A moment later Mountain of Virtue entered, her arm in Lieutenant Chi's. The heart of every man leaped erratically, seeing her. Virtue was beautiful enough to put ten thousand flowers to shame. Lieutenant Chi could have also put something to shame. In honor of the Tai Erh Chwang victory, he wore his full dress uniform. On one lapel was pinned a CIO Transport Workers button which had somehow gotten into China.

Sergeant Sun hurried through the beer-hall arrangement of tables to the stage where he busily spread out an assortment of objects on a small desk. The evidence. Among the objects were: a derringer pistol, a dried bit of red clay, a capsule of heroin, scattered envelopes probably containing chits, time schedules and other evidence. The sergeant then went about the bare, projecting platform stage lighting oil lamps, which flickered with the slightest draft. The flames made the crimson interior of the theater glow with mobile unreality.

Suddenly a string of firecrackers exploded, dancing upon the stage. The theater filled with powder smoke. Tate sat up suddenly. As everyone in the theater, he appeared very tense.

"Hello, Tate!" a voice spoke at his side.

Tate looked up, somewhat startled. He stared at the huge figure of Sir Oliver Quist. The ambassador eased himself upon a stool beside McKay.

"Really, I thought I'd be late," remarked the ambassador.

Tate smiled pleasantly and started to introduce McKay when a terrific roll of drums reverberated in the theater. Almost immediately, Quinto walked out on the stage. In the dramatic light he looked picaresque, Gargantuan and very Mexican. His cotton clothes hung on his huge body like a circus tent on John Bunyan. For an instant his smoky black eyes rested on Virtue, then they brushed over the audience.

"*Companeros y companeras,*" he began. "Tonight Teng Fa will make an arrest—the murderer of Clive Firth! But before such an arrest is made I am going to show you why." He paused effectively. "For a week Gimiendo Quinto has been a detective. Today I am a playwright . . . .

"My guerrilleros will give a play about murder. It is in the form of the Chinese theater with the usual pantomime and gestures. Because some of you do not understand Chinese the play will be pantomime. . . I shall merely add detail and suggest who among us is a murderer!"

Quinto stepped back while a new string of firecrackers exploded. His dark eyes again brushed over the audience and paused momentarily on Sir Oliver Quist, who, by this time, had seen Mountain of Virtue. A queer expression darkened the ambassador's broad face. He looked like a man who had just discovered he has been playing with loaded dice.

Suddenly a group of Quinto's guerrilleros raced into view, staging a magnificent battle in the style of Yang Hsiao-lou, the famous Pekin military actor. They tumbled, gyrated, somersaulted and wielded broad swords with fantastic enthusiasm and agility. Then they all fell dead in assorted poses.

Presently, a guerrillero, dressed as an invader officer, entered the battlefield and stole large placards marked "Bank Receipts" from the fallen heroes. From the opposite side of the stage two equally sinister figures entered. One wore a yellow trench coat. The other was a primly garbed foreignstyle officer with an elaborate mustache. He had three noisy alarm clocks fastened to his wrists. The two sinister men shook hands with the invader officer and all three turned to the business of stealing cardboard placards. As the scene ended, the dead Chinese heroes arose, turned their pockets inside out to prove they had been robbed.

Quinto bowed to his actors as they withdrew. The audience, whose first reaction of surprise had by now changed to eager watchfulness, listened.

"That," said the Mexican, "was only the first scene, the Wang-Nohuri Receipt Ring in action. The Receipt Ring was what you call the complicating factor in our mysteries at Lingtung Pavilions. Teng Fa, who will perhaps make a hundred arrests, can tell you that for years certain traitors to China, as well as the invaders, have made themselves rich by robbing Chinese bodies. They are what you call *zopilotes*—buzzards."

Quinto paused, glancing across the theater at Wang, who glared back in cold rage.

"You haven't even a shred of proof," Wang charged.

"I haven't, eh?" murmured Quinto.

"No. I deny all."

"*Oye, hombre*, a few days before Harrow died, do you not remember sending him to Pan Tao to pick up a shipment of receipts from an invader agent who had penetrated our lines. The Nohuri cipher tells me this, no? *Entonces*, upon Senor Harrow's return to Lingtung, I have a feeling you called a meeting in the cave upon the mountain. You would divide the spoils of the Receipt Ring, eh?

"But this meeting didn't work out because a very strange thing happened on the cliff above the cave . . . *Mira.* . . ." Quinto waved his hand toward the stage and stepped aside.

A chair had been placed in the left quarter of the stage. In the Chinese theater, chairs and tables are normal symbols for mountain tops and cliffs. This chair was a cliff. Ten feet to the right, a guerrillero stood with his back to the audience. He supported a sandwich-board to show that he was a cave.

Presently, Harrow, still decked out with alarm clocks, marched across the stage. He approached the chair, lifting his knees high at each step in the accepted gesture for mountain climbing. He passed the cave and mounted the chair, then stood, gazing down at an imaginary, beautiful Wei Ho Valley.

Suddenly a grinning guerrillero scurried around the rear of the stage on his hands and knees, tooting and whistling as he went. He was the Lunghai Express.

Harrow took his coat off and slung it over his arm. Then, for the benefit of the audience in the Little Garden Theatre, he set each alarm clock at a distinct time. Almost in the same instant, another prancing guerrillero actor leaped across the stage, puffing mightily to indicate that he was a South Wind. He blew, huffed and puffed at the Harrow figure, finally blowing the latter off the chair and down the imaginary mountain cliff. The Harrow actor groaned and died with true Oriental eloquence. A moment later the Lunghai Express chugged close to the chair on his hands and knees.

A buzz of excitement ran through the Little Theater. Chairs scraped and tea pots tinkled. The Chinese in the audience cheered delightedly that a villain with a mustache was killed. Among the Europeans there were nervous coughs and sighs of relief.

Quinto raised his hand for silence.

"*Bueno*," he said. "You see, Senor Abe Harrow was not murdered as we all imagined. While waiting for the hour of the Receipt Ring meeting, he went to the cliff. It has a good view. He stood too close. You remember, it was very windy that day. This is the only explanation."

"Say, Quinto," Tate called out from his table, "but what about those other footmarks on the cliff? Wang's?"

"Ah, the footprints," murmured Quinto glancing over his huge shoulder toward the stage again. "It comes in scene three."

An actor wearing a long black gown and carrying enormous bank ledgers under his arms marched toward the chair-cliff. It was Wang the banker. He mounted the chair, stamped his heels upon it to indicate that he was leaving footprints. Then he looked over the cliff while his face expressed mingled astonishment and disappointment. He lingered there a moment, then returned toward the sandwich-board cave.

Suddenly he glimpsed a figure who wore red suspenders over a military uniform—Firth. The Firth figure was spying on two other strangers near the cave. The latter two were dressed in the manner of Mr. Yellow Coat and Papa Wier. They also wore red suspenders, which are the usual theatrical badge of a foreigner.

At length and with much exaggerated stealth, the procession of Wier, Yellow Coat, Firth and Wang descended the mountain. Abruptly, an actor dressed in plus-fours and two-tone golf shoes leaped across the stage and followed the procession at a respectful distance.

"Intrigue, eh?" Quinto commented as the scene ended. He stepped over to the little table containing the clues and filled himself a glass of Pedro Domecq.

Doc McKay, having watched the third act closely, now waved his arm toward Quinto.

"Look here, laddie," he said. "There were enough folks on that mountain with enough good motives for killing Harrow. Why blame an innocent wind?"

"Ah, *claro*, you want a deduction, eh?" asked Quinto.

"I want something reasonable," grinned the doctor.

Quinto flicked his hand as though the matter were of no importance.

"Senor Doctor Mac," he explained. "It is very simple. Do you remember when Harrow left the Gardens for the mountain?"

"Somewhere after 10:15 that morning, wasn't it?"

"*Si, quate*," continued Quinto. "And it takes an hour and a half to reach the cliff, so Harrow did not get there until after 11:45. Of his three watches, all which stopped at the instant of his death, the one which stopped at 11:50 was perhaps the most correct. You understand, no?"

Doc McKay murmured something to himself. Meanwhile Quinto paused, glanced at the stage which was being reset, then let his smoky, alert eyes wander over the audience. The people in the theater watched, fascinated. Even the guests, the Mayor of Lingtung, the Military Governor of Sianfu and Sir Oliver Quist, listened intently—aware that a closely woven web was turning into a net to trap someone. But who?

"Please, Gimiendo." It was Virtue speaking. "Please tell them how you come to have only one mystery. That is the cleverest."

"But first I must tell Doctor McKay about the clocks," Quinto smiled. "The business of 11:50 is very important. *Por que*, you ask? It is because Senor Harrow was the only one who could be near the cliff at that time. Why? First, because it takes a half hour to walk to the cave. Second, it takes another hour to walk to the cliff. Third, it takes thirty-five minutes to come down the trail from cliff to cave. Fourth, to walk from the cliff to the Pavilions takes over fifty minutes.

"*Entonces*, here is why nobody was with Harrow. Nevada was on the mountain but he returned to the Gardens at 12:30. If he had been on the cliff, he must have started down before 11:40. Harrow was still alive. The others were near the cave at noon and afterward. They could not possibly have been near the cliff at 11: 50."

"But Wang was on the cliff," Tate protested. "The heel marks."

"*Es verdad*," Quinto answered, a little annoyed. "Wang was there, but he didn't arrive on the cliff until well after midday. Chi saw him pass the cave a little before noon. Wang does not walk very fast. But when Wang realized that Senor Abe's footprints, and maybe his life, ended on the cliff, he returned quickly. Then he saw Firth spying on Wier and Mr. Yellow Coat." Quinto looked toward Wang again, smiling wisely. . . Eh, Senor Wang, you became suspicious? You think perhaps that Firth killed Harrow and took the bank chits Harrow was carrying. Is this not so?"

"The single mystery, Gimiendo," Virtue prompted.

"*Si, chuela*, my pretty, I come to that part. It is only this. Instead of two mysteries, we have only one—Senor Firth. The matter of Wang suspecting Firth of having the receipts is the thread which connected these two deaths. *But Senor Firth's murder had nothing to do with the Receipt Ring!* There is yet another motive for his murder. . . ."

CHAPTER 28
The Truth—Suggested

A TREMOR of intense interest ran through the little theater, while anxious eyes shifted swiftly from Quinto's expressionless face to the stage, which had been reset.

A reed chair was placed diagonally upon the stage. It was the actual chair in which Firth had been murdered. Nearby were a typewriter, a file cabinet, a small table with two glasses of whisky on it. Two grinning guerrillero actors stood nearer Quinto. They represented the door of Firth's villa. On the opposite side of the stage another guerrillero was bent double, hands and feet planted on the floor in the accepted symbol for an air raid shelter tunnel.

"The time is now midnight," Quinto announced. "It is Firth's room."

Firth, still wearing his uniform and red suspenders, crossed the stage and entered his room by way of the two door-guerrilleros. A moment later, a second actor wearing Mignon Chauvet's hospital uniform followed him. Both began waving their arms violently and eloquently, making the conventional gestures for a heated argument. Suddenly the *tan*, female impersonator, departed. Left alone, Firth pounded his chest and exercised to indicate that he was still alive.

Quinto watched the scene with satisfaction, then turned toward Mignon Chauvet, who had watched tensely. Quinto smiled pleasantly.

"*Digame*, Senorita," he said. "It was like that, yes? You left Senor alive, although you argued a little bit?"

Mignon nodded but said nothing.

"You sure about that?" McKay asked with evident relief.

"*Eso es*—that's it. But how do I know?" asked Quinto. "*Mira*. You remember when you examined his body, there were two glasses of whisky on the table. Each had been half drunk. You finished them in the morning, is it not so? Well, Mignon does not drink. So someone else drank with Firth after she left the room."

"Who?" McKay demanded.

"*Quien?* Maybe Senor Firth's wife."

There was an intake of breath throughout the Little Theatre. Amazed expressions crossed a dozen faces. Mignon Chauvet sat rigid, her eyes wide. Mary Wier paled slightly.

"His wife?" Tate gasped.

Quinto nodded toward Mary Wier. All eyes shifted in her direction and an excited murmur ran through the audience.

"*Ai bueno*, but let us finish the play," said Quinto. "It was known that Firth was very rich, *muy rico*. If he died, Senorita Wier would inherit his wealth, for a will was written in her favor. She had a fine motive for killing him. She did not love him. Instead, her heart was made for Nevada, eh? Let us see what Senorita Wier did at 12:30 the night of the murder."

A firecracker burst upon the stage.

An actor representing Firth sat stiffly in the reed chair. Some red soya bean oil had been spilled on his chest to give the impression of a first-class bullet wound.

Papa Wier, still wearing his red suspenders, approached the door and entered. An elaborate, shocked expression crossed his features and he began staggering about upon seeing the dead man in the chair. Suddenly he picked up a derringer pistol from the floor and examined it in a bewildered manner.

A new guerrillero, announced as Mary Wier and wearing something which resembled a ballet skirt, entered upon the scene with mincing steps. The new character took the part of what is known on the Chinese stage as *ching-i*, that is, an honest girl. Promptly setting to the business of dropping enormous paper tears on the stage, the girl and her father then took the gun, left the room and hid the weapon under the stomach of the air raid shelter.

There came an interval of cheering from the audience as the two characters left the stage. Suddenly another character appeared.

"*Ole*," Quinto interrupted, "watch closely."

The figure of Wang the banker crossed the stage and entered Firth's quarters by the two-guerrillero doorway. He looked surprised upon seeing Firth dead. Then he stopped to smell the two glasses of whisky and turned his nose up in an appropriate WCTU gesture. Finally, and very methodically, he turned the typewriter over, emptied the file cabinet, scattered papers all over the stage, ripped the mattress of an imaginary bed. For his last gesture, he took a chunk of red clay from his shoe and deposited it carefully on the floor. With a look of mixed anger and disappointment on his face, he departed.

Quinto shook hands with the Wang actor as the latter left the stage. He seemed delighted with the high quality of acting done by his students.

"*Tres piedras*—unusually good, eh?" he murmured.

"According to the show," Nevada spoke, "Firth is already dead. Who done it?"

"The play is only proving that neither Papa Wier, Mary Wier or Wang murdered Senor Firth," explained Quinto. "You will remember, on that same night Virtue entertained a number of men. The poetry-reciting lasted until two o'clock. Yes, Papa Wier was there, but he left early because he was ordered to search for the receipts."

"Wang?" asked McKay.

"Yes. Papa Wier was under the control of Wang, who supplied him with heroin."

"And Papa Wier found Firth dead," Virtue put in.

"*Bueno*," continued Quinto. "Then Senorita Mary also came to see Firth. Perhaps to beg for a divorce so that she could marry Nevada. Is that not so, *chuela?*" Quinto beamed toward Mary Wier.

The girl nodded, timidly.

"I saw father with the gun," she said, as Quinto prompted her. "I thought he had done it. I was terribly confused. To protect father, I hid the gun in the air raid tunnel. But I didn't notice the capsule father had dropped in the room."

"That's hardly proof of innocence," Tate cut in.

Quinto glanced at Tate, somewhat annoyed. "*Mira, hombre,*" he said quickly. "I have two reasons for making them innocent of murder. *Primero*, Papa Wier and the Senorita do not drink whisky, which means someone else who drinks also visited with Firth. *Segundo*, Wang does not drink."

"How do you know Wang came in after the Wiers?" asked McKay. "He didn't tell you, did he?"

"No, he did not. But after the poetry that night, Wang was surprised that Papa Wier did not report back. So, after leaving Virtue, he went to Firth's room to search for himself."

"It was perhaps two-thirty," Virtue interrupted.

"Two-thirty," Quinto repeated. "*Entonces*, Wang left a piece of red clay which had stuck to his shoes when he looked over the cliff where Harrow died. It was this clue which seemed to connect the two deaths.

"Wang also made a little tornado in the room because the Wiers said it was in perfect order when they were there. So it was Wang who came in last. Senor Firth had no other visitors after two-thirty. We have good excuses, or as you say, alibis, for everyone else. Mr. Ho had his opium. Doctor McKay and Chi gave mutual excuses."

"It doesn't make sense," said McKay. "Someone had to kill him. I pulled out the bullet."

"*Claro*," murmured Quinto. He pulled out a paper and tobacco, rolling himself a cigarette. "There are still a few bits of evidence which must fit in," he said as he lit the cigarette. "Perhaps Senor Tate can help."

Quinto waved his cigarette toward Tate. "Senor Tate," he asked. "Can you tell us who left a tiny shred of burned cloth? Who drank whisky with Firth between midnight and twelve-thirty? Whom did Firth know well enough to admit to his room? Why was Firth calm in his last moment?"

"Me?" Tate gagged. "I-I-I don't . . ."

Quinto's smoky eyes shifted from Tate to the others in the theater. A sharp edge slipped into the tone of his voice as he went on.

"You see, *companeros*, I have taken suspicion from the members of the Receipt Ring. So now we must look for another motive for killing Firth. Perhaps something that has been hidden by our discovery of the Receipt Ring. Was there anyone here with another motive? Yes, *seguramente!* Senorita Woodford . . . ."

Four Chinese guerrilleros appeared on the stage, rolling like cartwheels. One of them chugged in imitation of an automobile motor. Suddenly an outlandish creature with a long putty nose, a tweed dress and a corset tightly laced over the tweed, stepped into a space between the cartwheel guerrilleros. It was Lingtung's idea of Mildred Woodford driving off to Sianfu. She was accompanied by a caricature of John Tate, who sported the usual red suspenders and an arm wound with a few hundred yards of linen bandage. Abruptly, the entire entourage, cartwheels and caricatures, rolled offstage amidst tooting of horns and roaring of motors.

Quinto squatted on his haunches at the edge of the stage, grinning at Mildred Woodford. "You like it, yes?" he asked.

"Like it?" replied Mildred. "It's bad taste. I don't look like that and I see no reason for your dragging me into this at all."

Quinto blew forth a feather of smoke.

"Ah, you were drinking in Sianfu that night, but you are still a very good suspect. You have the motive we are looking for. You are not a suspicious journalist. No. You are an artist."

"Artist, nothing," snapped Mildred.

"*Buenos, pues*, you were Clive Firth's cousin. You are the Lady Goodwin, is it not so?"

"Listen here, Quinto! You can't implicate me in this. I *was* in Sianfu!" Mildred screamed. She leaped to her feet, upsetting her tea table. Her face was beet-red as she glared at the Mexican.

Quinto leaned forward, a pantherish casualness in his poise.

"You are this Lady Goodwin, eh?" he repeated.

"I am not."

A booming voice from the rear of the theater seemed to smash Mildred down. It was Sir Oliver Quist's. "She's Lady Goodwin. Damme, she hasn't changed a bit."

Mildred swung around, got one good look at the ambassador standing next to Tate, then sank back upon her chair, features sheet-white.

"Good Lord, Quinto," McKay gasped.

"What's Lady Goodwin doing here?" the British Ambassador demanded.

"Ah, *companeros*, you see, we have a motive now. Lady Goodwin, who is nothing but a former Lady Goodwin, and Senor Firth were the only two living members of the Firth *familia*. Now, when Lord Firth died in Scotland, perhaps this Mildred Woodford got to think that if Senor Clive were to die also, she would inherit the family fortune."

"Great guns, Quinto, you'd better be sure of yourself," said the ambassador.

"Gimiendo is always sure," Virtue smiled.

"Ah," Quinto continued, despite the hubbub in the theater. "What Lady Goodwin thinks is like a book which I read *con facilidad*. She thinks, where can young Firth die without creating alarm? In a war, naturally. So she comes to China with a new name—Woodford."

"She pretended to be a spy, but I knew," grinned Teng Fa. "I always know."

"*Bueno*," said Quinto. "She thinks no one will suspect a slightly enemy agent to be related to Senor Clive, a hero. She fools us with the talk of Harrow. A good disguise, is it not? Then she faints when she hears Harrow is dead. *La senorita es muy pinto*—very shrewd. It gives her an excuse to remain in her villa so that Firth does not see and recognize her. Then she writes in her diary that Papa Wier committed murder. She knows it is not the truth. It is only something to add to the confusion. But now, let us watch how Senor Firth was murdered."

Quinto swept his eyes over the audience and the result was a responsive ripple of excitement. Sergeant Sun had moved to where he stood directly behind Mildred Woodford. Wang was looking amazed and distraught, having discovered too late that Firth had been worth a fortune himself.

"Did she . . . ah . . . kill Firth?" McKay asked doubtfully. "I thought she was in Sianfu that night?"

"*Ai que chi*," Quinto smiled. "She was there. It is true that Senorita Woodford did not murder Firth. Only now do we see the real murderer; the visitor in Senor Clive's villa between midnight and twelve-thirty."

A burst of firecrackers danced across the stage. The reed chair re-appeared, the file cabinet, the typewriter, the two-guerrillero doorway, then Firth. He exercised and did a handstand to show his good health.

"Mignon Chauvet has just left," Quinto commented.

A moment later, the actor representing John Tate raced up to a point near the doorway in his four-human-wheeled auto. Stepping out, he approached the doorway, meanwhile pointing vehemently at his bandaged right arm, then flexing his left arm to show that he could drive a car with it.

With a typical Tate waddle, he entered Firth's room. Both he and Firth drank from the two whisky glasses with much formality before Firth sat in the reed chair. Once again, the Tate actor grinned at the audience as he pointed at his bandaged arm then, abruptly, a gun exploded from within the bandage. Firth stiffened, toppled over on the stage to indicate death, then got up and sat in the chair, meanwhile breaking an ampule of red soya bean oil against his chest.

Tate immediately went to the file cabinet and after a moment of methodical searching in which he disturbed nothing, pulled out a huge sheet of paper marked "WILL." This he shoved into his pocket. Finally, he slit the bandages on his hand with a small knife, drew forth the deathdealing derringer pistol and dropped it on the stage.

He glanced around once more with gestures of elaborate precaution. Then, quickly, he departed through the doorway, entered his four-guerrillero automobile, and raced offstage.

The incredulous stillness which had gripped the little theater during the scene abruptly terminated with the crash of a table and the cascading din of breaking pottery.

Heads and bodies swerved, eyes leaping to the rear of the theater, toward the table which McKay, Sir Oliver Quist and Tate had occupied. That corner of the hall was in an uproar. McKay and the ambassador were on their feet. Tate was flat on his back upon the floor beside the overturned table.

"Jimminie!" cried McKay. "He's fainted!"

"Fainted—hell," the ambassador roared. "I knocked him down. Was trying to get away."

The ambassador lifted Tate to his feet, then dropped him on a chair. After a moment, the latter opened his albino eyes and blinked miserably. "I knew this w-w-would happen . . . ." he began weakly.

"What now, G.H.Q.?" called Sir Oliver.

Quinto smiled a bit sadly, reached into his pocket for more tobacco, and spun himself another cigarette.

"It is time for Teng Fa to do his arresting," he murmured.

CHAPTER 29
Two Persons of the Same Mind

FOR FIFTEEN minutes following the last act of Quinto's play, the Little Garden Theatre was in a state of turmoil. Guerrilleros rushed back and forth, setting up tables on the stage, firing cannon crackers with immense delight, and carting in great quantities of food.

Sir Oliver Quist, the ambassador, watched the banquet preparations with glowing eyes.

The guerrilleros brought in huge bowls of steaming chicken-rice, plates of tiger tendons, Yunnan hams, *tsung-tse*, noodles, shark's fin soup, fried snails, tender black edible beetles, pumelos and mangoes. Last, but not least, came mountains of baked pork. Pork is the favorite food in China, for no one there has ever been able to discover any other use for pigs.

A number of guerrilleros went about, serving cups of strong rose-petal gin and warm brown wine.

"It is always good to have a little something to eat," explained Quinto. "Senorita Woodford and Senor Tate, after Teng Fa takes them away, will remember us not as judges but as good hosts."

"But how did you know they were working together?" asked the ambassador. "What on earth ever made them think they could do it?"

"*Ai*, ask Lady Goodwin," murmured Quinto, nodding toward Mildred Woodford. The Englishwoman looked too sick at the moment to even take the rose gin Teng Fa was offering her.

"Where'd she meet Tate?" McKay put in.

"Hankow."

"You mean they planned it from there?"

"*Nada mas*—nothing less than that," replied Quinto as he juggled a snail with his jade chopsticks. "Tate arranged that the Ministry of Information should order him to guard Senorita Woodford. He convinced them she was a spy-journalist. I think maybe they came to Lingtung without any plans because everything depended on whether the lady would meet her cousin and be recognized."

"So if they had met, Clive might not have been murdered as he was," suggested McKay.

Quinto nodded wisely. Glancing to his left along the table, he saw that the portly Mayor of Lingtung was having trouble with his snails, constantly dropping them—a trouble which even experts come up against every once in a while. Quinto, the good host, stepped over to the mayor and helped him save face.

"My poorly offered snails have wings," he murmured in Chinese. "I beg of you to overlook their waywardness."

The mayor beamed.

"May you have a succession of honorable sons," he said.

When Quinto returned to the table of the ambassador and McKay, he found Mountain of Virtue explaining: "When Mr. Tate and the lady arrived in Lingtung," she was saying, "they discovered Harrow had died. It seemed to be murder. It was very appropriate, for they were able to make it appear that the second crime connected with the first. It seemed as if the same person had killed both men, or that both crimes were committed because of the same motive. But actually, the only real connection is that the second murder hid behind the skirts of Harrow's mystery. You can see now why it took Gimiendo so long."

"*Oye,* it did not take me long," Quinto cut in. He flashed Virtue a hurt expression. "I had the clues, didn't I? There was this bit of burned cloth." He exhibited the envelope containing the bit. "There was the whisky. But most importante, there was the derringer gun and the expression of calm on Senor Clive's face when he died."

"No wonder he didn't see the gun," said McKay. "It was wrapped in that bandage."

"Ah, but even you forgot that with a broken arm Tate could still move his fingers enough to shoot a gun. The derringer was very interesting, yes? The next day, during the air-raid, Nevada was shot by the same gun. Why?"

Doc McKay shrugged his shoulders.

"There was no reason, eh?" asked Quinto. "But then I remembered. A derringer shoots very badly at more than fifteen feet. Perhaps it wasn't aimed at Nevada. *Si, claro,* Mary Wier was standing beside Nevada and the ballet was for her."

"The will. Clive Firth's will," said Virtue.

"That's right," added Sir Oliver. "The girl was named heir. Goodwin and Tate had to get her out of the way. Clear as ice, isn't it?"

Quinto's smoky eyes leaped across at Virtue, frowning because of the slight smile she gave the ambassador.

"But wait a second," Sir Oliver added. "Tate couldn't have seen the will. It was in the mail and didn't arrive in my once until the day you came, G.H.Q."

"No. But Tate saw the carbon copy," replied Quinto. "He took it, in fact, from Senor Clive's file the night of the murder, but he forgot that carbon paper in Lingtung and China leaves traces that carbon copies have been made. Since the beginning of the war our carbon paper has been crudely made. It has carbon on both front and back and when a copy is made, it leaves an imprint on the copy and also a reverse imprint on the back of the original paper. When I saw the will Senor Clive sent to the Embassy, I knew someone had the carbon copy and that somebody was the murderer. Clever, eh?"

Quinto smiled rather proudly and gulped down an extra large cup of brown wine.

Tate, whose feet were tied to the legs of a stool, and who had been placed at the table between Wang and Nohuri, had recovered enough to protest.

"Quinto, I was in Sianfu that night. You've made a mistake," he cried.

The huge Mexican made a little "tsking" noise with his lips and shook his head. "*Es verdad*—that's right," he said. "You even telephoned me from Sianfu, didn't you? But remember, you and the Senorita went there alone. Without military escort. Sianfu is but ten to fifteen minutes' drive by fast car. You drove back alone with one hand. It is possible, no?"

"No."

"Ah, but you admitted you could drive. You offered to chase Wang the night the banker ran from Lingtung. *Ai, bueno*, so you came back to kill Firth. This was the only chance you had to take unless someone saw you. You climbed the South Wall. Your clothes were very dirty the next day. You see, I have good eyes. You knew Firth, so he was not surprised to see you. You shoot him quick, eh? Then you go through his files to make sure there is nothing about Lady Goodwin in them. Perhaps a picture."

"So he found the carbon of the will," interrupted the ambassador.

"*Ai, quate*," Quinto nodded. "But he did something else. I think he is afraid of search by military police in Sianfu. He cuts enough of his bandage to take out the gun. It is much safer to leave it in Lingtung. *Comprende?* But he leaves a clue—the shred of burned cloth!"

"From the bandage?" asked McKay.

"Yes. When the bullet fired through the bandage it burned off a tiny bit. *Que idiota, eh?* Tate goes back to Sianfu, and with Senorita Woodford he puts on a fresh bandage. They make the mistake of throwing the old one where it would clog up the Guest House plumbing and make China lose face. Teng Fa has saved me the evidence. . . ."

There was a gasp from both Tate and Mildred Woodford when Quinto went over to the small table which held his collection of evidence and lifted a long, rumpled strip of bandage. It was torn and scorched in two or three places.

"Who shot at Mary Wier and Nevada? Tate or Woodford?" Doc McKay asked.

"*Creo que Senor Tate*—I think Tate. He made me a list of where people stood in the *refugio* tunnel when Nevada was wounded. Mr. Ho and Wang were put at the west entrance, Senor Doc and Senorita Chauvet at the other. At first I could not see why any of these four were interested in shooting at Nevada. *Despues*, after seeing Firth's will in which Mary Wier is named, I began thinking that Tate had rearranged the list. He was hiding himself. He was at the east entrance."

Quinto glanced toward Tate, who was looking whipped and bewildered.

"He does not look like a murderer, eh?" continued the Mexican. "He is very weak. But in the poker game he showed a certain character. He is what you call the cautious plunger. If he thinks all the cards in his hand are high, he bets heavily."

"What was Tate going to get out of it?" asked McKay.

"*Ai, muy poco*, very little."

"That's no reason to murder."

"He had reason," Quinto replied. "Once when we were talking of Senor Clive's bravery and the way he died with a calm face, Tate said, '*I doubt if I could sit by calmly while someone waved a gun at me, even if it were my wife or mother.*'"

"Well, maybe he's not the type," McKay grunted.

"*Bueno*, but only a married man would use such a word like 'wife' in such a manner. This is not the way a single man thinks about women..."

Mountain of Virtue touched Quinto's arm.

"The clothes, Gimiendo," she reminded him.

"Oh yes, the clothes," said Quinto. "When I brought Senorita Woodford's clothes to my *yamen* after the drinking, Tate recognized her dress. Now the Senorita had only worn tweeds in Lingtung and while travelling. Only Sergeant Sun and Quinto saw her wearing this new dress, the cream-colored one. Perhaps Tate had seen it before, while she was packing a suitcase in Hankow, or in her room at the Guest House."

"Which made you suspicious," said McKay.

"No. It only makes me think they are married."

"Married?" It was Sir Oliver. He stared at Woodford as though he were seeing her for the first time. "I'll be dashed if you might not be right. She did marry an American."

"It is not important," murmured Quinto. "You can check on it if Senor Tate doesn't tell us first. Perhaps the little American wished to separate from the lady. He needed money to study his calligraphy. So he takes this chance, eh? Perhaps they made some agreement in which they would separate and he would be given a fine reward for murder. I think so."

Sir Oliver Quist glanced at Quinto somewhat puzzled. In between gobs of rice which wallowed around in his mouth, he asked: "I say, how'd you find she was Lady Goodwin?"

"You identified her."

"But before. You must have had some idea?"

"*Si, claro*, when you send articles to the New York and London *Times*, do you send them to London or New York? No. You send them to their offices in Shanghai and Hankow. Senorita Woodford is such a poor journalist she does not know the papers have such offices in China. But it was this morning that Virtue gave me a final proof . . . .

"In Senorita Woodford's diary there was a picture of Nevada in modernistic, cubistic style. The Lady Goodwin in Firth's Will was once a student of Picasso—a cubist. *Comprende?* It is not very often people with a talent for drawing think in cubes."

"Think cubistically," Virtue prompted.

"Yes, cubistically. It is a matter of training. So Virtue said, 'It is Lady Goodwin.' Meanwhile, I asked you to come here because I thought the will would produce something.'

Quinto sighed a little, noting that the food was running low.

"They were very clever, those two," he commented. "Had it not been that Gimiendo Quinto was here, they would have had success. My brain is sharp, yes?"

Virtue sipped her wine and watched Quinto from beneath the sweep of her long lashes. There was something very strange about her, for it reminded Sir Oliver Quist of an old Chinese proverb which says, "If two persons are of the same mind, their sharpness can divide metal."

CHAPTER 30
The Lotus Eaters

THE MORNING following Quinto's startling theatrical, the Pavilion Gardens were bathed in golden sunlight and filled with the delicate odors of jasmine and camphor. There was still a great deal of noise, for the celebration of Tai Erh Chwang had been so successful the guerrilleros had voted to keep it going another day.

Flags waved above villa tops with a gay, brilliant abandon. Firecrackers exploded here and there in the gardens. The ducks in the canal added voice to the festive atmosphere.

Following breakfast, a long black sedan pulled up at the North Gate near Sergeant Sun's pink brick guardhouse. Five people got in the back of the car—Colonel Nohuri, Banker Wang, Papa Wier, John Tate and Mildred Woodford. Then Teng Fa, resplendent in his olive uniform, seated himself in the front beside the driver and the car roared away along the road to Sianfu.

As the sedan swung into the East-West Road, Teng Pa glanced over his shoulder at Mildred Woodford. The sight of her Yorkshire nose made him wince a little. Then, as if for relief, his thoughts turned to Mountain of Virtue. He was a bit saddened by the prospect of leaving her behind with Quinto. Suddenly he frowned.

"The one blind spot in my files," he murmured reflectively. "I must come back and find out how she always turns up three queens at poker. Could it be that she . . . ah . . ."

In the rear seat, squeezed uncomfortably between Wang and Woodford, Tate looked out upon the sunny landscape as the car rolled along. There was a pained expression on his round face and a certain bitterness evident in his watery eyes. The pain was the result of Mildred's corset stays jabbing into his thigh. The bitterness came from thinking of Virtue.

It had been Mildred's idea to wind the derringer in the bandage. She had thrown the bandage down the drain at the Guest House. She had drawn the cubist picture of Nevada.

Bitterly, Tate contrasted her with Mountain of Virtue. If he had had Virtue to work with, everything might have gone off smoothly. He would never have been caught. Virtue would have seen to that. She was as capable as she was lovely.

As the sedan spun along the road, racing to catch its own elongated shadow, it passed a low hill. Upon the crest of the hill, a silk-gowned figure watched the passing sedan.

It was Mr. Ho. His friendly, complacent gaze shifted from the speeding car to the broad rippling field of poppies that extended as far as his poor eyes could see. Mr. Ho sighed pleasantly as he estimated the size of the prospective opium crop. He was extremely happy.

Lieutenant Chi leaned over the billiard table in the *yamen* Pavilion. He looked very morose for a man whose army had just won a thumping victory at the Grand Canal Front. On the billiard table were spread a half dozen copies of the *St. Louis Baseball News*. Chi shook his head sadly and spoke to McKay, who also glanced at the news items:

"Looks very bad season for the Dodgers," he said. "We'll be in the cellar again this year. What we need is a new manager and somebody like Dean. Since we got this Heinie Manush we go to sixth place last year. He hit .333. If we got Dean we could see fifth place."

Doc McKay grinned, eyes twinkling from under tufted brows. "Yi, laddie, you should worry as much about baseball as you do about the war."

"But with China, I don't have to worry," replied Chi with utter confidence. "We'll win. We're only fighting the Japanese. With the Dodgers it's different; they're faced with Cincinnati and the Giants."

McKay smiled tolerantly. His eyes rolled toward the spirit screen where Sergeant Sun appeared. The sergeant was grinning cockily from ear to ear as he hurried over and handed the doctor a pot containing a brilliant blue-flowered cineraria plant.

"Here chop chop new kind just grow you ask for Doc Meeki," said Sun.

"Thanks, laddie," replied McKay.

He took the plant, smelled its flowers and then hurried outside toward the garden path where he knew Mignon Chauvet was strolling. As he went, he suddenly recalled that it was Mountain of Virtue who had once suggested to him that a gift of flowers might make Mignon happy.

That was very interesting, because now, as he carried the flowers, a pleasant sensation of warmth and happy anticipation filled his own being.

Of all the citizens in the garden, Nevada was the most serious and practical on this particular morning. As he breakfasted alone with Mary, in the Wier villa, he tried to put things straight.

"Listen, Mary," he drawled, fitting his thoughts and words together carefully, "Teng Fa is gonna get the military court to be easy on your pa. He'll get him paroled to you. Quinto says I gotta leave China. He says we oughta go to Nevada and get us a ranch and take your pa. Then the ambassador guy said he would fix it so the Firth money could buy the ranch . . . ."

As Nevada spoke, Mary fingered a tiny jade wedding ring on her finger—a gift from Virtue. There was a certain tenderness to her thoughts, for she was thinking of how Quinto had arrested Nevada, brought him back to Lingtung, and then had had the Mayor of Lingtung perform the wedding just before the theatrical. Nevada had looked embarrassed and somewhat amazed, but he had said, "Yes."

With such thoughts in her mind, she stared at the lean cowboy. Absently, she raised her hand and felt the slight swelling on her jaw.

Nevada stopped talking. He forgot all about being practical when Mary touched her jaw. He realized she was very beautiful. Even the gesture was beautiful. He had seen it somewhere, exactly so. Yes. He remembered: the Chinese princess, the one who creased her brows with the pain of toothache. Virtue had done that.

Toward noon a dazzling sun looked directly down upon the sawed-off crest of Running Wind Mountain. Its rays picked out two familiar figures walking arm in arm against the mild breeze that combed the mountain top. One figure was huge, and dressed in something pea green.

The second figure was strictly *hsiaochieh*. It was Virtue, of course. She wore a jacket and trousers of jade-silk which contrasted prettily with the brightness of her lips and the wind-swirled blackness of her hair. There was a smile on her lips as she and Quinto came to a halt upon the mountain cliff.

For a moment, both stared down upon the Wei Ho Valley, seeing the spread of green, the rolling poppy beds, the orchards and the turquoise ribbon of river. Then Quinto sighed contentedly.

"There is just one little mystery I haven't solved," he murmured. "The Generalissimo's teeth!"

"The teeth? Oh!" Virtue smiled mysteriously.

"*Hola, chica*, I thought you knew something about those teeth," said Quinto. "You were in the *yamen* when they disappeared. So?"

"Lieutenant Chi holds them."

"Chi?"

"Yes. He took them." Virtue nodded prettily. "He had fine reason.

The lieutenant is suspicious that there might be a trace of Japanese workmanship or material in them. He is a patriot also, and since it has been rumored about that the Generalissimo might want these particular teeth back, Chi stole them. He feels that with the present teeth, which are all Chinese, the Generalissimo can bite better. It is very important for China's bite to be strong."

"When did you learn this?" asked Quinto.

"Oh, I saw Chi take them."

Virtue slipped a delicate hand in her pocket and brought forth a lotus pod. Breaking the pod she slipped a few seeds between her lips.

"I am thinking," said Quinto, "that since everything goes well at Lingtung again I must do something. My guerrilleros have reached such a point in their training that they are ready for what you call the graduation exercise. I know what it will be. For a long time I've had the ambition to capture a Japanese Cabinet Minister. Yes, perhaps two Ministers."

Quinto smiled at the sound of his own words and he blinked gently upon the valley spreading below him. Suddenly, from the distance, came a half belligerent and somewhat carefree whistle. It was the Lunghai Express, clattering toward Lingtung. The camouflaged car was now securely coupled behind the engine to prevent it from going off on its own again.

A vaguely troubled look crossed Quinto's sunny face as he turned to Virtue. He suddenly remembered what the ambassador, Sir Oliver, had said about Nanking and about Mountain of Virtue.

His mouth opened a trifle as he stared at his strangely beautiful companion. He was on the point of asking her a question about Nanking. A very important question. It would have to be put delicately.

Then he found her staring back at him. Her lids drooped for an instant, dark lashes sweeping her golden cheeks with an air of bland innocence. She seemed to be reading his very thoughts for a smile curved her lips and she handed him a pod of lotus seeds, saying:

"To enjoy their fragrance, Gimiendo, you must think of nothing, absolutely nothing."

The End

AFTERWORD
About James Norman

EVEN IN AN ERA known for its colorful literary figures, James Norman Schmidt stood out. Born in Chicago on January 10, 1912, James Norman (the name he used on his novels) visited or lived in many countries as an artist, a writer, a journalist, a soldier and a teacher during a long life that was filled with many incidents as exciting and as odd as can be found in his mysteries.

Raised a Catholic, Norman attended Loyola University in Chicago where he was expelled when he and some friends tied the Jesuit boarding room supervisor to his bed so that they could sleep late the following day. Thirty years later in 1953 Norman finally completed his bachelor's degree at Mexico City College. He received his master's in 1957 from the University of Guanajuato.

After he was thrown out of Loyola, he worked as a reporter for the Chicago *Tribune* (1932-33) and United Press (1935-36). In 1937, he went to Madrid to cover the Spanish Civil War for the Paris edition of the *Tribune*. He quit his job with the *Tribune* and joined the 14th International Brigade, which was composed primarily of French anti-fascist volunteers. Norman manned a cannon battery during the war and as a result suffered a partial hearing loss.

While at the front, he came down with typhus and spent several weeks with high fevers alone in a cabin, surviving only because composer Conlon Nancarrow (who died recently in Mexico City) walked several kilometers a day to bring him aspirins and potatoes. Invalided out of the army, Norman served as a government newscaster for Madrid radio station EAQ.

During the war, he also met Ernest Hemingway and although in print he claimed to have been impressed by the American writer, he told his children that Hemingway was frozen with fear during bombing raids. When Franco's fascist troops overwhelmed the loyalists, Norman fled Spain from Valencia to France with other International Brigade members on a British ship.

Norman had already spent some time in France where he learned

French and studied art at the Ecole des Beaux Arts in Paris. An accomplished sculptor, he supported himself in Paris as an ice carver, a profession he took up again in the U.S. from time to time when writing jobs were scarce. Following the war, Norman returned to Chicago where he served as the sports editor of the Chicago *Record* (1939-40) and as the editor for *Compton's Encyclopedia* (1941-42). It was during this period that he wrote for the pulps and published *Murder ,Chop Chop*.

With wife Judith Schoenberg he moved to California, where his son Paul was born in 1942. When his dog Leo refused to allow Judith near baby Paul, Norman offered the German Shepherd to the army's K-9 corps. Norman himself served as a combat correspondent for the U.S. 6th Army in Luzon. A first lieutenant, he was a member of a plane crew that flew low-level missions over the Philippine jungles, dropping supplies to guerrillas. Following the Japanese surrender, Norman served as the cultural attache for the 6th and 8th Armies in Kyoto. Norman received a bronze star for valor and a special commendation for his work in the press corps. Both he and Leo received honorable discharges in 1946.

Back in Hollywood, Norman was a scriptwriter for the *Herald Theatre* and the *Loretta Young Show*. He was beginning to get movie script assignments when it was revealed that he had been a member of the Communist Party in his youth as well as a member of the International Brigade. Sen. Joseph McCarthy's red witch-hunt was focusing on the entertainment industry and Norman found himself blacklisted. Unable to make a living in the United States, Norman moved his family to Mexico where many of his old friends from Spain, including Albert Maltz, were then living in exile. While in Mexico, he and Judith were divorced; he married another writer, Margaret Fox, in 1962, who had a daughter, Melissa, from a previous marriage.

He remained in Mexico for many years, working as a freelance writer and as a lecturer at the Academia Hispanoamericana until 1965, when he was asked to join the faculty of the creative writing program at Ohio University in Athens as a lecturer. In 1968, he was made a full professor, and in 1982, he was named professor emeritus. He died in Athens on Sept. 16, 1983.

In his youth, Norman was an outstanding athlete and was a member of the U.S. water polo team at the 1932 Los Angeles Olympics. In 1933, he trained Charles "Zimmy" Ziblemann, whom he had met in Africa, to swim the English Channel. Zibelmann reportedly didn't like to train and Norman tempted Zibelmann with glasses of champagne. What made Ziblemann's channel attempts unusual was that he had lost his legs in an auto accident in Chicago while escaping from the mob

(Zibelmann had run afoul of the mob when he refused to accept a secret arrangement between them and the Hearst Corporation to control the unions). Three times Norman coaxed Ziblemann into the channel: one time they drifted out into the North Sea and two other times Zibelmann got seasick, once ten and a half hours out of Dover.

Norman was something of a practical joker, as his Jesuit boarding room supervisor could probably testify to. For whatever reason, Norman had it in for film star Greto Garbo and once convinced several friends to collect moths in paper bags which they released in a theater showing a new Garbo film. The moths immediately flew to and covered the entire screen.

An excellent cook, Norman enjoyed entertaining and people were always trying to wangle an invitation to his house for dinner. But if Norman didn't like the guests—often friends of new wife Margaret—he would gather together the dirty dishes after the meal and place them on the floor for the dogs to lick clean; then he would pick them up and put them on shelves in the pantry while the unwelcome guests watched with wide-open mouths. Few sought a second dinner invitation. After they left, he would retrieve the dishes and wash them. "I think even Margaret enjoyed it," son Paul said.

Dogs were always a passion. Whatever the breed—cocker spaniel, visla, Doberman or mongrel—Norman trained them as retrievers for duck hunting. At the time of his death he was working on a gourmet dog cookbook which was to be filled with stories about famous people and their dogs as well as recipes. After Margaret's death in 1979, Norman tested many of these recipes, often sharing a meal with Chuco, the last of his dogs, who reportedly was very fond of escargot.

—TOM & ENID SCHANTZ

The editors wish to thank James Norman Schmidt's friends in Athens, Ohio, and, most importantly, his son Paul Schmidt of Mexico City, for their help in putting together this biography.

About The Rue Morgue Press

The Rue Morgue Press was founded in 1997 by Tom & Enid Schantz with the intent of bringing back in print some of the books they have enjoyed calling to the attention of their customers during the nearly 30 years they have operated their mystery bookstore, The Rue Morgue (which opened in 1970 as The Aspen Bookhouse).

The books chosen for publication by the press (with the exception of *The Mirror*—see previous page) aren't necessarily immortal classics but rather are books that mystery bookstore owners might have pushed into the hands of their customers back in the 1930s or 1940s had such stores existed then, explaining: "This just came in. I think you'll get a kick out of it."

For example, 1942 saw the publication of Raymond Chandler's third novel, *The High Window*. In that same year James Norman's *Murder, Chop Chop* was released and although it was very popular with the readers of the day and earned praise from mystery critics, then and now, it has been unavailable for almost as long as *The High Window* has been in print.

The press hopes to eventually issue one book a month. Write to

The Rue Morgue
P.O. Box 4119
Boulder, CO 80302

for information on future titles.